I0612173

Children of Earth
Part 1

U'tanse Explorer

Wizard of Mars

Henry Melton

Children of Earth
Part 1
U'tanse Explorer
Wizard of Mars

Henry Melton

Wire Rim Books
Hutto, Texas

WRB

Children of Earth Part 1 © 2025 by Henry Melton
All Rights Reserved

Printing History
First Edition: November 2025
ISBN 978-1-935236-93-1

ePub ISBN 978-1-935236-94-8

Website of Henry Melton
www.HenryMelton.com

Printed in the United States of America

Wire Rim Books
www.wirerimbooks.com

Acknowledgements

As I bring the Project Saga to its conclusion with this Children of Earth trilogy, I'm grateful for the special early readers, some of which have been helping me from the beginning, decades ago. This time, it was a big ask, seeking help with three books at once.

Jim Dunn, Linda Elliott, Todd Hartman, Mike Lynch, Scott McNay, Tom Stock

Contents

U'tanse Explorer

Wizard of Mars

Abe's Hand-drawn Starchart #5: Betelgeuse Nebula Region from Earth View

B - Betelgeue Nebula
R - Rigel (blue giant)
S - Sirius (White, brightest visible star, 8 lightyears from Sol)

U'tanse Explorer

The U'tanse were humans, they kept telling themselves that. They had been isolated so many generations that their stories of capture and enslavement by the Cerik were more mythology than history and the allure of long lost Earth was part of their religion.

They had much to celebrate. They had taken over the technology of their captors and had long ago shaken off their chains. They had built their own cities and left the Cerik as primitive predators roaming their prairies.

But everyone knew U'tanse were different, with psychic gifts inherited from their ancestral mother. They knew that there might be problems if they ever rediscovered Earth, and they knew that in spite of their ineda mind blocking skills and the tradition of breeding every tenth male to be non-telepathic, there were problems that threatened their existence—unless they could relocate the lost planet of their origin.

The Notice

"It's ridiculous, Ohen!" Grant told him. "You're a great designer. Why in the world would you give that up to go drive a boat that you designed? You're meant for greater things."

Ohen bar Clay of Chase-on-Ha was, himself, stunned at his notice. He'd applied on a whim. This could change his life. Telling his boss had been his first impulse, but Grant didn't see it the same way he did.

Ohen was accepted as lead boat operator on Starship Leonardo's next trip. He had one month, just thirty-five days, to turn over his position and report to the Cluster where the starships were based.

"Grant, you don't really need me here. Nell is ready to take over."

Grant's ineda had his thoughts locked down tight, but his face was easy to read. He'd been expecting Ohen to be lead designer for the light passenger boat that the company had just won the bid from the Chase government.

There was a knock on the door. Ohen could tell it was Nell. His ineda must have slipped when he saw the notice. It was hard to keep secrets when everyone could read minds, even if everyone was supposed to keep their mental shield up.

Grant sighed. "Come on in, Nell."

She entered, her eyes were wide and looking stunned. "You're going?"

He nodded. "How can I turn this down? It's the first expedition to hunt for Earth in nearly fifty years. The Council has gotten very cautious these days."

He was surprised at how his heart was racing. He couldn't turn this down, but he would be giving up an important position on this whim.

She nodded at his words. The U'tanse had seven intact starships, but generations of research had unveiled an uncomfortable truth. The leap engines in those seven remaining ships, inherited from the Delense, the extinct slave race of the Cerik, weren't locally invented. They had been purchased from some other galactic race. Humanity didn't have that technology. There was no way to build more. They couldn't be risked lightly.

There had been others, but those derelicts, torn apart in the battles that had ended in the extinction of the Delense, had been examined in detail by U'tanse scientists. The leap engines had been identified, but once dead, they could never be revived. Without a leap engine, the trip to another star would likely take decades, and needed enormous energies to get such a ship up to a reasonable velocity.

Ohen sighed. If he was giving up his position, he had to leave it in good hands.

"Sit down. You don't have to stand all the time."

Nell was five-foot-eight and Ohen was seven-foot-two. They were hardly eye-to-eye now, with her standing, but he was annoyed when she tried to even them out like this.

Ohen nodded toward their boss. "Nell, Grant will put you in lead designer position. What do you need from me in the next five weeks to get ready to take over?"

...

He blinked as the stars shifted in his view. *They told me my helmet was optically perfect.* The planet Ko was the largest thing in sight, its red-tinged atmosphere plainly visible around the edge even on the dark side of the crescent. Ha, the moon, his whole world for most of his life, was a much smaller orb in the distance. *I guess any world or moon is huge when you measure everything by your own footsteps.*

Ohen frowned as he edged his boat ever closer to the starship Leonardo. Because of his body size, none of the standard commercial spacesuits would fit him, so once he attained his adult height, he'd had to purchase customized suits. *They're all too expensive.* He flexed his fingers again. This new one didn't feel right, yet.

Normally, he just managed without suiting up. Yes, he lived on airless Ha, the primary moon of the planet Ko, but the whole city of Chase-on-Ha was a sealed maze of domes and passageways, and all the boats entered and left through airlocks to pressurized docking areas. He rarely went out into vacuum, except to attend the astronomy club meetings.

The club had a site in a crater to block the lights from Chase so they could see the stars in all their glory. There were a few telescopes at the site, but Ohen most often appreciated the spectacle only obscured by his suit helmet's glass.

He always took a good look at the Betelgeuse Nebula, the remnant of the supernova that brought the Cerik to Earth in the first place. The Cerik, the apex predators and still the dominant species on Ko, and saw the expanding shockwave of the supernova as an opportunity to weaken potential prey.

Ohen glanced again at the planet. Down on that single continent, the Cerik still roamed.

They still think of themselves as the master race. No U'tanse wanted to remind the predators that their former slaves had usurped their whole technological base. *Let them chase the grasslands for their prey and have their endless tribal wars.*

The few U'tanse still on Ko mainly lived on island settlements far from any Cerik. The rest of Ohen's people lived in space or on settlements on other worlds.

Just as the Cerik didn't like to think about the loss of their technology, the U'tanse avoided thinking about the generations they'd lived as a slave species themselves, under the claws of the Cerik. The previous slaves, the Delense had sought their freedom in a surprise attack on the Name's of all the Cerik clans. The strategy had been to wipe out their leadership as the Delense attempted a mass escape from the planet. It hadn't worked.

The U'tanse, instead, had bought their way out of slavery, stealing the technology that powered the planet and then one by one, trading power cells for freed U'tanse.

Now, only the U'tanse had spaceflight capability. Ohen had never seen a Cerik in real life, although there were plenty of photos and videos of them.

Ohen and the designers before him and had made great strides in making new and better ground-to-space boats and the best of those were being loaded into Leonardo after an extensive set of tests. And the tests mandated that he pilot the craft with his spacesuit on, clumsy gloves and all.

Ohen tapped the pads. *No more hack and slash.* The original boats built by the Delense had a set of controls designed to be used by their Cerik masters. They only had claws totally unsuited for delicate work. Ohen had been amazed when he learned of how the Cerik could fly the boats by slashing their claws through the air, intercepting light beams with the computer interpreting those motions as real piloting commands. The Delense had been good engineers and were very clever in accommodating the masters that had eventually killed them.

The view in front showed the starship Leonardo growing in size as he approached. The large hull had also been built by the Delense, over the primary framework purchased from some other species. The hull appeared to be a set of whitish eggs of various sizes melted together into a roughly spherical cluster.

Ohen had been in deep research mode since the day the letter arrived. Archeologists had discovered the actual design plans for the starship hull and it had appeared that the cluster-of-eggs design was a compromise due to the limitation of how large a single hull could be manufactured on the Delense manufacturing facility—what was now old-town Chase-on-Ha. The Delense had to make their hull of smaller pieces and merge them together into a larger space.

In recent years there had been a proposal to retrofit the starships with a more human-friendly design. Interior fittings had been converted over time, but such a major change but was considered too risky.

Ohen requested docking and the indicator flashed. He removed his hands from the controls. Everything was automatic from this point on. The outer airlock port opened and automated tractor beams carefully guided the boat inside. Short-range beams gave the illusion of gravity and the boat settled down to its landing spot. There was the sound of winds as air was restored to the landing dock.

The huge docking space, actually a huge airlock, had offended Ohen's engineering sensibilities. He would have preferred a smaller airlock, only large enough to hold the boat, so that less air would have to be pumped in and out, but the Delense engineers had worked around the larger volume of air by using pressor beams to force the air out of the docking bay into storage tanks without needing a large volume vacuum pump.

If a starship was ever redesigned, he'd put in his opinions, but he had to live with the existing design for now. He was just a pilot, not a designer anymore.

He checked the instruments as the outside air quickly stabilized.

"Hey, Ohen!" a voice over the boat's shouter echoed in the cabin. "Stay put and I'll be there in a minute."

"You got it." The familiar voice brought a smile to his face. Gabriel was a navigator, and the man had been in the same introductory class he had attended. They shared a lot of interests.

Ohen took the opportunity to shed the space suit and make his log entries.

There was a tap on the hatch and Ohen opened the outer door of the airlock—just large enough for two people, or one person and a big bundle of gear. The boat was a much smaller vessel than the starship. The original Delene boats didn't even have airlocks.

Gabriel entered, looking around. "Spacious."

Ohen chuckled. "Hey, I was the designer for this boat! I wasn't about to build one where I'd have to duck my head all the time."

"I bet all the giants will appreciate it. How many of you are there, I wonder?"

Ohen shrugged. "We're rare enough, I guess. I know about a dozen, but most of them are in my family."

"And a very distinguished family it is at that."

Ohen gave him a look. "Okay, what's with the compliments? What do you want?"

Gabriel stretched out on one of the seats. "Ohen, just how difficult would it be to install a new telescopic camera on one of these boats?"

"A retrofit now, at this late stage? We're leaving in two weeks, right?"

He nodded. "Yes, but you know my problem, right? We've got to calculate each jump precisely. I can aim the leap engines in any direction and specify the distance to travel, but we're going into unknown territory. I can pick a star from the map and aim it accurately enough, but we don't have distance measurements worth anything. A star in the sky is just a point of light.

"It takes trigonometry to get a distance measurement. We look at stars from one side of the orbit and half a year later look at them again. The ones that shift position the most are closer. We also have records from all the previous flights, back to the Cerik exploration age, but the Cerik never took pictures.

"When we arrive at a new star, we'll take more pictures and try to estimate star distances from that, but it would also be helpful if we had a better way of estimating distances.

"We could send a boat with a good camera out some distance from the starship and that would give us a baseline to look for closer objects, like planets and moons in that system."

Ohen nodded. "Moving the starship a short hop would be too expensive."

"Exactly. We've got the energy for only ten leaps. Nine exploratory and the final one to get us back home. Yes, we can always make short hops to get closer to an important target planet or something like that, but if we could make more accurate leaps by taking more pictures using your boat, then it'd definitely be worth it."

Ohen considered it. "Do you have the telescopic camera already?"

"Oh, yes! We have several spares for the ones already installed on Leonardo."

He sighed. "Okay, give me the physical specifications and the interface requirements. If it's possible, I'll get started once you get Captain Foster's permission."

"Great!"

Ohen frowned. "I thought I was going to get a few days to relax once I finished the final tests. You'll owe me for this."

Gabriel beamed, "Of course. I'll get the data to you within the hour."

A New System

"That felt smoother," Ohen said.

Kerry, the ship's white-haired master healer, nodded from across the lunch room table. "Less chop," she said.

Leonardo's second interstellar leap was different. Ohen couldn't feel the telepathic snap of distant connections being severed this time. When they left the Ko system initially, there had been that familiar feel of endless minds—the telepathic leakage from the population of Ha and Ko. And then at the jump, it had all vanished abruptly.

Their initial target star, Prom-34, had been a previously documented destination from one of the Cerik expeditions and close enough to be occasionally visible from Ko. It was chosen because it was ninety degrees off from the vector towards Betelgeuse, and because astronomers on Ha had gotten a decently accurate distance measurement to Prom-34 from their star parallax studies over the years.

While he was involved in finishing up the installation of the new camera on boat B3, Gabriel and the crew of astronomers and navigators were taking detailed star images. Specialized computers could compare star maps from Ha and Prom-34 and get distance measurements from any of the lights that appeared in different positions between those locations.

Ohen finished his meal. "Did you join the betting pool?"

Kerry shook her head. "I really don't think we'll find Earth, not for years yet. The sky is just too big."

"Then why did you join the expedition?" He had asked that of several people. Getting to know his crewmates better was his way of trying to fit in.

Whether it was his size or his family, it often took a while before he stopped feeling like an outsider.

She chuckled. "Well, we have to find Earth. I think the U'tanse will stagnate without contact with the rest of humanity, but even if it takes hundreds of years to find it, we have to start now. Like I said, the sky is big, but if we keep at it, eventually, we'll find it. I'm just along to make sure that nobody dies in the process."

Gabriel entered the lunch room and waved at them. "Hey, Ohen, we need you."

"What's up?"

Gabriel nodded to Kerry and sat down beside her. "Well, this isn't the right system, but I hadn't expected to find it yet. We're not in the right zone."

Kerry frowned, "Zone?"

Gabriel nodded. "We have clues. We know from historical records how many years ago that the Betelgeuse supernova appeared in Earth's sky. When we get an accurate enough distance measurement to Betelgeuse, then we'll have a spherical zone where Earth has to be."

Kerry waved her hand. "That's math stuff. Not my specialty."

He nodded. "But once we reach a yellow star where the pattern of other stars around the Betelgeuse Nebula matches the constellation Orion that Abe drew in the Book, then that'll be our prime target."

Ohen said, "I take it that you don't see Orion?"

"The first thing I looked for. I can always find the Betelgeuse Nebula, but the stars around it aren't even close to what we're looking for.

"But, our secondary mission is to map these new star systems we visit, and that's where you come in. My team is scanning the sky looking for any planets, but if we could get you to take your boat a million miles away so we could get some parallax to work with, it would help."

Ohen nodded. "I knew this was coming. Good thing I ate."

. . .

He chose to take B3 ten light-seconds away, thrusting hard against Leonardo, since the starship was the only other mass in range his pressor beam could push against. He had to coordinate the maneuver, both acceleration and deceleration since it would also move the larger ship somewhat and disturb the photography. He pushed hard and decelerated the same way, coming to a stop an hour later.

Gabriel's group got a precise measurement of the distance between the two vessels using a low power pressor beam just to measure the round trip speed-of-light lag, and then Ohen was on his own to map the stars around him while the starship was doing the same job on their end.

It's quiet out here.

Ohen's boat was a four-sided flat wing, with tractor/pressor engines at each vertex. The design was a compromise mainly designed to travel through the atmosphere, but perfectly capable of pure vacuum travel between planets, moons and the starships. One other constraint was that it had to easily fit into the starship's loading dock, just like the original triangular Delense boats.

Ohen had chosen four engines, steerable in all three dimensions, for extra stability in the atmosphere, and they could all push together for situations like this where he needed a strong acceleration.

The camera was mounted near the center of mass. Ohen set the boat into a very slow roll, giving the camera nearly two hours to take pictures of the whole sky without too much motion blur.

Traditionally, the voice channel between boats was called the shouter, but that was just a translation of the Cerik name for it. The Book called it radio, and that's what the technicians called it. The camera's data was streaming back over radio to Gabriel's people to be analyzed.

Ohen's job was to sit quietly and wait until the astronomers were happy with the results. He had been told not to move around too much, since even that would introduce some wiggle in the star patterns. He sat strapped into his seat with even the floor gravity turned off, reading a book.

The book, recommended by Kerry, was an analysis of U'tanse population density and the probability that a hiver outbreak would happen.

It was disturbing. The author's analysis was that any U'tanse community over ten thousand individuals was more likely than not to have the nucleus of a telepathic hive mind. The list of historical events tended to back that up. During the slavery period when Cerik controlled all of the U'tanse communities, there were incidents where only a few isolated and despondent U'tanse merged telepathically.

Chase-on-Ha had a population just over eight thousand. Ohen wondered just how much danger his home town was in.

In contrast, the Book told of an Earth with billions of people, with cities numbering in the millions of inhabitants. The book he was reading made the case that a high density population of telepaths was self-limiting. All it took was a cluster of people who had lost hope for the people involved to give up their individuality and cling to the comfort of shared thoughts and become a hive. Once their numbers reached a critical level, then to preserve the hive, they aggressively recruited the unwilling to join their numbers, and the combined minds of the hive had formidable telepathic powers that could overwhelm others.

Ohen hadn't given it a lot of thought before, but over their history the U'tanse scattered thinly. Those on the planet Ko lived on numerous isolated islands. The moon of Ha had several cities, but Chase-on-Ha was the largest of them. The various space-based installations were all small communities.

He'd never really wondered why there was such a strong push to find habitable planets and found new colonies when the total population of the U'tanse was probably under two million. He guessed someone had been thinking about the hiver problem for a long time. It was a distasteful realization that there just might be a design problem with the U'tanse people. They had to spread out to thin their population or they would self-destruct.

There were two major colonies on the native planet of the Uuaa. The Ba had welcomed the U'tanse as well, but their massive oceanic world wasn't really suitable for more than just a diplomatic outpost. During his lifetime, there was always news of a new space colony either in the Ko system, or in one of the systems explored by the Cerik. But it had never occurred to him why people would move to whole new star systems when there was plenty of space on Ha just by expanding the size of the existing cities.

After four hours, there was a shouter message from Gabriel.

"Ohen, we've got good data, but my assistant Mary wants another pass. Are you willing to hang in there for another two hours?"

"Yes, I'll wait. It's nice and peaceful out here. Maybe I'll take a nap. Let me know when I can come back home."

"Okay, thanks. By the way, we're already seeing probable planets. The big scope has already checked out two of them. Gas giants out of the habitable zone. But maybe there are more candidates."

"That's good news. Now go away, I'm reading."

...

Four days after returning to Leonardo and doing an extra check of B3's systems—just to be safe—Ohen was in the Display Room with his crew, all three of them.

Abel bar Trook was his primary assistant and he'd wanted a look at the new planets. Paul and June wanted to come along as well.

The Display Room was a lunchroom right next to the command deck. It had the main display mirrored on a ten-foot-tall wall so that even on break, the captain and others could keep an eye on their status.

Of course any of the starship crew could come there as well if something interesting was going on.

"It's a water planet," said Pam the cook, as she fixed their plates. "They're looking for islands."

The big blue planet, capped with white ice at the poles, was a colorful spectacle. One of the navigators from the next table over said, "It's an oxygen/nitrogen atmosphere very close to what we're looking for. We'd have never discovered it without the boat's mapping. Thanks."

Ohen asked, "Are we going to attempt a landing?"

"That's up to the captain, but I don't know. Without land, it would be risky."

Paul said, "We could always land on the ice caps, I suppose."

Ohen had his own thoughts. The whole point of discovering a new planet was to find a place where people could live. Settling on an ice cap would need lots of support to protect people from the low temperatures and provide greenhouses for crops. Floating islands might be a possibility in warmer zones, but either option had problems. Were there any advantages in living in such protected habitats on a water world, compared to the space colonies they'd already tried? Without land where crops could be grown and metal ores mined, it would be expensive to expand.

It was a little disappointing that they'd already used one of their leap engine hops just to get closer to this planet, rather than move on to a new star system, but that hadn't been his call. All they could tell from their original position had been that it was the right sized planet with an oxygen atmosphere in the habitable zone. He'd have probably made the same decision.

He said, "It might be a paradise planet for the people who come back to explore the planet more closely. But we're a different kind of exploratory mission. I'd bet we take lots of pictures and move on."

And it wasn't long before the word came. Navigation needed to finalize their next leap projections. Gabriel's crew hurried off to take another look at their star charts. Those tasked with documenting the new planet hurried to gather as much data as possible. Maybe another starship would return to this water world someday, and they would need as much data as possible when they did.

Spores

"Get back inside!" Ohen yelled over the boat's shouter. Dell and Stan hurried back to the airlock door. Stan was coughing hard, overloading his spacesuit's oxygen system.

The two men got in and Ohen sealed the outer door and rinsed the interior with a water shower and pumped up the pressure inside to make sure nothing was leaking in.

"Hang on! I'm taking off."

With the two men trapped in the airlock, Ohen lifted B2 off from their landing site. The cameras outside showed a circular cloud spreading away from them as their engines grabbed air from above and threw it down to the ground.

As soon as they were up and on course for higher altitude, Ohen said, "Dell, stay in your suit. I'm going to be flushing the airlock to get rid of the spores.

He pumped more water and air through the system, venting it to the outside. Ohen got into his own spacesuit. No telling just how toxic these spores were, and how much they might infiltrate the boat.

Dell said, "Stan looks bad. His eyes are rolling."

"Go ahead and get his helmet off. I've got fresh air moving through the airlock, moving ceiling to floor. Keep him upright as much as possible."

Ohen glanced at his consumables. He could keep exhausting air to the outside for another two hours at best. He'd need to start pumping the air through the filters and hoping that the spores were large enough that they could be contained that way.

Captain Foster's voice came over the shouter, "What's going on?"

The starship was about five light-seconds out, beyond this planet's three small moons.

Ohen reported, "Stan got a sniff of the local air and determined that it was full of aromatic spores. Just a few seconds later, he started coughing and is still in distress. Both Dell and Stan are in the airlock and I've lifted off. I'm flushing the airlock and using the rinse to get rid of as many of the spores as possible."

After the radio delay, the captain said, "It was toxic within a few seconds? How bad is it?"

"I don't know yet. I'm going to be letting them inside where we can give Stan some medical aid. Dell and I will be staying in our suits."

He opened the inner door and helped Dell move Stan to the couch. He was still coughing. Ohen frowned. Contaminated phlegm was being splattered all over. "Get a breathing mask on him." Dell moved to comply.

Ohen and Dell deliberately dropped their ineda so telepaths on the starship could see through their eyes. Almost immediately, Kerry was in his mind.

"How good are your healing skills?"

Ohen sighed.

"Practical training."

"It will have to do. Can you risk getting skin-to-skin contact?"

Ohen winced and unsealed his glove. He put his hand on Stan's face. The man's body was burning up.

"Dell, help me get his suit off."

Dell took the suit and stashed it in the airlock while Ohen followed Kerry's instructions, probing into Stan's body with his clairvoyant sight. Kerry gave him directions, which he struggled to follow. The spores had triggered a violent allergic reaction and Stan's body was doing everything it could to expel the intruders.

The problem was that the reactions were so extreme that Stan's breathing and heart rate were overreacting. Ohen had to use his psychokinesis abilities to inhibit certain immune responses and to calm down the tensed muscles.

Kerry tried to explain what she was asking him to do, but he'd never received that training and the words were nonsense to him. Luckily, connected mind to mind as they were, it was as if she were doing the work using his skills. He'd not be able to do it without her, but together they got Stan down to a labored, but stable, breathing and heart rate.

Ohen washed his hand carefully and slipped his glove back on. He didn't feel any reaction to the spores, but he'd have to be alert for any sign.

The captain said, "Ohen, I know we need to get Stan back on Leonardo for better medical care, but I cannot risk bringing a load of spores back into the ship."

"I understand that. Dell and I can stay inside our suits for as long as we can keep replenishing our air from the boat's supplies, but I'll work on how to sterilize the boat."

With Dell monitoring Stan's situation, Ohen checked on the boat's autopilot. They'd climbed a third of the way out of the atmosphere. He slowed them to a hover. Until he knew what to do next, they didn't need to be traveling.

Carefully, he opened the inner door to the airlock and collected a thick dollop of Stan's phlegm from inside his spacesuit helmet and sealed it in a specimen container. He stowed the jar and then stared at Stan's suit for a moment. He regretted the loss, but he wrapped the suit tightly and propped it up against the outer door. The inside of that suit would be the hardest place to clean. Better to just get rid of it. There was a spare in the boat if they needed it.

He went back inside.

"How is Stan?"

Dell shrugged. "He's breathing a little better, but he's unconscious."

Ohen nodded. Kerry had predicted that reaction.

He triggered the shouter. "Captain, I'm going to jettison Stan's space suit and do what I can to clean the boat. After that, I'll rendezvous with the Leonardo."

"Good. I'll see what we can do to help, but until I'm satisfied we aren't letting something deadly into the ship, you'll have to quarantine in the boat outside the dock."

"Got it. I'll keep you updated."

He didn't blame the captain. It was simple math to preserve the fifty or so people aboard the starship over the three of them. It would be up to him to make sure they stayed alive until all the questions were answered.

...

Just above the atmosphere, Ohen opened the outer door and sent the spacesuit tumbling out into the vacuum. They were a bit slower than orbital velocity, so he knew it would burn up in the atmosphere.

"Strap yourself in, Dell. We're going back into the atmosphere ourselves."

Ohen guided the B2 into the atmosphere at a shallow angle, flying the wing until the atmospheric friction caused the hull to glow red. Carefully, he rotated the ship so that each side got to be the leading edge and the entire hull had been scalded.

Dell asked, "Has anyone named this planet?"

"Not that I know of. Why?"

"Well they call it the Fires of Koee when a boat burns up in Ko's atmosphere. I just want to be sure."

Ohen eased up on his angle. He shook his head. "We aren't going to burn up. I've got this under control."

There was a shriek as the high speed blast caught some imperfection on the hull. Ohen changed the angle again and accelerated, pushing out into thinner air.

Dell nodded. "Just keep telling me that."

...

As they approached the starship, Ohen brought the B2 to a halt about fifty feet from the Leonardo. A man in a spacesuit floated over and when Ohen opened the outer airlock door for him, he retrieved the sample bottle with a grappler arm and took it back to the ship for examination.

Ohen and Dell settled in for a long wait, hoping their suit's water and food paste would hold them long enough.

Half a day after they arrived, Stan woke up and Dell gave him food and water.

"You're still ... *cough* ... in your suits?"

Dell said, "Well I'm not about to get your spit all over me."

There was another coughing fit, but he got it under control.

Over the shouter, the captain asked Stan questions.

"Yeah, I knew the instant I smelled it and my nose wrinkled up that it had been a bad idea to open my suit. I tried to seal my helmet but it was just too strong."

Foster sighed. "We're writing the exploration procedures as we go along. You'll have a whole chapter talking about how stupid that was."

"Sorry."

And after that, it was a long wait. Ohen disassembled part of the air recycling system to extract an ultraviolet tube and made a portable gun with it. With Stan's face blindfolded and Dell and Ohen's solar filters in place, they sterilized every surface inside the boat and inside the airlock.

And then he had to put the air recycler back together again.

On the next day, Ohen asked, "Captain, may I have permission to remove my spacesuit? Dell can last a bit longer, but I've used all the food in my suit and I'm starving. Stan doesn't seem to be getting any worse."

Captain Foster chuckled. "I can imagine, what with your size, but hang on just a little longer. Kerry is coming here with the results of the lab tests on your killer spores."

"Don't take too long."

It was another few minutes. Kerry spoke over the shouter, "We got the spores Stan coughed up into the lab and tried everything. Some we took apart down to the molecules and I've got to say, about two thirds of the proteins are close relatives to what we have, but some are totally different. The good news, I guess, is that we could not make them sprout. They were totally inert in all kinds of growing media, including a close analog of Stan's lung tissue."

Stan gave a weak cheer.

Ohen said, "Then it was just an allergic reaction?"

"Probably. The alien spores had enough common features with our own allergens that Stan's system reacted strongly to them. Stan isn't going to start sprouting mushrooms and infecting other people."

Dell asked, "So we can come in?"

The captain said, "You can, in your spacesuits, but B2 is going to be staying in this system until a better-equipped exploratory mission returns. Ohen, I'll want you to power the B2 down. Drain the water tanks and leave just a low-power beacon running. We might want to find it again in a few years."

Ohen couldn't object to Foster's precautions. They had four boats and rarely used more than one at a time. They had wasted three of their hops on this system; one to get to the star and two more to get close to the planet. It had looked so much like their idea of Earth that it had been so tempting, but if U'tanse couldn't breathe the air, then it was time to move on, and that meant just three more hops before they had to go home.

Stan, in a new spacesuit, was helped across the gap by Dell as Ohen moved the B2 to a safe distance and began dumping the water and making sure that the boat, even after being frozen solid abandoned in space, would still be able to come back active if necessary. He started a simple radio beacon, a simple ping broadcast every ten seconds. It ought to last thousands of years.

Lastly, he made a log entry on paper, describing the situation with the spores and Kerry's analysis and left it sticking out of a cabinet. If the person or entities who discovered B2 could read or decode English, then it would give them a head start.

He shut every other system down, including the lights and floor gravity, and floated to the airlock. He bled the air down to vacuum with the manual override and left the outer door open.

He was about a thousand feet from the Leonardo.

"This is Ohen, I'm going to jump back to the ship. If I miss, I'll yell."

"Don't miss."

"Yes, Captain."

The Shattered System

Gabriel was sweating. After the last fiasco, when they leapt from the Spore system, something had been off in their calculations. They'd arrived much too far from the target star. After four days of remapping and recalculations, they didn't find any planets demanding a closer look.

So Gabriel pulled out all the stops, examining the closest stars, looking for a yellow sun in the direction his constellation simulations indicated.

He pointed. "I think that blue star is Rigel from the Book. I can't prove it, but Father Abe knew a few astronomy details. Of the four primary stars of the Orion constellation, Betelgeuse, before the supernova, had been a red supergiant and Rigel was a blue supergiant. Betelgeuse was at the upper left and Rigel was the lower right as viewed from Earth. At the short distances we've been covering with the leap engines, this blue supergiant has been moving closer to the Betelgeuse Nebula and although none of the other stars match Abe's hand-drawn map, I do think we're getting closer to Earth's neighborhood."

"How close?"

Gabriel winced. "Somewhere in the closest hundred stars. But still, we know Sol, Earth's sun, was yellow and not a binary. Cross your fingers Ohen. Either this leap or the next, we've got to either find Sol or have a strong pointer for the next expedition."

Ohen sighed. The next expedition just might take another fifty years to be approved. After the mistakes they'd made already, the Council might not be willing to risk a new expedition with the same people.

The captain's voice rang out, "Leap in ten seconds."

Ohen stared at the stars on the display and then there was the faintest of glitches. He could see that some of them had shifted.

Gabriel reached for the telescopes aiming controls, centering the view on the Betelgeuse Nebula. There was a groan. The star pattern sort of looked like Orion, but there were too many bright stars in the view.

Ohen looked at Gabriel, ready to give him supporting words, but the navigator had his eyes glued to the image.

"Ohen, I think one of those is a planet and if you ignore that bright white star, Orion is very nearly spot on. I've got to get your boat out there to give us better measurements. How quickly can you be ready?"

The captain approved and Ohen was back on B3, pushing out to ten light-seconds again.

This time, infected with Gabriel's enthusiasm, Ohen spent the time watching the star field slide slowly by as his telescope took its pictures and radioed them back.

After a bit, he got on the shouter. "Gabriel, is that red star a planet?"

Twenty seconds later, he replied, "Which red star? But Ohen, the initial analysis says this is a very cluttered system. I've already got five planets marked and there are numerous smaller dots. I'm going to ask you to stay at it a little longer. I hope you brought dinner."

"Well, keep me updated. It's quiet out here."

"Will do. But busy… later."

A few hours later, Gabriel sent him a star chart with local items annotated. There were indeed several planets. Two gas giants had ring systems. There were three rocky planets close enough to the star to be in the habitable zone.

But it was disturbing to see all the possible asteroids. A lot of those little lights were just numbers, indicating rocks of various sizes, and they were in all directions.

"Gabriel, did we just leap into an asteroid belt?"

"It looks like it. Some of them are pretty close. Captain is sending out B1 to visit one that's maybe five miles in diameter. Dell is in charge, with some geologists along for the ride."

"Tell them to go slow. I wouldn't have pushed off as fast as I did if I'd known how cluttered it is out here."

"Already noted. Can you do two more sweeps and then make your way back?"

"Yes. Did you notice that red planet? It looks funny."

"That's because sometime in recent history it was slammed hard. It's glowing red. The whole surface is molten. Our spectral readings of its atmosphere contains a lot of sulfur and iron vapor in addition to the usual stuff.

"I suspect this whole system was recently disturbed and it's still in the process of settling down. I doubt any of the worlds are habitable."

...

Ohen took most of a day to return to the starship, glued to the radar indicator that just might warn him of rocks in his path. If space was full of asteroids, then there wasn't any guarantee it was clear of smaller rocks. Even a pebble would be disastrous if he hit it at high speed.

I was just lucky on the way out. My pressor beam was pushing against the Leonardo to speed me up, and it might also have been pushing the clutter out of my way ahead of me. By the time I decelerated, that column of space had been cleared.

But the tractor beam pulling him back to the starship might also pull any rubble that might have wandered back into that zone of space toward him. It just wasn't a good risk to move fast in the middle of a new asteroid belt.

By the time he reached the ship, he had to wait for two hours outside the docking doors. B1 had returned from its geology survey and the dock was filled with people wanting to get a look at all the samples they had collected.

When the dock was cleared and he settled B3 down beside B1 and they restored the air, people were already coming back to look.

Dell waved him over, with a smug look on his face. "Ohen, you've got to see this."

B1 was stacked with several hundred pounds of rocks. Harter and Don, the geologists that had gone on the expedition to the asteroid were carefully working through the pile and sorting their samples.

Harter picked up a rock and grinned. "I think this is copper. Add it to the common stack." Don nodded, peered at it carefully. "There are traces of other metals here as well." He tossed it into a bin already containing similar samples.

Ohen asked, "Lots of metals?"

Harter sighed and shook his head. "That's just the tip of the iceberg. The asteroid we visited is just a rock pile. Some catastrophe shattered some planet-sized body that had already formed metal and mineral lode bodies. It's like a whole planet has been mined and the results tossed out here in the vacuum for us to pick up. I've seen gold, silver, copper, iron of course, ruthem, what looks like aluminum compounds, titanium ore, and what looks like a lot of the gold family."

He picked up another. "I just bet this is sliferium traces. There's no telling what's out here."

Ohen nodded, although he wasn't sure what sliferium was. In the Book, Abe had listed and described about thirty elements, but said that he was sure there were nearly a hundred found naturally on Earth. As the U'tanse had discovered some of the unknown elements that didn't match Abe's list, they had to be named and categorized. Ohen knew his boat design relied on titanium and magnesium and there was even some technical debate if the elements called by those names were the same that Abe had listed.

But Ohen immediately realized just how valuable a discovery this was. The vast reaches of Ko were Cerik hunting grounds and off limits to mining. While there were mines on Ha, many elements were very expensive.

Don said, "I'm going to ask the captain to make sure that asteroid is marked on the star charts. We've got to come back with another expedition and fill up the holds with this stuff."

Ohen said, "If one asteroid has so much riches, then there are probably others."

Don nodded, beaming.

Probably this one discovery would make the whole expedition a success, even if they never found another planet.

By the time Ohen made his way to the Display Room, Captain Foster was there waiting for him. He waited until he got a plate from the cook and sat down with him.

He was straight to business. "Can you boat designers make a larger, cargo-oriented boat that will still fit the starship docks?"

Ohen nodded. "Yes, certainly. I took a good look at the dock specifications before I ever built this current set. A boat could be three times taller, twice as wide, and up to ten to twelve times longer and still fit through the hatchway into the dock. The general purpose boats would have to be moved out of the way, but a much larger, cargo-oriented boat is certainly possible.

"There are some very old designs of larger boats still in the system that were considered back during the Ba repatriation voyages. They were never built because the larger Ba that wanted to return to their home world chose to separate into smaller versions of themselves. Yes, it certainly can be done."

Foster nodded. "I want as detailed a proposal as possible on hand when we return to the Ko system. People are talking like access to this much metal could boost the U'tanse economy several times over. There are cargo holds on the Leonardo that have never been used, and I can imagine having them filled with treasure would make the Council much more welcome to the idea of another expedition."

Ohen nodded. "Be sure to name the system something glamorous, like 'Treasure Star' or something to catch the popular attention."

Foster winced. "Maybe something a bit more elegant than that. But, you're right. We need popular support for something like this."

"I'll see if I can mock up a design for a cargo boat before long."

The captain nodded and hurried off to some other urgent task.

Ohen waved down Abel, his assistant, and as they ate, they discussed the kind of cargo boat that might be useful for mining transport, both here in this system and to get the cargo to the manufacturing sites in the Ko system. Abel was enthused with the idea and Ohen told him to get started on it.

A new boat was always an exciting project, but he was happy to let his assistant take the lead. For some reason, piloting the boat himself and getting out here in the stars had become more intriguing to him than engineering. It just might be a let down to return to boat design.

Constellations

Gabriel wasn't at the ship-wide meeting to discuss the mining opportunities and to name the system.

Ohen found the navigator peering over his computer display, comparing different views of the star field and making annotations.

"This star is now named 'Glitter'."

He nodded absently. "There were people with their ineda down. I heard."

"What would your vote have been?"

Gabriel shrugged. "Doesn't matter. I'm still looking for Sol."

Ohen peered over his shoulder. "Have you located it?"

"I'd stake my reputation it's one of these five yellow stars." He highlighted the choices.

Ohen looked at them. "I can't tell any difference between them and the rest of the stars. There's just too many of them."

"Yeah. But with all the mapping we've done, I can know with confidence that these stars will have nearly the same view of Orion as we have right now."

"I thought Orion was wrong."

"Yes, but if you remove all the planets and asteroid dots, then the only big flaw is this big white star in the way. Now, it looks like all the major stars of Orion are hundreds of light years away, or more, so it should look nearly the same for all of these close-by yellow star candidates."

"And the white star?"

Gabriel smiled. "It's pretty close as well, and what's more, in the Book, in the star charts Abe drew, there's another constellation near Orion and it has a bright white star in it called Sirius. From here, I don't really see that constellation.

"Maybe, just maybe, this one is Sirius. I've tried to calculate what Sirius would look like next to Orion in each of these yellow stars."

"Is there a winner?"

Gabriel shrugged. "Not a clear one. And really, I only get one chance. If we had more energy in the power cells to make more leaps, I'd visit all of them in turn, but we don't."

Ohen frowned. "Couldn't we use the planets here to set up a charging beam and collect enough energy to charge Leonardo enough to make more jumps. I realize that's not in the missions plan to make more than ten leaps, but technically—"

Gabriel shook his head. "I already had that discussion with the captain. He vetoed the idea. This system is just too cluttered. Setting up a charging beam from this location wouldn't be ideal in any case and we're too likely to suck up a stray rock and damage the ship.

"He promised me that if the next leap doesn't land us in Sol system, then he'd consider it, as long as we don't land in the middle of asteroids again."

...

It was frustrating, Ohen realized, to be able to see your target star and to be able to aim the ship at it precisely, but then knowing that the actual distance to leap was just a guess. Their triangulation efforts using a ten light-seconds baseline reduced the uncertainty a lot, but it still wasn't enough, as their poor showing on this expedition showed.

While Dell and the geologists made three more trips to that asteroid, loading up rocks to take home, Gabriel was checking and rechecking his calculations. Ohen took the opportunity to re-read parts of the Book.

Abe the Father had tried to learn everything he could about the starships and what the Cerik had done with them, just so he could write it all down for future generations.

The Cerik had been poor navigators, after they had exterminated their technical slave race, the Delense. Any star leap logged from a previous trip was easy to duplicate, but getting to a new star took trial and error when they overshot their destination, or fell too short. There was a comment in the Book about the Cerik mission that had located Earth. The Cerik had exhausted their leaps as well, only finding Earth at the last. It would have been an unsuccessful mission if Tenthonad, the Name of the ship, hadn't seized the opportunity to make the captured humans into a replacement slave race and formed the U'tanse.

Considering all the places they'd visited during this mission, Gabriel was doing a lot better visiting unknown stars than the Cerik, but it was too easy to compare the flawless leaps using previously logged coordinates with the error-prone leaps to unknown distant points of light.

The log of the original visit to Earth had obviously been scrambled by Abe or Sharon and that had been lucky for the human race, preventing the Cerik from ever duplicating that trip, but it also put the pressure on this mission. Only someone like Gabriel, tirelessly calculating distances from multiple maps, would ever be able to reconnect the U'tanse to the main body of the human race.

...

The groan in the Display Room was no different than on the command deck. When the image showing the Glitter star shifted, showing the new yellow star. It was if it shrunk. They had landed too far from the target.

Ohen sighed, "That's it then."

Kerry said, "I don't understand."

"The star looks tiny, but it's the same size star as Glitter, so that means we've landed so far away from it that we're well beyond the habitable zone. We've done that before, but corrected by making a small leap to get closer in. We can't do that this time because we have only one leap left—the one to take us back to Ko."

"Oh." She sounded disappointed. "How far out are we?"

"I don't know. But I bet it's my job to find out."

He got to his feet and went to speak to Gabriel before he came hunting for him.

Gabriel looked a lot more excited that he expected. The navigator glanced up as he walked in. "Can you see it?"

"The star?"

"No, the constellations! Just look at them." He brought up photographs of some of the maps Abe had drawn and put them up beside the images of the stars outside.

"Here is Orion, and it's perfect! There is Canis Major, with Sirius. Over here is the Big Dipper. There's Leo, and Cassiopeia, and Pegasus. Recognizable constellations in all directions.

"We have to be right on top of it. Either this star is Sol or that one over there."

Ohen squinted at the crude black on white images and tried to see them in the star fields. He could almost see them, but there were so many stars that sometimes the marker stars of the constellations were swamped out by the others.

Still, Gabriel was confident.

"So, you want me to take B3 out for a walk?"

"Oh yes! Identifying the right planets would cinch it."

...

This time, they were so far out that Ohen doubted there was even a speck of dust anywhere within range, so he had no fear going out to his designated distance at high speed. Soon he had the telescope sending images back to the starship.

He settled down at one of the viewports, looking at the stars with his bare eyes and trying to compare them to Abe's maps in his personal copy of the Book.

Orion was indeed unmistakable. Canis Major was supposed to represent a dog, some kind of slave-like hunting animal that was following Orion the Hunter.

Cassiopeia was supposedly a queen sitting on a chair, but in practical terms was just a big W in the sky, just like Pegasus was just a big square. He had no idea what a flying horse was supposed to look like. Or a regular horse for that matter.

I wonder if the fanciful images are more realistic when filtered through an atmosphere to remove all the lesser stars.

He was a little disappointed by it all. If this really was the ancestral human sky, shouldn't it resonate a little more? *But I guess star fields aren't encoded into genetic memory. They probably even shift over millions of years.*

He turned his head to look at the yellow star. It was plainly the dominant star in the sky, but it was so distant that it wasn't painful to look at. Somewhere close to it was the habitable zone—the region where the sun's energy would keep a planet warm enough for liquid water to flow.

He hoped the telescope on his boat would let Gabriel locate all the planets. Abe had described Sol's planets in some detail, so if they could match everything up, then that would bring a return starship expedition in short order, even if their current position made it impossible to go there themselves.

Ohen knew the math well enough to realize it was hopeless to recharge the leap engines from their current location. The whole point of recharging was to get positioned in between two much larger masses, like planets. Then, you set up a pressor beam or tractor beam to counter their relative motions. The planets' momentum overwhelmed your beams and caused a back-pressure that forced energy back into your energy cells.

But at their current position at the far edge of the star's system of planets, all of those planets would be on one side of the starship. There was no way to get in between any two of them.

He sighed, still staring off at the yellow sun.

He frowned. He shook his head. For an instant he thought he might have sensed thoughts off in that direction. But it was so far away.

Over to the side, there were thoughts leaking from the Leonardo's crew. An all-adult crew, with everyone practicing their ineda, meant there weren't a lot of thoughts leaking out, but there were always some. Unless telepathy was needed in an emergency, it was just common politeness for everyone to block their thoughts. No one would go around without ineda any more than they would walk the halls naked.

He focussed his thoughts back on the yellow sun and the area around it. *Maybe.*

If there were planets, there just might be intelligent beings living on them. Maybe even humans. But it was just a trace. Not something he could be sure of.

If this was Sol, and Old Earth was circling there nearby, then maybe this could be proof!

Solo Mission

Back aboard the Leonardo, they discussed their options.

Captain Foster shook his head. "We've got too many opinions and not enough proof. Gabriel claims to see all the constellations of Abe, but there are just so many stars that it could just be wishful thinking. Ohen claims to sense thoughts from the habitable zone planets, which is a really incredible claim at this distance, but no one else on the ship can sense them. Mary can see four gas giants, one with rings, which matches Abe's description of the Sol system, but only three central rocky planets, whereas Abe says there should be four."

Gabriel shook his head. "At least three! One could be behind the star, or too close for our telescopes to resolve it next to the glare of the star."

Foster continued, "And Kurt says he can't detect radio signals. The Book says that Earth was so radio-noisy that the signals should be detected far beyond the planetary system. So even if Ohen could detect thoughts, it's possible this is a different star system with different life-forms."

"But the constellations!"

"Give it a rest. Gabriel." The captain sighed. "Perhaps we might just consider that we've relying too much on notes that were written well over a thousand years ago. We all revere Abe, the Father of us all, but he was just a man and he said so in the Book he wrote. He made a special point of it.

"He was a man who was caught up in extraordinary events and had never planned to be the progenitor of the U'tanse. He hadn't studied ahead, as he said, and could only write about the 'common knowledge' he had in his head at the time. He said his constellations could be in error. It's written down there in the Book, but we have a tendency to believe that everything Abe ever wrote was perfect and error-free.

"But we're here now. We're stuck here and can't go closer for a better look. The only option we have is to push the button and go home. We have a successful expedition, what with all the new planets we've located and all the asteroid riches around Glitter."

Gabriel said, "I thought this mission was to locate Earth."

Foster nodded, "If we could. Only a few people thought that was ever a real chance, what with the information we started with."

Gabriel said, "Give me more time. If I can nail it down that we really have located Sol system then it won't just be a successful mission, it'll be historic. Really, what do we have to lose by waiting a few more days to push that button."

Foster sighed. "I suppose, but the geologists are itching to get home."

As the meeting broke up, Ohen went with Gabriel back to his computers. Ohen sighed, "Everyone wants to go home and show off the pretty rocks."

Gabriel grunted. "Abe once mentioned 'gold fever' in one of his essays, but never defined the term. I suspect it's like this. Everyone is itching to show off the treasure and it's like a fever."

Ohen shook his head. "I wish someone else could have sensed the distant thoughts like I did. But I can't even duplicate it now. The ship is too noisy with our own thoughts. Nobody believes me."

Gabriel glanced around at the empty room. "I believe you. I have to."

"What do you mean?"

"I can understand what the captain said. Abe's constellation maps did have errors, I know that."

Ohen frowned. "You said it was perfect."

The navigator shook his head. "In general, it is. But Foster was right, it was a hand-drawn map based on Abe's memories. The thing is—I've seen Abe's memories as he looked up at the night sky, and believe me, we're in the right place."

"You've seen his memories?"

Gabriel did another look around, but most of his people were taking a break, after long hours making the maps. They were a little burned out.

"Ohen, you see, my telepathy is a little slippery. Don't tell anyone, but back in my ancestry, there was a man who could see the future a little. I guess I've inherited some of that. All my life I've occasionally felt thoughts from other times. One time, I deliberately stretched my limits and made a brief contact with Abe himself."

"Then you could ask him!"

Gabriel shook his head. "No, never. For one thing Abe wasn't a telepath—no two-way conversation. For another, if I ever made deliberate contact with someone in the past, that would give them a glimpse into the future and open the gateway to all kinds of paradoxes. It's much too dangerous. I'm content to live under my ineda and pretend to be a tenner.

"But that one glimpse—his memory of the night sky from Earth—changed my whole life. That's what got me into astronomy in the first place. I've come to feel like my whole purpose in life was to locate our lost home planet. And now, to be so close to unlocking the mystery and have to turn around and go home—it's unbearable."

Ohen could sympathize with him. Perhaps it was his chore to take his boat out to map the stars. Perhaps it was that maddening hint of other thoughts in the far distance. Right now Ohen wondered what his purpose in life had become. He was jealous of Gabriel's sense of destiny. Ohen had been good at designing boats, but this search for humanity's home was so much more visceral. He really wanted to know the truth. He wanted to see Old Earth for himself.

He would love to know that finding it was his destiny.

But was it really impossible? Had they reached the limits of their capabilities and come up short?

...

Abel brought his new boat design for critique. Ohen nodded and then made a few suggestions.

"You've worked with Nell bar Hook at the Boat Center?"

Abel nodded, "She probably doesn't remember me, but I worked on her commuter-boat design."

"Well, keep her in mind as you make these plans. Sooner than you realize, you'll probably have to present them to her. She'll be the one to give the approval."

He frowned. "You won't go back to your position?"

Ohen paused. "Maybe not. Whether it's the followup mission back here, or some other expedition, I may just give up on the design business." He grinned. "Flying the boat is more interesting."

Abel shook his head. "Not for me. But if Nell is the person I have to impress, then I might want to make a few changes to the command console."

"Like what?"

Abel bent over the diagrams and explained.

...

Captain Foster frowned as he sat at his desk. "It sounds crazy."

"I think it's reasonable." Ohen was confident. The plan had come together in a dream and he was excited about it.

Foster shook his head. "The star is a long ways away. A boat could never make it on its own."

Ohen tapped his computer display. "I've run the numbers, and I know this boat better than anyone. With one person to support, I can stretch the food, water, and air to more than a year.

"If the Leonardo uses its beams to give me an initial boost, I believe I can make the habitable zone within four to six months. B3 has the good telescope. Just as soon as I can get a closer look at the inner planets, I should be able make a definitive call whether this is Sol System or not, and I can use the shouter to give you that information to take home."

"But you'd be stranded here! We can't go to your rescue, and we couldn't wait for you to return either—our supplies won't last that long."

"I can survive, especially if there really is a habitable planet with intelligent life on it. I can last years if necessary. And to be honest, I'm sure the Council will okay a return mission to Glitter in short order. You can come track me down then. I'll have the best boat ever made with all the gear I'll need.

"Really, we risked a boat and three men to go visit Spore's planet. This is much less of a risk with a much more important goal. Don't you think the U'tanse deserve this chance to find their home? Our home?"

...

It took days to convince the captain, although half of the crew thought he was crazy and that it was a suicide mission.

Gabriel gripped his arm. "You'll go crazy living by yourself all that time. I should go along with you."

"The numbers won't work with a two-man crew. Besides, you need to stay and analyze the images I send back to you. And, by the way, keep the captain from pushing that home button before we've gotten our answers."

Gabriel gave a long sigh. "I'm already pretty unpopular for delaying our return. I hope they get used to this longer delay."

Ohen nodded. "Help me load this crate." Air could be recycled, as could water, but unless he wanted to set up a hydroponic garden, he'd need as much food as he could pack.

...

Ohen couldn't feel a thing as Leonardo's pressor beam engines gave him that initial push, but the view out the window was gut-wrenching as the starship vanished almost instantly. Almost was the key. He could just barely detect it as their distance separated so quickly.

Well, that's it. I can't back out now.

Leonardo had pushed B3 with engines powerful enough to move the starship from planet to planet, but the starship was so much more massive than the boat, giving the major velocity change to the smaller mass.

After the initial push, he was racing towards the yellow sun fast enough to get there in seven months. It was up to his own engines to speed that up somewhat.

But first, he wanted to take a set of pictures of the planets. He needed to do that on a regular basis to keep his promises. Gabriel wanted them taken when he was just cruising, not under acceleration, so he'd have to chop up his boosts into sections.

An hour later, he radioed the images.

"Thanks, Ohen. I'll be doing what I can at this end. Best of luck."

It was already so far from the starship that a conversation was out of the question. Ohen carefully aimed his four engines at the largest of the gas giants, Jupiter if this was indeed Sol system, and engaged the tractor beams. It would take some time for the beams to connect with the planet's mass and begin the actual acceleration. Nobody could beat the speed of light—except that unknown alien race who made the leap engines.

Sorry

"I'm sorry," the distance made Gabriel's voice sound a little noisy, "It's not Old Earth."

Ohen nodded to himself. He'd tried to find any excuse for what he'd seen in the telescopic images. But after getting better images each time he turned the engines off, he couldn't deny that the blue and white planet he so hoped was Earth actually had three moons—one big one and two smaller ones. Abe was very clear that Earth had one large moon, and that was it. He'd written about it several times, comparing it to Ha, Ko's single large moon.

Gabriel continued, "In addition to the three moon problem, Mary's analysis shows that the primary moon of the blue planet has an atmosphere and Abe said it was airless. In addition, the red planet also seems to have a thick atmosphere, and Abe had mentioned only a thin, nearly nonexistent atmosphere on Mars.

"When you add the other anomalies we've seen, like that highly elliptical cometary belt that was mentioned nowhere in the Book, I have to admit this is not Sol system. It breaks my heart, but I can't deny the data. Sol has to be one of the other nearby yellow stars." He sighed. "We'll have to wait until the next expedition to find out for sure."

Captain Foster took over the speaker. "Well, you gave it your best shot, and I'm sure the Council will appreciate it. But we really can't wait here any longer. I'll wait for your confirmation, and I'd appreciate it if we double-checked your beacon code, so we can hunt you down when we return, but then, we'll be leaving."

Ohen said nice words in return, trying to let them leave with a clear conscience.

But then, they were gone. He was still close enough that he sensed when all those minds vanished. *I'm really on my own, now.*

He let himself soak up the isolation. How did he really feel about it, now that it was far too late to change his mind?

Surprisingly, he didn't feel desolated at being left behind. Maybe he was just an outsider at his core. This wasn't too bad.

And his job was to stay alive until they returned. He'd still take pictures for when they came to pick him up, but he had to focus on remaining alive even with dwindling food stocks.

But there were people of some kind up ahead. Alone in his boat, the distant murmur of thoughts was more distinct. He certainly couldn't tease out the thoughts of any one person, but he no longer doubted his senses. If there were people of any kind there, even if it was another Ba planet with swimming armored plates, then there should be an ecosystem with food of some kind. All he'd have to do is find out what was poisonous and what wasn't.

I just hope it's not another Spore planet.

But the problem now was that he was traveling too fast and aimed wrong. Pulling at the Jupiter-like planet had altered his path so that he would pass the sun too far from habitable zone planets. He'd zip past with only the opportunity to take some blurry photos. He had to kill his speed if he was every going to be able to land.

He did some vector diagrams and plugged in some numbers. If he could push off the ringed planet, the Saturn analog, then for as long as he could store the energy that would generate, he could slow down and bend his path back toward the inner planets. Once he got closer he could choose which of the four (the innermost planet had finally appeared) looked most inviting, and refine his path more at that time.

Ohen set up the beams and started a pressor beam, pushing at the Saturn-like planet. But in its orbit, the planet was moving toward him and his puny little beam couldn't stop a planet, so just like a spring being compressed, his beam began building up energy, which was quickly shunted over to the boat's power cells.

He could keep that up for four days before reaching his power cell limits. After that, he'd need a new strategy for getting rid of his speed.

...

Gabriel had been right that a man could go crazy traveling alone in a boat for months on end, but Ohen had some tricks up his sleeve.

Part of his confidence was that he'd done it before. During the design phase of building these boats, Ohen had spent weeks at a time living in various prototypes as they refined the design. He was already used to the limits of walking around in tight quarters, and this was his design. It would have been much worse on a boat designed for smaller people.

Another problem was exercise. Ohen was already committed to pacing and weight lifting under the floor gravity of the boat, powered by a matrix of small, rapidly cycling tractor beams that gave the illusion of planetary gravity inside the cabin of the boat. But although the default gravity was the surface gravity of Ko, which even was standard in the Ha cities, Ohen wanted to be ready for when he reached his target planet, probably the blue one that most closely resembled Earth. And he could only guess what its surface gravity would be.

Since his astronomy skills weren't up to estimating the density of the planet, he could only plug in some probable numbers. At the upper range, gravity on the blue planet just might be 1.3 times the gravity of Ko. So Ohen adjusted the boat's floor gravity to 1.4 and just lived with it.

Muscle aches gave him a clear conscience to concentrate on other parts of his journey.

...

At other times in his life, he'd been isolated, but not quite as much as this time. His size, and the reputation of his family worked to his advantage at times, but in day-to-day life, he'd been slow to acquire close friends. There were telepaths that took no effort to block their thoughts and their buddies knew every thing that concerned them. Others, like Ohen, had learned ineda at a young age and lived like tenners, keeping their mind blocked off and not really trying to listen in to other thoughts.

It had helped him academically to have a disciplined mind. People judged him on his results—good grades, productive product schedules, and on his creative boat designs.

And he made friends, school friends, work friends. But when he left school, he left those friends behind. When he left Boat Center, he left those co-workers behind as well. Perhaps he'd meet them again, but he wasn't the kind of guy who kept in touch telepathically with those he left behind.

He'd made new friends on the Leonardo, and now those friends were out of range as well. It might just be a long time before he had the opportunity to make a new circle of friends.

He'd been isolated before. He could handle it. He still had work to do.

He fed his astronomical photos into his computer's memory, and they were tagged with date and time, but as far as his daily routine, he quickly lost track of the calendar. Day followed day. The deceleration beam aimed at the ringed planet filled up his power cells and so he just coasted for a while, until he could get into position between two planets at the right time to make another adjustment.

He was really grateful for the cometary ring, which was out of the plane where all the planets moved. Using his beams on it allowed him to move his boat into the planetary plane.

But sometimes, he just sat for hours looking out the window with the internal lights turned off, just watching the stars and the planets with his own eyes.

He came to recognize the constellations as easily as Gabriel had, and yes there were some differences between what he could see and Abe's drawings, but it was trivial.

At his closest approach to the ringed planet, he could actually see the rings without telescopic help. He began to identify the largest of the moons around the Jupiter planet.

And he was fascinated by the crescent phases of those inner planets. He recognized it was just a natural part of sunlight falling on a planet closer to the star than he was.

He was staring intently at the fuzzy red planet, just making out the big ocean at the top when it happened.

There was a thought, clear as day. A farmer out in his field, well past sunset had gazed up at the sky.

I wonder if there are any people living out there among the stars.

And just as quickly as it came, the brief telepathic connection vanished.

Ohen gasped. He was sure that had been a human, a real human, who had that momentary link.

How can that be?

He grabbed his copy of the Book, a thick volume containing all the essays Abe had written for his descendants. It wasn't too hard to locate what had been written about Mars.

It was all familiar. Mars was the fourth planet out from Sol. It was smaller than Earth with a surface gravity roughly one third of standard. Studied via telescope and even remote probes sent there by rockets, Mars had a very thin atmosphere, but had ice caps that changed with the seasons. A human couldn't live there without a space suit. The red color was probably because of iron oxide. There was no surface water on Mars.

Ohen pulled up his latest telescopic image of the red planet. While it definitely had a red tint, much of the surface not obscured by clouds was brown and green, hinting at vegetation. And it definitely had a large ocean, and maybe a couple of large lakes.

And that farmer was just standing out there on the surface breathing the air.

Either this wasn't Mars, or something very strange had happened to it in the years since Abe was captured by the Cerik.

Ohen was deeply puzzled.

Perhaps Abe was just very, very wrong in his description of Mars, and indeed the rest of the Sol system. But he had been fairly accurate in his description of the other sciences. U'tanse scientists had filled in many of the gaps, but they hadn't usually found anything wrong with Abe's essays.

Perhaps this was not the Sol system and somehow in the last millennium, humans had managed to travel to this nearby star system that shared so many likenesses to the Sol system and colonized this Mars lookalike. Maybe humans had invented their own starships. There had been billions of humans on Earth. In all that time, humanity's technology could have grown vastly more sophisticated than what the U'tanse had managed.

Or perhaps something radical had happened to change the planets of the Sol system itself. Something that he just couldn't imagine.

But the fact remains that there are humans living on this Mars. If my primary goal is to stay alive until the U'tanse come for me, then I can't do better than go there.

He had to change plans. His new target planet was the fourth planet. He needed to make course corrections as soon as possible to get there quickly and safely.

Planet of War

B3 was still going much too fast. The problem was that he had too much energy in his power cells. That boost the Leonardo had given him had greatly shortened his travel time, but he still had to get rid of all that energy.

I don't want to have to burn it off in the atmosphere.

He'd done it once on the Spore planet, but he didn't like it. And he had so much velocity now that he'd have to make multiple passes through the Martian atmosphere to get rid of it, and one mistake could convert the B3 to glowing gas.

The only other way he could think of was to use the boat's engines to speed something else up.

He carefully charted the current position of all the planets in the system. There were several intersection points, where B3 would be in line between two planets. There was one coming up soon. He'd be between the blue planet—he still couldn't quite bring himself to call it Earth—and the big Jupiter-like planet. An inner planet always traveled faster than the outer planet, so he could slip between them and waste his excess energy pushing on the blue planet to make it go every so slightly faster. It was just the opposite of making a charging beam. By the time he moved out of position, he could have the energy cells down to half-power, ready to be charged back up as he slowed down approaching the red planet.

He set a timer and had everything aligned. He started the beams.

Just minutes into the process, just before the beam was fully established, something happened.

The lights flickered. A status alarm went off, and the beam collapsed.

"What?"

He almost startled himself speaking out loud. He'd gotten out of the habit.

He stumbled to the controls and tried to make sense of it all.

The energy cells, which had been so full that it was nearly dangerous, were now totally empty. B3's lights and environment systems were running on batteries alone.

If my beam system is dead, then so am I. He'd sail past any possible rendezvous with any of the planets and his batteries would run out well before he had any chance of being rescued.

How long can I live on the batteries? It was only weeks, he knew. Rather than design the boat to carry massive batteries, the system was designed to keep the smaller batteries topped up by converting a trickle of beam energy into electricity for charging. But now all that beam energy was gone. Where did it go?

The big puzzle was that if his beam system died, then it should have gone out with a bang, adding a momentary bright new star to the night sky of those planets. But he was still here.

Was the beam power still there, but just hidden by an instrumentation glitch?

It was time to run extensive diagnostics. Luckily, he'd built the ship and written the manual. He knew how to start.

...

Ohen had to feed a little of the battery power into the main power cells, just to make the status board read anything at all. It still looked like zero power, but at least it was talking to him. The power cells, which stored power as paired beams in conflict, just appeared drained, but still functional.

Energy vanishing with no reason was something that would drive a physicist crazy. It was impossible.

Ohen was more of an engineer than a scientist. He'd had physicists tell him in all seriousness that tractor/pressor beams and the leap engines were totally impossible as well.

Energy vanishing without a trace was a major puzzle, and very annoying, but as long as impossible things played by the rules and he could build things that behaved as predicted, he was happy.

He could set aside the impossibility of what had just happened and work toward getting the boat functional.

The window where he was aligned between the two planets had passed. But now, if his power cells were empty then he could put a braking beam on any large mass.

He chose the second planet, because he needed a push in that vector to get him closer to the Mars planet.

Very cautiously, he set up a weak beam that barely attempted to slow him down and monitored the back surge of power very carefully.

He waited through the speed-of-light delay with his finger hovering over the button to cancel the whole thing if the system showed any instability.

But then the trickle of power arrived and B3 slowed incrementally. He took a deep breath. Everything was working properly. There was just one big mystery, not a failure of his systems. He could work with that. He increased the braking beam and power flowed back into B3's system.

...

Ohen stared out the window at the Mars-like planet. But under the thick atmosphere showing various weather patterns, he could see a polar ice cap, a single large ocean and a couple of smaller seas or lakes and many rivers.

And just as the sun hit the land at the right angle, he could see a dotting of cities and agricultural lands. There was enough bare red land to give the planet a reddish tint at a distance, but up close, it was a colorful, vibrant planet full of life.

The everyday thoughts of humanity drifted across his mind; hunger, love, worry, and rage.

There were battles.

Ohen frowned. People were fighting other people. They were definitely not U'tanse.

Telepaths had conflicts—sometimes bitter ones—but it never escalated into physical battle. When the pain you inflict on someone else instantly rebounds on you, there's a strong aversion to taking out your anger on some-one's body. Everyone learned that as a toddler. It was instinctive.

The most deadly threats to the U'tanse, the Cerik and the hivers, had both been isolated and contained. There had been no battles—not since one of his ancestors had wiped out a hiver outbreak at the cost of his own life.

That was the tradeoff. For a telepath to choose to kill, it was a path to suicide.

Ohen carefully put the B3 into an orbit above the atmosphere. He really didn't want to land in the middle of some conflict. It would be bad even if he tried to stay out of the fighting.

But he would need to make a decision. He would need food eventually. He couldn't orbit forever.

...

It was a hard choice. From orbit, he couldn't easily follow individual thoughts, certainly not for long. But it was clear enough that war was an ordinary part of life. There were dozens of nations, all with borders that could change at any time.

Nations had been mentioned in the Book. There were groups of people with some common history or ancestry or language who identified themselves as distinct from the people on the other side of the river or some other boundary. At various times in Earth's history, wars over resources or land or some other issue had been common.

If the U'tanse show up here in significant numbers, will we be considered another nation to be fought?

Ohen had never really considered the problem. Obviously, the U'tanse would need land to live on and their own resources to support them. At least on this planet that was an instant danger flag.

I guess it's naïve to think we would be welcomed like long lost cousins and invited to stay.

Maybe it's my job to scout out the situation and find some kind of solution for when the Leonardo or some other starship arrives to collect me.

It helped to look at it as a technical problem to be solved.

Step one was to cobble together a radio beacon from his repair stores and put it in orbit. If he was going down to the surface, he needed to leave his marker on this planet for the searchers to find.

When he pushed it out the airlock, the little radio device broadcast the signal that he'd agreed to use, but it also included a warning:

"This planet is filled with humanity in conflict. Any landing must be done with extreme caution. One mistake and the U'tanse could find themselves at war with the rest of humanity. I'm going down to try to scout out the situation."

...

Finally, he had no more excuses for delay. After many orbits, he located a large plateau far from the more populated coastal cities. It was a place where there was more worry than rage. He chose a time where there were patches of clouds over his target zone and began the slow descent through the atmosphere.

It was interesting that this atmosphere was deeper than he'd experienced before. He wondered what led to that situation. The gas giants had immensely deep atmospheres, but the other planets he knew like Ko, and the home planets of the Uuaa and the Ba, and presumably Earth, had thinner atmospheres.

He guessed it was lucky. This Mars-like planet had less gravity, and breathable air demanded a certain pressure of oxygen at the surface. If it had a shallow atmosphere like Ko, the air would be too thin to breathe.

When the B3 settled down to subsonic speeds, he eased it into the clouds and coasted along so that he wouldn't be visible to the people on the surface.

It was nightfall when he located a forested area above a farming settlement. He eased the B3 down in a little meadow hardly larger than itself. The trees were high enough that the boat would be invisible from a distance.

He was down. Although he'd never used it before, his design had included an anti-tamper lock on the outer door. He'd intended to use it on trips to planets like the Uuaa world, where the naturally curious natives might get hurt by accidentally activating some system—but keeping possible hostile humans out might be a good idea as well.

The instruments said the air was breathable, so he left his spacesuit in its locker and went into the airlock, trusting in his instruments.

Now or never. He stepped outside on the new world.

Xanthe Kingdom of Mars

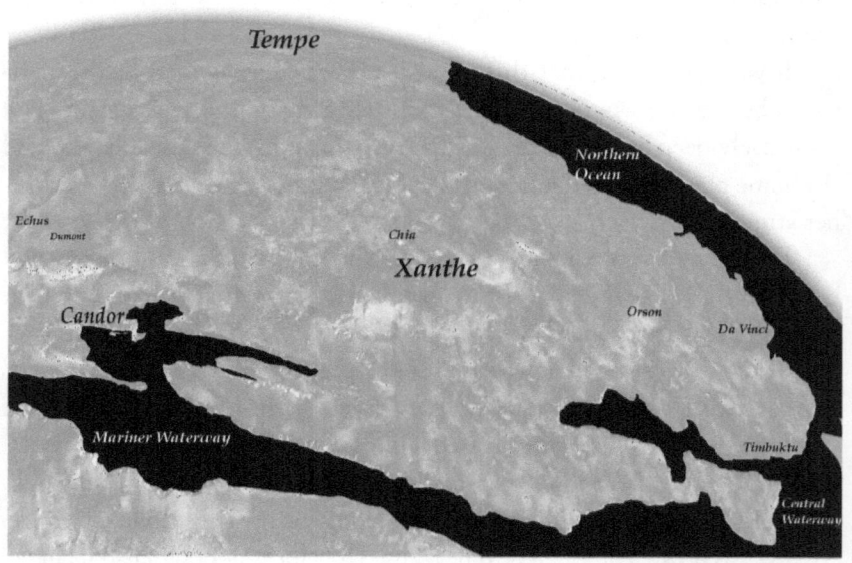

Wizard of Mars

Meeting other humans had been a long time dream of the U'tanse, even becoming part of popular fiction. Even if this wasn't Old Earth of legend, the humans were real and the situation would fire the imagination of any U'tanse.

It was probably silly to believe that first contact fantasies would work out as planned.

First Steps

It was a pleasant place, and the air was aromatic, like something he'd only smelled in the greenhouses on Ha. At least it wasn't filled with spores. He wasn't going to be another Stan, felled by alien allergies.

Plants were everywhere, not like a greenhouse at all. Everywhere he looked, there were different kinds of vegetation. It was numbing. He couldn't even focus on one kind, when another crossed his view.

A few steps and he almost stumbled. The gravity was very light. Mars supposedly had a gravity that was only one-third standard. This felt like it.

He grinned and jumped. And after sailing through the air, he crashed and tumbled. He patted the mat of green vegetation that had protected him from the rocks and got to his feet and jumped again.

This must be what the Cerik feel like, leaping across the landscape, hunting down their prey.

It was addicting. He'd never been on a light-gravity world. Even in his home town on Ha, everywhere was covered by the relatively cheap floor-gravity generators. Back in the early history of Ha's settlement, the decision was made to live under one standard gravity so that there would never be a time where one branch of the U'tanse would be separated from another by the gravity they could tolerate. Every new building put in floor gravity just as they put in lighting.

He had visited orbital stations, but the zero gravity was just another transient obstacle, like the airlock, before the station's floor gravity took over.

It took him a couple of hours before he felt comfortable leaping across the countryside, although he managed a few scrapes from the rocks and the stinging slap of an unexpected tree branch in the face.

He reached an overlook. It was getting dark. The sun had gone down and there were flickering lights in the valley, clearly marking the settlement. He paused and listened to their thoughts.

That's clearly English. Although, if he had just been listening, he might have trouble understanding the very different accent. Telepathy would be necessary to understand them easily. But it wouldn't help him speak with their accent. That might be a problem.

Although everyone was concerned with the harvest, there was a constant worry about raiders from west across the Echus River or the new threat from the canyon lands to the south. Anyone not from the settlement was likely dangerous. Children around the fireplace were warned to be alert for strangers.

Ohen shivered. It was getting cold. He'd been bouncing around, keeping warm, but once he stopped, the wind was cooling him off.

I never thought of that. In the Book, he had read that Earth and Mars both had an axial tilt that caused different season as the sun alternately warmed the northern and southern halves of the planet. Growing up in a climate controlled city on Ha, and with Ko having very little seasonal variation, he hadn't planned for it. There were no extra thick clothes to provide insulation.

He did have his space suit, but that would immediately flag him as a stranger. His ordinary clothes were simple in design. Maybe he could pass as a local.

But his original plan to go visit the village and walk around, listening to their thoughts, was not practical now. It was already getting dark and he'd have to climb down the slope with not much visibility.

Maybe I should just go back to the boat and warm up, have a good night's sleep, and explore the village in the morning.

He shivered. He nodded.

Looking around in the dark, he realized he'd come quite a distance, and for someone without clairvoyance, it would be hard to find his boat.

But that's not me. He sensed the B3 in the distance and took a solid leap in that direction.

Cold stinging rain caught him in the face and he stumbled, rolling down the slope and splashing into a small, but very cold, creek. He was soaked.

He got to his feet, confident he didn't have any broken bones, but he'd need to move more carefully. This was unknown territory and he didn't have the experience.

The rain increased, and he was surprised by tiny ice pellets. He put up his hand to protect his face and tried to run.

He almost slammed into a simple fence made from log rails. It was too dark to see it. There wasn't even any starlight anymore.

I don't remember a fence. Am I going the right direction?

He could still sense the boat, but he must have traveled erratically on the way out.

There was a farmhouse up here on the hillside. And there were animals.

He could hear them in the darkness, making a low call. Seeing them with his clairvoyance, he could tell that they were stocky, likely slower than the runners on Ko.

And they could also sense him. They were startled and keeping their distance, edged up against the fence.

All but one. His breath was harsh and snorting. The animal's thoughts were fierce. He thought Ohen was a predator and he would protect his harem from any intruder!

As it stomped closer, Ohen could see the dangerous looking horns on its head. It charged.

Ohen jumped, sailing over the fence. In panic, he jumped again, and cracked his head against a large tree branch. Everything went black.

. . .

It was a struggle to think. There was light, dim, a flickering. His head throbbed with each heartbeat. There were voices.

And the thoughts were suspicion and they were worried.

People. They found me.

"No weapons on him."

I'm hurt. Head injury. Concussion?

He didn't seem in immediate danger. Not from the people who had found him. He was stretched out on the floor, some cloth under him. He was indoors, out of the rain.

But his head hurt.

Self-aid training came to mind. He needed to check his injury.

Talking to the people who had found him could wait. A head injury could be life-threatening.

As hard as it was to concentrate, he had to focus his clairvoyant sight inwards. Training had allowed him to sense details within his body. This was the basis of the healing skill. He'd never match a trained healer like Kerry, but self-aid could be critical, especially if there were no other U'tanse healers available. He needed to check his head wound.

It had been a hard hit. He had probably jumped with all this strength and hit a tree limb. The scalp was lacerated, but it was already scabbed over. He must have been unconscious for more than an hour.

There were micro-fractures in his skull, but those would heal on their own. More serious was the cerebral hemorrhage. He used his psychokinetic abilities to assist the blood clotting, careful not to block any of the blood vessels. He'd have to monitor it regularly until it was all healed.

He did nothing for the pain other than regulate his breathing and ease the muscle tension in his neck. His self-aid training instructors had been clear—at his healing skill level, it was better to do too little than too much.

As he relaxed, the voices around him came into focus better. He was getting better understanding the accent.

"Never seen a git as big as this'n."

"Where's he from?"

Ohen blinked his eyes. Four men were standing around him. They were holding farm tools and knives, held like weapons.

He tried to speak, but his voice was raspy. "Hello."

"Foreigner!" One spoke, but the others thought it. Foreigners were dangerous, probably spies or warriors sent to attack their village. There could be others. They were desperate to know more.

Ohen swallowed, "Where am I?"

They almost couldn't understand his words. He tried again, "Is this Mars?"

A couple of them laughed.

A man holding a hammer said, "Of course, where else?"

Another asked, "Where are you from? Why are you here?"

Ohen struggled with the pounding in his head. It was hard to keep track of their words and their thoughts.

"I was … hunting for Earth."

"Well look in the sky before dawn! It's the morning star, right now."

Ohen nodded. They thought this was Mars. They had no doubt. Gabriel had found the right yellow star. It was just the planets that were messed up. They'd changed.

"I need to go to Earth."

The man with the knife put it in his sheath. "He's delirious. Still out of it."

Another said, "Stranger, you can't go to Earth. Nobody can go to Earth, even if you had a spaceship. It's been sealed off for centuries."

A woman elbowed her way through the men, holding a mug. "Can't you tell he's out of his head? Hold him up. I've got to get this tonic down him. And then let him rest."

The helpful hands were rough and just made his headache unbearable, but he swallowed the warm broth and closed his eyes when they set his head back down. Sleep came quickly.

...

The cart's large wheels hitting rocks on the rough trail bounced him awake.

The sun was in the sky and it was much warmer outside.

But his hands were roped together, as were his legs. The next bounce was worse, and he really couldn't hold himself steady.

The cart was being pulled by the same sort of beast that had tried to attack him, although this one seemed docile. One man was sitting on a bench, controlling the beast with leather straps. Another man was walking easily beside the cart. They weren't traveling very fast.

Ohen's head was clearer now. A quick check of his injuries showed them healing nicely.

But it was plain that he was a prisoner, and the thoughts of the men carrying him were concerned with how long it would take to get rid of him and get back home.

B3 was still hidden in the forest. Tied up as he was, there was no chance of escaping and making his way back to it. Staying calm and healing a bit more seemed the wisest choice at the moment. He worried a bit about having left the lights and heating on. He'd need to get back soon if he didn't want to drain the batteries. Parked as it was, the boat wouldn't power up the beams to recharge the batteries on its own. He only had a couple of weeks left.

But he needed to know the local names and landmarks. If he were carried too far away, it might take ages to find B3's hiding place again. He needed to focus on his own safety, so he closed his eyes and concentrated on the men's thoughts.

Their village, named Marion, was caught in a vise. While they had been settled by descendants of the Spanish from the Maja region, they had to worry about the settlers from the Candor Valley to the south that were outgrowing their fields and looked to the highlands. And then from the west, across the Echus River, the Malay people made periodic raids, stealing animals and grain stores.

The locals didn't know who the new giant represented, but their easiest way out was to turn him over to the Dorsa military as a gesture of friendship. Maybe they could figure out where the spy came from.

Ohen frowned. It looked like he was getting deeper and deeper into trouble.

Captive

The Dorsa guards were in drab blue uniforms, guarding a barricade on the road. It looked like this was a narrow pass between mountains. The villagers gave the guards their story and the guard seemed to be taking them at their word.

"Who are you and where do you come from?"

"I am Ohen bar Clay from Ha."

"Where's that?"

"It's a moon."

He was about to try to explain, but the guard shook his head. Ohen didn't detect any sympathy from the man. It would be a waste of breath to try to explain the U'tanse or interstellar travel to him.

Ohen was manhandled from the villager's cart into a different one and he was off again, although this was on a smoother road and the beast pulling the cart was a different animal, one more sleek and a lot faster.

I really am bad at this. I should have held off and researched my first contact situation for weeks before choosing to reveal myself.

And it was really stupid to knock himself out and nearly kill himself in the first few hours on the planet. Nobody was friendly, but he couldn't blame his situation on anyone but himself.

Unless something improved, he'd have to find a way to escape from his captors.

It was discouraging how quickly he was being separated from his boat. Even if they turned him loose, it would be a long walk back.

My priority is to stay alive. I need to still be here when my people come for me. And the more information I have about this kind of humanity I can give them, the better for the U'tanse.

Several times one of his many captors had entertained the thought of just killing him while he was still weak and injured. These people had killed before and the idea was repugnant to them, but often necessary.

How am I going to escape?

They entered a larger community. There were more buildings than the dozen wooden structures he'd seen in the village, and some were stone.

They all looked primitive to him. He'd grown up in a technological city where buildings were designed to support life on an airless moon. Stone and wood looked like piled rubble, although he was aware that his perspective was skewed. This was a habitable world, where people could live with the efforts of their bare hands.

I have to be careful. Even this technological way of looking at things could turn them against me. It won't take much to push them over the edge.

The people he could see all looked smaller than him. Although their height was not out of the ordinary for the U'tanse, they looked thin. Likely the lower gravity demanded less of their muscles.

And that just makes me look more dangerous. I need to act meek.

The cart pulled to a stop. There were five men in uniform outside a stone building. He could sense many more inside. The driver went inside to report. When no one watching him, he tested the ropes, but he was bound tightly. He'd need something with a sharp edge to cut through the twisted fibers. If he could get his hands free, then he could untie his legs.

But the soldiers spilled out of the building before he could do more than plan. One man flourished a knife, and before Ohen could do more than inhale sharply, he cut the leg ropes and urged Ohen to stand.

He was a little wobbly, still weak and with his muscles cramped from the journey. But with pokes and the threat of sharp knives, he was escorted into the building and immediately put into a small stone room with a narrow slit of a window up at the ceiling.

"Sit."

Ohen sat in the chair indicated. It was a little small, but it was better than being bound up in the cart.

From the sound, the door was barred with a sturdy board. And there he sat, alone for a while.

The walls were too thick to consider escape. There might be something abrasive to wear through the ropes around his wrist, but if he couldn't immediately turn that into an escape, it would just brand him as an unruly captive, not worth keeping alive.

Abruptly, he sneezed. His first impulse was to fear spores or other allergens in the small cell, but a quick look inside his body found bacteria rapidly growing in his sinus passages. His body had been weakened by the cold and the injury. Something in the air was trying take advantage of his foreign immune system.

He needed to remember everything about fighting infections from his self-aid training. He closed his eyes and concentrated on killing off those bacteria.

. . .

So, once he had brought the first infection under control, he spent the idle time in his confinement listening to the thoughts of everyone in the area.

Hardly anyone was thinking about him. There was a military operation underway. The Candor troops were moving into the area from the south and since the city of Dumont was at the far end of the Xanthe zone of control, they were in danger of having their roads to the eastern cities cut off. Many suspected that an evacuation might be ordered. It was an open question among the soldiers who would be pulled back to the Xanthe-controlled lands and who would be left to try to hold Dumont. The farmers knew they would have to stay, but no one knew whether the Candor invaders would want to just capture the land, or kill all the farmers so their own people could settle here.

After three hours, the door was unbarred and a man in uniform walked in, carrying a thin board with papers bound to it.

Ohen stood up.

The man waved him back down. "You're a big one, aren't you?"

Ohen cleared his throat. "A little over seven feet."

There was confusion in the man's mind. "What?"

"I'm over seven feet tall." Again, the words didn't make sense to him.

Ohen shook his head. "It doesn't matter. All my family have been large."

"Who are you, and where do you come from?"

"My name is Ohen bar Clay." The man wrote down on his paper, "Owen Barclay." In his mind it was a foreign name, but nothing unusual.

Ohen decided it wasn't worth correcting him, especially since he couldn't see what the man had written with his eyes and he shouldn't have been able to know what was written. He knew any psychic gifts had to be concealed. There was a whole section on that in the Book. Normal humans felt threatened by any evidence of psychic activities.

He continued, "I'm from the city of Chase-on-Ha."

The man wrote and frowned. "I've never heard of it. How far away is it?"

Ohen sighed. "A very long way."

"How many kloms?"

It was Ohen's turn to be puzzled. But then he put the pieces together.

The Book had mentioned that on Earth, there were two systems of measurements, the English system with feet and miles, and the French system with meters and kilometers. Abe had been raised with the English system and the U'tanse had used it. Apparently the people on Mars, and maybe the rest of humanity had gone with the French system.

He sighed. One more system to learn. The U'tanse used the British system, but anyone in a technical job had to be familiar with the Delense measurements based on a unit that was about eight inches long and a base-8 number system. Anyone who dealt with the Cerik had to be familiar with the trinary system they used. It was unsuited for large numbers, but the Cerik never needed to count very high.

Ohen said, "Ha is very, very far away. It's on a moon around another planet."

The man wrote down what he said, but obviously didn't believe a word of it.

"How did you end up in the village of Marion?"

Ohen was cautious, but he'd already claimed to come from another world.

"I came from the sky and that was the first place I saw."

The man sighed. "You're not helping yourself. I don't have a lot of time to waste on fantasy tales."

Ohen nodded. "I understand. I'm not from Candor, if that's what you're worried about."

"How do you know about Candor if you've fallen from the sky and have never been here before?"

"I overheard some soldiers talking."

His questioner nodded, but his thoughts said otherwise. He was judged a liar, and likely some kind of spy from Candor. That nation had access to the trade on the Mariner Waterway, and any kind of foreigner could have been recruited. He just couldn't understand what kind of game Owen Barclay was playing with his fantasy tales.

"That's enough for now."

Ohen asked, "Do I get to eat?"

The man debated with himself, then nodded. "I'll send something in. Don't try anything."

Ohen shrugged. "I'm just one man and I don't know how to fight."

That cinched it in the investigator's mind. Barclay was a liar. Everybody knew how to fight.

. . .

A milky soup was offered, and although he didn't care for the taste, he quickly finished it off. He hoped for more. His appetite had always been healthy, and now he was getting only a little to eat, with no way to hunt or scrounge for more on his own.

He filled his time with more telepathic listening.

There was no one who believed him and he had no sympathizer. The wars they'd been in had run for thirty years and everyone had lost family. Just recently, the Candorians had started a major push, greater than anything they'd tried in the past. If he was branded a Candor spy, then killing him was the obvious thing to do. There were even some who visualized it. Seeing himself beheaded was shocking.

As an exercise, Ohen stretched his senses to the south, locating some Candorians. They were a little more optimistic than the Dorsa. But they were hardy any more sympathetic. They had their war losses as well, and some time back, they had established farming communities in vacant land in the highlands, but the Dorsa had pushed back, wiping them out.

Ohen sighed. There wasn't a clear innocent side to this conflict. If he'd contacted the Candorians first, likely he'd be in their prison instead.

He needed to escape. But how?

The Computer

Ohen was moved from the investigation room to a place more suited to hold people. It was a cell with iron bars and a mechanical lock. There was a bed, although his feet stretched off the ends. There was pot for his excrement and a small table where he could eat his meals. His cell was one of three, but he was the only prisoner.

But with his hands free and the ability to move around in the small area, it was a lot more comfortable. There was a guard in the same room as the cells, positioned where he could watch everything.

But although Ohen was stretched out on the bed with his eyes closed, he was watching the guard as well. The guard, named Will, was bored. They had emptied out the jail not a week earlier, executing one of the prisoners and turning the other five loose. With the Candor forces getting closer, they didn't want to waste resources taking care of them. The jailers were assigned to regular forces and sent away.

But now this spy appeared and Will was stuck with the job of watching him. He was going slowly crazy, with nothing to do but carve at chunks of firewood with his knife. Sadly, his animal figures looked like nothing recognizable and the block of wood slowly turned into a pile of kindling chips.

"What are you carving?" Ohen asked.

Will heard him, but ignored the question. He had been ordered to avoid getting involved with the spy. He was just bored.

Ohen was getting bored listening to the guard's thoughts as well. He probed other minds in the military base.

He was intrigued with the shouter box in the commander's office. Several times during the course of a day, someone would go to the box, type in a code, and then either with the keyboard or by voice, communicate with someone. There were peak times, when many people used it, and slack times when it was not used at all.

When the voice replied, Ohen could sometimes, but not always, get a sense of the remote speaker's location. Many times, it was someone hundreds of miles to the east, probably at the capital city or maybe a regional center.

But it wasn't consistent. Sometimes it was like a conversation, other times there was a delay, much like when Ohen was many light-seconds away from the starship. But these were all relatively local—just hundreds of miles at the most.

He didn't understand the delay at first, until one of the soldiers, waiting in line for his time at the speaker box, was fretting that the moon would be gone from the sky before he had his turn.

Ah, the moon is a relay.

Stuck as a prisoner for three days, he had nothing to do but be the spy they claimed him to be. He worked it out.

The speaker box wasn't a simple radio. It was a sophisticated store and forward system. One of the moons of Mars was in a fairly low orbit and passed by maybe twice a day—he hadn't worked out the period yet. If the moon was visible, the signal was relayed quickly. If it wasn't then the messages would be delayed until it reappeared in the sky.

He got the impression this the local soldiers couldn't plan their response without constant contact with the leadership elsewhere.

I guess quick distant communication is critical to a kingdom where travel is limited to how fast a horse can travel. He'd identified the sleek animals as horses and stocky ones as oxen. Both could drag wagons, but horses could be ridden by individual people.

The box, which they called the computer, had to be a rare item, if only the military could use it. He had no sense there was any other in the city.

I have computers on the B3, but those are all U'tanse-made. I doubt the technology is the same. It's impressive how well the Martian one can accept voice commands.

On the fourth day, he had to revise his impressions of the computer up another notch.

During one of the times when the moon was not in the sky, an elderly man went to the computer and spread out his papers. He typed in his code and began to ask questions.

The answers were immediate, and Ohen realized that the man wasn't talking to someone far distant. He was talking to the computer itself.

The computer was doing calculations. The man was planning a trip, with multiple wagons. Ohen realized that this was an evacuation, with several wagons containing important people, but the man was deciding how many more wagons containing supplies and support soldiers would be needed as well.

Some of the questions the computer answered had to do with distances on the map to intermediate destinations and also reports on the last known location of Candorian troops.

That computer has a lot of data.

Ohen wondered if he could ask it questions.

Nobody wanted to talk to him, a suspected spy. Ohen could read people's thoughts, but rarely did they think about topics he was interested in. He really had nobody to talk to.

But could he talk to the computer?

Will, the guard, could request someone to take his post for meals and when he was ordered to some other task, but for the most part he was as confined to the jail as Ohen was. He even slept in one of the empty cells when he had a chance.

There was a knock on the door well after sunset.

Will answered. It was Joseph, a friend of his. There was a raised eyebrow. Will glanced back at his prisoner, who appeared to be sleeping. Will knew what was being asked. He nodded, and in the darkness, the two crept off to join the game a couple of buildings over. Ohen got the impression of some game of sticks and pebbles and coins exchanged over the results.

Ohen was quickly to his feet. He went to the lock of his cell. He'd spent some idle time probing the interior with his clairvoyance, but he'd never attempted to do anything with the knowledge while Will was watching.

But now, he strained with his psychokinesis, attempting to move the metal parts inside. He had the skill, but it was limited. He could manipulate cells within his body, but he couldn't fly or lift anything more than a few ounces.

Still with a few taps on the lock box to shake up the parts inside, his skills quickly moved everything to the unlock position.

He opened the door to his cell, grateful that the hinges didn't make much noise.

The darkness assisted him, too.

I'm free. Should I just escape?

He really needed to get back to the B3, if only to shut down everything properly so he wouldn't be left with a dead battery when he returned.

But this Dorsa computer's skills nagged at him. He might never get this chance again.

Telepathy told him when lookouts were staring off at the hills in the distance, rather than down at the streets below them. Ohen made his way to the building where the computer was held.

There were indeed soldiers working deep into the night by candlelight, but Ohen suspected that if he talked quietly, no one would notice him over on the other side of the building. He'd just have to risk it.

"Computer, could you answer a few questions." The machine lit up a display screen at the first word.

The voice was like a young man, not resonant, but with very little emotion. "I do not recognize your voice."

"Um. How do I introduce myself?"

"Speak or type your name. If you have an identity registered elsewhere in the system, enter your ID code."

"I am Ohen bar Clay."

On the display appeared, "Owen Barclay."

"No, that's not how my name is spelled." He typed it in. The keyboard was obvious, although the letters were in different positions than the ones the U'tanse used.

"Do you have any other ID code?"

"No."

A string of letters and numbers appeared. "Please note down your ID code."

Ohen, like most of his ancestors, had a flawless memory, but he paid special attention to the code.

"What do I use this code for?"

"Others can communicate with you via your name or a public code. Only you can receive messages for you with this code. There are a wide variety of other uses. Do you wish a list?"

"Not yet. Tell me. Do you understand miles?"

"Yes, the British Engineering System unit of measurement. Also known as Imperial measurements. One mile is equal to 1.609344 kloms."

"Good. Give me a quick list of the conversion factors between BES and units commonly used here." The list appeared on the display.

Ohen hadn't had a chance to figure that out himself, but if he knew the conversions, he could get up to speed with the local units.

"Now, how many nations exist within a thousand miles of here?"

Ohen spat out questions as fast as he could think of them, with the computer displaying the results. He really didn't know how much time he had before someone noticed him, and he'd really be executed as a spy if he were discovered talking to the military's computer.

But the results were fascinating.

He had speculated that humanity with its billions could advance scientifically more rapidly than the U'tanse with fewer numbers. It appeared spot on.

Earth had recovered from the Betelgeuse supernova flare and quickly returned to space. With their technological advancements, they had chosen to terraform new worlds where humans could live with no extraordinary life support. Mars was given an atmosphere as was Luna, Earth's moon.

The U'tanse created habitats, bubbles of breathable air where we could live. Base-line humanity created whole worlds!

Mars had been colonized by carefully chosen representatives of over thirty nations. Luna was on the verge of being settled with preference given to other nations when the Plague happened.

This brain fever attacked all of humanity at one time, killing the vast majority of humanity and disabling the survivors. All interplanetary travel ceased. The carefully planned communities on Mars were scrambled as survivors went where the food was. Within a generation, new nations had appeared. The worlds of Earth and Luna were places of legend, visible in the sky, but no one traveled there anymore.

Ohen asked, "And the computers?"

Computers were relics of the pre-Plague times. There were many of them, but when they ran out of power, they went silent. Only a few were left.

Ohen had so many more questions, but off in the distance, Will lost the last of his coins and realized he needed to get back to his post.

"One last question. What about Earth? Someone said Earth is locked off."

The computer spoke, "That is true. After the Plague, many attempts were made to return to Earth. No attempts succeeded."

Ohen, frustrated, wanting to ask so many more questions, had to sneak away. The computer went dark.

Evacuation

Ohen had to race back the jail to get there before Will. He considered just heading out of town, but there were a lot of soldiers that could be called up quickly, as well as guards watching on the roofs. They'd definitely see him running for the hills and know right where to hunt him down. A man on a horse could catch him quickly.

He'd wait for a second chance if Will went gaming again.

He barely got back into his jail cell and closed the door in time. He definitely didn't have time to lock it again. Luckily the hinges were sticky enough that the door didn't open on its own.

He was back in bed when Will walked in, grumbling about his luck.

Ohen calmed his breathing, trying to look like he was sleeping, thinking about what he'd learned.

That computer was something special. We've barely made ones that could recognize single word commands, and I couldn't afford to use those in the boats. This one was able to hold its own in an unstructured conversation with me. I couldn't detect a single error.

If he'd seen that back on Ha, he would have suspected a hidden human operator staying silent under a tight ineda. But this was real—a computer that could talk.

And none of these technologically primitive people thought it worth a comment.

It certainly felt unusual to Ohen. Even when talking to people with tight ineda, he could still feel the living mind behind the words. A talking machine was disturbingly unnatural to him.

But that machine had easy access to an extensive history of humanity. What else did it know?

Ohen hoped Will would sleep so he could fix the lock, but it didn't happen.

Just as the dawn light started creeping through the windows. The door opened and three military officers walked in.

Ohen got to his feet.

Uh, oh. They're here to decide whether to kill me or take me with them on the evacuation wagons.

One of them was his initial interrogator. He had his papers with him.

"The prisoner is named Owen Barclay and has not been able to give a satisfactory explanation of how he was discovered in the nearby village of Marion. The locals captured him and brought him to the nearest Dorsa guards. He's been here for five days now."

The man with more metal on his uniform said, "Mr. Barclay, what do you have to say for yourself?"

Ohen shrugged. "I'm an innocent traveler that accidentally stumbled into your area. I injured my head when attacked by a farmer's bull. From that time until now, I've been held captive. I've done nothing against the people of Dorsa. I would happily leave this place and go in any direction you choose. I don't really know what it would take to prove my innocence to you."

There were shouts outside. Ohen could tell that a scout had arrived with notice of more Candorians nearby.

The highest ranking officer could tell what was happening as well. He'd been expecting it. He fingered the sword at his side.

"Guard, open the cell."

It was there on the surface of the officer's mind. If Ohen made a break for it, he'd be cut down.

Will reached for the jail cell door, and it opened before he inserted the key.

The interrogator said, "What did you do?"

Ohen shrugged. "From the beginning of my captivity, I haven't fought back. I've done nothing wrong. I'm doing the best to be cooperative, even if the door was left unlocked by accident. I'm not your enemy."

Evacuation

The officer in charge pointed to the guard. "Bind his hands and take him to the wagons." The man was still undecided, but Ohen's fate could be decided in Chia. That was where the important people were being taken to safety.

Will was furious at Ohen for implying that he'd failed his duty by leaving the cell unlocked. He bound Ohen's hands extra tightly behind him.

My arms are bound again. Luckily he'd realized it was coming and tensed his muscles while Will was tying him up. It didn't give him enough slack to slip free of the rope, but at least his blood flow wasn't constricted.

There were eight wagons in the train, some more finely constructed than others. Some were simple cargo wagons. Others held passengers. The officers and their families were being evacuated.

Based on the summary he'd gotten from the computer, Chia was over four hundred miles away to the east. There were several smaller towns on the route, but the Candor invasion was coming up from the south and their escape route could be cut off at any point.

It took Will a few minutes to realize he was being evacuated too, as Ohen's guard. He was reluctantly grateful, but he resolved not to let it show on his face.

Some of the soldiers were expected to stay behind and hold the city of Dumont. When they saw the computer being loaded into the wagons, they realized how dire their situation was. They needed communication with the rest of Dorsa, but the officers couldn't risk the computer being captured by the Candor forces.

Keeping his face passive, Ohen used his clairvoyant sight to view all the wagons. In the middle, the officer in charge who'd ordered him to be brought along was sitting with his wife and three small children.

The officer had a last-minute discussion with the local commander. Ohen picked up their names. Wallace was the local commander. Baron Rusher was the commander in charge. The Candorian forces were less than three hours away. They had to get moving.

The wagons moved out. Ohen was grateful for the Dorsa's smooth roads as they picked up speed. He and his guard were wedged into a wagon filled with wooden crates. He sat on a crate of documents. Will was sitting on a box of household goods owned by one of the families.

The humans had a mix of emotions at leaving, but the horses were eager to be moving. They'd done this many times before and they knew food and water were waiting for them at the end of a good day's run.

Ohen was intrigued by the idea of domesticated animals. On Ko, the Cerik considered all animals as prey, with the exception of a few small pets. Growing up on airless Ha, Ohen had only seen many of them in videos. Certainly he'd never thought to sample their thoughts.

When Ohen turned his thoughts to the countryside, he sensed the Candorian forces relatively close. Baron Rusher worried that the guards he'd brought along might not be enough if they were forced into a battle. It had been a hard call when the Commander Wallace needed every one of them if he was going to hold Dumont. Rusher had no confidence in the city's local fighters.

Ohen sighed, even if they had no confrontation, he'd still be a captive hundreds of miles from B3. He could just hope that none of the fighters would discover the hidden boat. They might not be able to get inside, but they could still cause damage. He'd just have to face the fact that when he did manage to get back to the boat, he'd have to find a way to recharge the battery. He was stupid to have walked away without shutting everything down.

He still had hopes he could get himself out of this mess. It would be embarrassing if the starship returned and found him tied up in a local jail.

He had to keep his eyes open and his senses active if he were going to get free.

...

An idle thought about Foster's Pass caught his attention—Foster like the name of the starship captain. Foster must have been one of those names that survived both on Mars and among the U'tanse. Long, long ago, they had a common history, after all. He wondered what the captain would think about it.

Ohen used his sight to probe ahead on the road. They were still an hour away from the pass, but he was curious.

He took in a sharp breath. Candorians had already taken the pass and were waiting to ambush Dorsa traffic.

He looked at his guard. Will noticed and frowned at him.

Nobody is going to listen to my warnings. Will won't even pass them on to the soldiers.

Ohen felt a stab of fear. He was heading into a battle, where people were going to be hurt and killed. Even if he personally came through without a scratch, the overwhelming pain and fear of the others would be more than he could bear. It was a telepath's worst nightmare.

I have to get free.

He looked at Will, idly thinking of friends he was leaving behind. There was no help for it. Will would try to stop him.

I hope this works. He focused on Will's head and tried to induce the cells in a certain area in the front of the brain to fire at a certain pace, about a dozen times a second. He'd done it once in medical training, but he never realized he'd need it.

Inducing sleep in others was a useful skill healers used, but Ohen had never considered himself a healer.

He was actually surprised when, a few minutes later, Will's head nodded and his breathing slowed.

Really? Now the ropes.

One of Ohen's cousins had ignited a candle wick with his psychokinesis as a party trick. Ohen had tried it before, but other than making the fibers warm, he hadn't succeeded.

This time, he had more motive.

Tied behind him, the ropes binding his wrists were course fibers twisted together. Mentally focusing on one particular spot not too close to his skin, he concentrated on agitating the molecules at high speed.

After ten minutes of effort, the whiff of a trace of smoke was the first hint that it was working. Deep within the tangle of fibers, some had reached kindling temperature and were oxidizing, the cellulose fibers decaying into carbon and volatiles. He kept at it, straining with his muscles, hoping the weakened fibers would give way.

And with a snap, they did. He hurriedly untangled himself and pulled the rope free. There was a visible char mark where the rope had snapped. A quick glance out the little window on the door and he dropped the rope outside. No one should ever see that. No one should ever know what he was capable of doing.

His wagon was near the end, and he was glad the soldiers on the wagon a hundred yards behind him were talking among themselves and keeping an eye on the terrain around them for enemies.

The road was winding back and forth as it gained altitude, approaching the mountain pass. Ohen gave one last glance at Will, still sleeping, and then opened the door. As they slowed to ease around a curve, Ohen jumped.

Concealed by the trees, he was free and the others on the wagons hadn't seen him escape.

His heart raced. He was safe.

But as the last of the wagons passed by, he frowned. Everyone in that train of wagons was racing into a trap, including the families of the officers, and even innocent Will, still sleeping away.

Could he let them all be slaughtered?

Battle at the Pass

The wagons were slowing down because of the steepening grade and the winding road.

This is stupid. I shouldn't be doing this.

He leapt from one boulder to the next, going straight up the mountain, his high-gravity-trained muscles letting him cut across the winding path to get there quicker than the wagons.

There. That's the baron's wagon.

He jumped into the trees a few hundred yards ahead and waited. When the wagon passed, if was just a quick hop to the running board.

The passengers inside were dozing, but baron snapped awake when the door opened, saw Ohen and grabbed for a small firearm in his pocket.

Ohen gripped his arm, and he was much stronger than the officer.

In a low voice, barely loud enough to be heard over the road noise, Ohen said, "I'm not a fighter. I'm just here to talk to you."

The others were waking up. A little boy squealed and gripped his mother's coat. Ohen smiled at him. "It's okay. I'm just here to speak with your father."

Slowly, he released the man's arm. Baron Rusher made no move for his gun. He was worried about his family. He asked, "What do you want to speak with me about?"

Ohen made up a story. "I could look out the window as we traveled, and when I saw the gap in the mountains ahead, I thought that maybe the road went through that pass."

Rusher nodded. "It does."

"Well, with nothing much to do, I kept watching every time the wagon was turned the right direction and noticed a cloud of dust up there that came and went. Do you have some troops stationed up there?"

"No, I don't."

Ohen frowned. "Hmm."

Rusher asked, "You saw dust up at the pass, just at the pass?"

"Well, from what I could see. And it came and went, like some people moved and then stopped."

Ohen was not going to tell him that he saw them with his clairvoyant sight. That would just brand him as a crazy man, or a magician, and that would be even worse.

Baron Rusher frowned. "I need to speak to my men."

Ohen realized there was a big risk that he would be recaptured and tied up again, but he nodded. Rusher opened the door on the other side and yelled to the driver to stop.

The woman asked, "What kind of cloth is that?"

Ohen turned his attention to her. She was concerned with keeping her children from panicking. He smiled.

Fingering his collar, he said, "This is fassail cloth, but I don't really know anything about the plant it comes from. Sorry I haven't had the opportunity to wash it." He wrinkled his nose. "It probably stinks."

The oldest boy, about twelve, asked, "Why are you so big?"

"All of my family are large. I had one ancestor they called a giant. There are legends about him."

Rusher climbed out and spoke to his men. He looked back in. "You. Barclay. Come with us."

Ohen nodded to the woman and her children.

Three of the soldiers that had collected around the wagon watched him carefully, but made no move to bind him again. The baron had stopped all the wagons and had sent a scout on horseback up ahead.

The scout wasn't long in returning. "You're right. Candorians hiding in the rocks above the road on the left side."

The baron nodded. "Half the men stay here with the wagons. Keep them bunched up. The rest of us will move in. They won't expect us to know they're there."

He pointed. "Get a horse for Barclay. He's coming with us."

Ohen winced. "I'm not a fighter. I don't know how."

"How did you get free of your guard?" Rusher was skeptical.

"I didn't lay a hand on him. He dozed. The rope was loose."

A horse stepped up beside him. The soldier leading it said, "Get on."

Ohen frowned. The horse looked at him suspiciously as well, but it did expect him to step into the stirrup on the side.

Cautiously, he put his toe in the stirrup, unsure if it would hold his weight.

Luckily, there were several minds waiting for him to take the next move, so Ohen at least knew what to do.

Getting up into the saddle wasn't hard, but it was uncomfortable. The seat wasn't built for someone his size. A soldier put the reins in his hand and everyone else mounted up smoothly. They headed out.

Ohen's horse didn't need guidance from the reins. It was just following everyone else.

The ride was painful. Ohen bounced out of the saddle and almost fell off twice.

He gripped the saddle tightly, in a panic that he'd fall and be tramped under the other horses's hooves.

"Hey, stranger. Don't blame the horse. That's a Donny. The best troop horse breed on the planet." Others laughed.

As they approached the pass, they slowed down. Experienced soldiers puzzled out how to attack the Candorians in protected positions. The soldiers had firearms, but they weren't terribly accurate. Some were better skilled with swords or spears. Ohen knew that some of the Candorians had firearms as well. If there were going to be chunks of metal flying through the air, no place was safe.

Ohen waved at the baron.

"Yes?"

"You're going to need to get them to leave their hiding places."

"I know that."

Ohen frowned. "What I'm trying to say is that maybe I could chase them out."

The soldiers didn't laugh, but they ignored him. He was obviously untrained at this.

It was frustrating. If he could just explain. Ohen looked up at the hillside. His sight could easily identify their hiding places.

Clumsily, he slid off his saddle and reached over to another soldier's horse, where a lance was sheathed in a leather bag at his side. He pulled the lance free.

"Hey, there!" the soldier objected.

Ohen turned and jumped, lance in hand. He was up the side of the rocks before they could react.

I need to be careful.

He needed to stay out of sight of the Candorians. They had seen the wagon train coming by the dust in the distance and were expecting their prey at any moment. He had to stay above them.

Climbing with the six-foot lance made everything harder. Jumping helped, but after landing on unstable rubble a couple of times, he tried to limit it. He hurried. The Candorians were wondering what was taking the wagons so long to get there.

The baron had an inkling of what he was trying to do and was getting his men into position, just out of sight of the roadway at the pass.

And then, Ohen reached his target, an old avalanche rubble field above where the ambushers were hiding. With the lance as a crowbar, he chose a few large boulders and levered them into position.

As quickly as possible, he pushed them all over the edge.

It was hardly a full-scale avalanche, but one boulder knocked others free, cascading the tumbling rocks down on the hiding Candorians. He kept it up, until down below Candorians began running to get away from the falling rocks.

The waves of panic caused him to freeze up. Ohen collapsed and held his head, screaming.

It just got worse when the panicked runners encountered the Dorsa troops. There sharp cracks as the firearms were unleashed and the Candorians started dying.

Ohen had been wrong. He'd hoped that by keeping his distance from the actual battle, he could avoid the mental damage.

It was far beyond what he'd imagined. It was one thing to intellectually understand the damage of feeling the death pangs of others. It was quite another to encounter it in real life.

All he could do was lay on the ground, weeping.

...

It was an hour later when he rejoined the Dorsa, climbing slowly down the mountainside, using the lance as a walking stick.

"There you are," Baron Rusher said. "We were about to leave you behind."

Ohen nodded, barely able to keep eye contact. He handed the lance over to the soldier he'd stolen it from. "I was wiped out. I can't handle a battle."

Rusher nodded. "Your guard said you were recovering from a head injury. Climbing that mountain so fast like that probably didn't help it either. Go back to your wagon and rest."

"Okay." He tried not to look at the bodies piled up beside the road. Some of the Dorsa soldiers were picking through them, collecting weapons.

Ohen hadn't killed them directly, but he'd certainly chosen his side and played a critical role in their deaths. It was hard to accept. He'd never thought he'd be in a battle.

Out of one of the wagon windows, a boy waved at him. He waved back. *Does it make it okay if I helped kill them if that boy is still alive because I did?* There wasn't an easy answer.

I can't stop these people from warring against each other. But I've got to make sure I'm far from any battle again. I don't think I can take it.

He wondered how all the others could deal with it. Sampling their thoughts didn't help a lot.

Some of them were life-long soldiers. They'd been through battles before and they were just grateful that it had gone their way so easily. The dead bodies piled up beside the road were not really people, just tokens in an endless game.

It must be great to be free of telepathy. Ohen had felt every one of those deaths. There was no doubt that they were all human, with their own hopes and fears. They had come here to make the land safe for their families.

Ohen paused. He would have vomited again if there had been anything left in his stomach.

He reached his wagon. Will looked at him as he climbed in.

"At least I don't have to tie you up this time." The guard was just grateful that the baron had taken his story at face value. He'd fallen asleep and when he woke, the prisoner had escaped.

Ohen nodded. "I need to sleep." He closed his eyes and used what self-aid he could to calm his body. He wished there was something he could do to calm his spirit, but maybe that was impossible.

Chia

They hit a rough patch of the road and it jostled Ohen awake.

"What happened?"

Will shrugged. "Just part of the Old Road that washed out."

Ohen got just the sense of it. "How old is the Old Road?"

Will did his typical sniff, annoyed at having to talk to him. "Pre-Plague. Really old.

So, hundreds of years old, before their technology collapsed. No wonder it's so smooth.

A couple of pieces came together in the vast puzzle he struggled with. Dorsa, which was just a region of the Xanthe Kingdom, was spread out over hundreds of miles, and connected with these superior roads. With the roads able to move troops at a fast pace, and with the computers to tie the spread-out populated centers under one central command, the Xanthe had been able to hold a large region for a few generations at least.

Towns like Dumont had grown up along the road, settled by the Xanthe people. Numerous smaller communities, like Marion, were settled from other places, but owed their allegiance to the stronger military presence of the Xanthe.

Only lately, the concentrated surge from the south had broken their control.

The wagon train had crossed paths with troops heading back the other way to support the endangered communities. Ohen had seen one set of dozens on horseback, and another larger group on foot.

Not a single powered vehicle among them. I guess that makes sense.

The Book had told what history of Earth Abe had been able to recall. The Roman Empire had held a large region by building good roads and moving its armies along them. When steam powered locomotives had been invented, troops could be moved even faster, and nations with easy access to oceans could transport their soldiers on large ocean-going ships. On Earth the terms boats and ships referred to water-traveling vessels.

With petroleum mining, liquid-fueled automobiles in all of their variations could be used to give even more mobility to troops.

But even though Mars was a pleasantly habitable planet, the coal and petroleum of Earth were fossil fuels mined from ancient deposits and Mars had none of those. The U'tanse and the Cerik had access to power cells, but those were all charged via beams in space. Mars didn't have that option either if they had no usable spaceships.

Mars had no ready source of portable power. The best they could do would be to chop trees for firewood. According to Abe, steam power, the first step into a powered age, was done with coal. Was coal more power-dense than firewood? He honestly didn't know.

Ohen frowned. Earth's space exploration was all done with rockets. Those used liquid fuel based on petroleum for the rocket's high-pressure engines. Did that mean that a world like Mars, with no fossil fuels, could never get back to space?

Just how advanced had base-line humanity's technology gotten before their Plague? Did they have tractor/pressor engines, or was all of this, including the terraforming of the planets done with rockets?

Supposedly, there were still spaceships in existence, but all were silent and probably drained of their fuel. He'd love to get a close look at one.

But that meant the only way off the planet was B3 and the only way he'd ever get back there was with help. The idea of sneaking away and walking back was out of the question now. He'd already traveled hundreds of miles, and it was now a war zone.

...

The mountain ridge to the west of the city of Chia showed the largest human-made scar that Ohen had ever seen.

"Is that a mine?"

Will shook his head. "You're really a foreigner, aren't you? That's the quarries. The best building stones on Mars are cut from there. I'd have thought everyone knew that. Surely you've heard of Chia granite?"

"Sorry, no."

Will sniffed. He had relatives in Chia and he wasn't above bragging about what he knew.

"It's an old crater wall, you see. A lot of it has natural fractures and skilled drillers can cut up the rest. Some of the blocks are shipped down the Maja River to the ocean and sold all over. Others are hauled on wagons to Orson. My people used to be drillers."

Ohen could hear the echoes of Will's mother's voice in his thoughts. Will had been raised in Dumont, but he'd heard stories.

As the wagons moved into the city, Ohen could see the buildings built with the local stone. Whether from quarried slabs or more patterned conglomerates of smaller rock, everything deeper in the city was trimmed with wood and looked like it would stand for ages.

There were wooded parks tracing the stream beds throughout the city. Ohen suspected the original city had been designed long ago, perhaps pre-Plague.

And then it was time to unload. Ohen volunteered to help before he was asked—anything to stretch his legs after the day's long journey. He really was considerably stronger than the others, but he didn't make a show of it. Helping might make friends. Showing off might make enemies.

Baron Rusher was there when he was done. "Come with me."

A junior officer took him to a barrack house and Ohen was told to wash up.

By the next day, he was fed, rested and getting used to his new clothes. The military tailor shook his head while measuring him, but managed to put together a blue outfit very much like the rest of the troops, but devoid of any trim or insignia.

The baron met him in the morning.

"You're still under suspicion, officially, but I have a feeling you'll be more valuable as someone to talk to rather than wasting away in a jail cell."

Ohen knew the baron had been talking about him with others on the trip. While he wasn't trusted, his initiative during the battle at the pass had impressed them. If they could just figure out who he was, they could finally decide what to do with him.

Ohen wasn't sure he wanted to be classified, not yet. With all the background information he'd been able to access from people's minds, he could probably put together a believable story. But although he hadn't sensed anyone who had traveled this whole world, there could be some, maybe in the port cities.

The instant his captors could definitely catch him at a lie, then he'd be killed or kept permanently in captivity. His story, whatever it was, had to stand up to repeated questioning.

He decided a simple lie would be the best.

The baron took him into a conference room. From the uniforms, he could tell at an instant they were all high-ranking military.

"Barclay, I'd like you to tell these people your story."

Ohen nodded. He told them his tale of being startled by the bull and hitting his head. Rusher confirmed the tale of his captivity and told of Ohen warning him of the ambush at the pass.

Gray-haired and with forty years of experience, Commander Kobb asked, "Why did you escape, just to warn the baron? That could have gotten you killed."

Ohen shrugged. "Well, I saw the dust."

"Yes, I heard. But why were you looking for it? We had experienced soldiers on that wagon train and they didn't notice the dust."

He nodded. "Well, yes, I was sort of expecting trouble."

"Why?"

"I'm new to this place. I've been keeping my ears open. This east-west road is critical to Dorsa's control of the region and the Candorians were attacking from the south. It just made sense to me that they would try to cut your access to Dumont and other places. Since they were coming up from the south, they had their pick of places to attack, and pinch points like that pass were obvious."

He gave a little chuckle. "Being a prisoner wouldn't save me from an attack, so I was on the lookout for any danger signs. Once I saw the dust, I realized my only safety was alerting the Dorsa troops."

He told them about how slow the wagons were moving and how he cut across the switchbacks to catch up with the baron's wagon.

The baron told of his ploy to chase the Candorians out of their hiding places.

Kobb asked, "What gave you that idea?"

Ohen paused. "I must admit, it was fear. The baron was dragging me into a battle and I don't know how to fight. I don't know how to use any of those weapons. I'd be the first to die in any ordinary fight. I haven't even touched a weapon other than that lance, and I used it as a crowbar."

"You haven't been in contact with the Candorians?"

"I've never even seen a live Candorian."

Other officers asked questions, but Ohen could tell that Kobb was the man he had to convince.

"Where are you from, really?"

Ohen said, "Do you have a map?"

"Yes. Maps we have." Out of a large drawer, they slid out a highly detailed map, protected under glass. Ohen could tell in an instant it was pre-Plague and based on photographs from space. There were even a few clouds recorded for all time.

Ohen put his finger down on Dumont. "I know I was here. And probably this is where the road to Marion goes, but I don't see it."

"The map was made before the village was settled, likely."

Ohen checked the landscape, and made a mental note of where B3 was likely hidden. "I'd guess Marion was here. I remember that place."

With a frown on his face, he traced his finger around several possibilities, then sighed. "I really don't remember."

Kobb asked, "You don't remember anything from before your head injury?"

"Oh, I remember my family and the town where I grew up, Chase-on-Ha, but recent stuff…." He shook his head. "All I know is that I was searching for Earth."

There were a few chuckles.

Kobb sighed, "What should we do with you, Barclay?"

Ohen shrugged. "Don't give me a weapon. I may be big and strong, but I'd be useless in a battle."

"Don't worry about that. You'll get nowhere near a weapon."

The baron asked, "Barclay, you seem to know what our strategic situation is. Do you have any opinions?"

"A few. That's about all I've been thinking about on the trip here."

He put his finger on a mountainous region just north of the road. "If they haven't done so already, I'd expect the Candorians to put a force here, slipping them across the road in between your regular traffic. With your attention focused on the south, they could mount an unexpected attack from here."

Several heads leaned over to look at where he was pointing.

Ohen had sensed some Candorian thoughts from those mountains as their wagons had passed through. Probably just scouts, but the plan was obvious.

Baron Rusher nodded, smiling inside. He knew Barclay had a good head on him. Better to keep the stranger close, and on their side.

Odd Man Out

With thousands of uncontrolled thoughts around him at all times, Ohen was lonely. Even Will was gone, quickly moved into a new military unit and sent back west. Ohen's guard barely had time to meet up with a cousin of his on the base before he was reassigned.

Superficially, it looked like they weren't even guarding the big stranger anymore. He was assigned a small room that was his to live in and given access to meals in the large dining area on the military base. He had a way to survive in this situation. Running away wasn't an option. He was stuck hundreds of miles from his boat.

His social status seemed to be above the ordinary soldiers and less than the officers, much like the personal servants that served many of the officers. *Better off than an actual prisoner, but I'm not paid.* He was unique, and the people around him knew it.

Ohen had always been a little bit a loner, just because of his size, but he'd rapidly climbed the ranks to achieve his boat designer position and had acquired many professional friends.

Better to exist in this culture on a technical level, if I can. Otherwise I'll just be made a soldier or a laborer, because of my size.

And the officers were interested in what he had to say. If he could continue to hide his clairvoyant and telepathic insights behind logical explanations, they'd be happy to keep him around the table.

During the night, he stretched his senses to detect anything the Candorians might be up to. During the day, he hovered over the maps, speculating about what the invaders might be planning to do. He made sure he wasn't flawless, often suggesting two or three conflicting options, but when the officers got used to him guessing right so frequently, they paid attention.

But outside the planning room, the regular soldiers were paying attention as well.

Ohen's telepathic scans were picking up a lot of speculation about him. His size quickly caught people's eyes and the knowledge that he'd been captured as a suspected spy was all it took to turn a lot of hatred his direction.

He was making the best of the morning meal in the dining hall, scraping the bottom of the bowl to get the last of the mush and relishing the plain bread rolls that he'd been able to double-up on while in line. Malnutrition was one of the things that worried him the most.

He was easily a foot taller than the rest of them, but his body mass was considerably greater, although the uniform did disguise that to some extent. He had muscle trained for a much greater gravity and a skeleton with the strength to support it all. He needed much more food than the rest of them, just to keep from dwindling. Back on B3 he had supplements that could help him through this time, but it did him no good here.

As a child on Ha, he'd perfected the skill of giving the cooks a grateful smile as they prepared his plate, but the cooks here never looked at the soldiers. Their job was to move the food, and the various hands that appeared in their field of view to take it away were only an annoyance.

At least getting a glimpse into their heads let him know when he could get an extra helping without being called on it.

"We'll take him down as he turns the corner."

Ohen jerked. The leaked thought was about him. There were three, no four men, planning to ambush him on his way out.

The hatred was like a knife in his head. All of the group had lost good friends in battles with the Candorians and were convinced that he was an enemy spy in their midst. They didn't understand why their officers were turning a blind eye to him, but they knew their duty—kill the Candorians.

Ohen knew very well that although he was stronger than any of them, that as long as he had to conceal his special abilities, a group like that would likely overpower him. They were trained to fight and had the will to hurt their opponent.

He had neither the training nor the will.

If this was at night in the fog, he'd find a place out of sight and jump past them. But this was a clear, sunny morning. The dining hall had one entrance and one exit, designed to funnel as many troops through as possible in staggered mealtimes. The only way out was right into the ambush.

If he had friends, he could leave with them, but the soldiers around him weren't friends. Many of them were just as suspicious of him as those that wanted him dead.

But perhaps there were other exits.

He picked up his tray and went to the cleanup station. There was a door the cleanup crew used to collect the dirty dishes. The latch was hidden, but not to his clairvoyance. His extra height let him reach over the half-wall and open the latch with his fingers. People were watching, but he slipped into the cooking and cleanup area. Cooks stared at the giant in their midst for the first time, but said nothing as he hurriedly went out the service exit.

But his escape was noticed and the four waiting for him weren't the only ones in on the plot.

"There he is! Get him!"

He glance back at the people running his way. Five of them.

There was no help for it. Ohen put on more speed. He tried not to jump in the low gravity, but he could at least use his muscles to advantage.

He reached the conference building and raced past the guards standing at the entrance.

Inside, he paused to calm his heart and slow his breathing. The ambushers had given up once they knew he was inside the officer's conference area. They would risk an anonymous attack, but they wouldn't confront the officers.

"Next time, we'll get him for sure."

Commander Kobb frowned at him. He whispered to his assistant. He wanted to know why Barclay looked flustered.

Ohen decided to say nothing about it unless questioned. He focused on business. His only safety was in the protection the officers provided. They only tolerated him for his help.

. . .

Ohen was thumbing through a logbook when Kobb spoke.

"What are you doing?"

Ohen shook his head. "Wasting my time, it appears. This log book was labelled with the naval logo. I was hoping to see what it said about shipping on the Central Waterway."

"Why?"

"Something about the raid last week bothered me. Troop Bray reported that the Candorian camp they destroyed showed that the invaders were poorly dressed for the season. Cotton clothing that had been worn bare is what they said. I thought Candor, being an agricultural center, would have been able to provide better clothing for their soldiers."

Kobb nodded. "Why does it lead you to an out of date naval logbook?"

Ohen leaned over to a wide view map of the region. "Candor is this protected valley on the north side of the Mariner Canyon. The Mariner Waterway and the Central Waterway would be their main commercial connection to the rest of the world. If Candor used to ship cotton to others, but doesn't now, then that would tell me that Candor's cotton crops had failed or that they had shifted from cotton to food grain, or something like that. I'm just trying to get a feel for Candor's economic situation."

Kobb nodded. "I see what you're saying, but I doubt the naval logs would tell you anything more than the number of Candorian ships seen. They wouldn't tell you anything about the cargo."

"So ... no one nation controls the Central Waterway?"

"Xanthe controls its ports. Margareta controls the ports on the other side. No one really controls the ships in between."

Ohen nodded. "What happens if a Xanthe ship encounters a Candorian ship in the waterway?"

Kobb shook his head. "That's not my part of the war. I haven't heard of ship battles, but there's no reason the king would send me a message about it, anyway."

Ohen sighed. "Well, if it's not you part of the war, then it's not mine either. I was just wondering ...."

"Wondering what?"

Ohen shook his head. "You've been at this for decades. Xanthe isn't going to give up. Considering how the Candorians are fighting in spite of poor supplies, they aren't going to give up either. I was just looking for a way to undermine Candor's will to keep fighting. If the economics changed— if the Candorians suddenly had a way for their future that didn't involve encroaching on the highlands, then both sides could go back to their original borders and people could get back to growing crops and tending their herds."

Kobb shook his head. "Funny way to defeat an enemy."

"I'm not trying to defeat the enemy. I'm trying to have us win."

The commander waved his hand. "Anyway, you're working late today. The dining hall will close soon."

Ohen shrugged. He'd planned to leave when it got dark, to make it easier to avoid anyone waiting for him.

It seemed that Kobb was aware he was having problems. "Do you know the people who chased you?"

Ohen shelved the log book and shook his head. "No. Just people who think I'm a spy that should be put down."

"You could probably take them in a fight."

"In theory, one on one. But I can't fight a pack of them. Besides, it's not my job to fight Dorsa soldiers. Even if I was justified, even if I was attacked first, I'm the outsider. So it's a bad strategy to fight, but I can run. I'm good at that."

Kobb nodded. "Well, I'm hungry, come eat with me."

Ohen knew it was a one-time offer, but he was grateful anyway. They walked over to the officer's mess. The meal was just what he needed, rich in protein, some kind of meat in a savory sauce, along with a potato dish and several fruits.

They ate at Commander Bordoloi's table.

Their host looked at Ohen, "You're Barclay, Baron Rusher's guy, right?"

Ohen nodded. "He took an interest in me, yes."

"Then, are you leaving with him?"

Ohen said, "I wasn't aware of the baron's plans." He chuckled. "I'm hardly in his private circle."

Kobb said, "The baron turned him over to me. I'll make a decision in a month or so."

Now that he was aware of it, Ohen could pick up the right thoughts. Baron Rusher was going back to support the defenders of the western cities, now that his family was safely taken care of. Rusher and Kobb had several conversations about him. Every recommendation he made that led to a successful battle made it more important to keep him working for them.

Black Patch

The Chia military base had a store that sold a variety of items to soldiers. Ohen hadn't spent much time there, not until Kobb gave him a servant's stipend and ordered him to buy a patch for his uniform that marked him as an officer's assistant.

This was Ohen's second visit to the store, and he really didn't like being there.

He had been woken at dawn by the distant, dying thoughts of Will. Their battle with the Candorians had been won, but not without cost.

I put him in that battle. He died because of me.

Usurping the Candorian hold on that one mountain made the Dorsa villages in the area a lot safer. It had been Ohen's plan, moving the Dorsa in from two directions at once and cutting off their escape.

The black patch was cheap and not an official military insignia, but they were very common on soldier's uniforms. Ohen bought his and sat on a bench to sew it in place with a few quick stitches. He'd do a better job later.

But with the black patch on his left shoulder, he walked over to a warehouse where supply wagons were stocked.

One of the workers looked at him and frowned. Ohen confirmed it was the right man by his thoughts.

Carlson asked, "Are you looking for me?"

Ohen nodded. "Yes, I am. I'd like to speak to you when you're off duty."

"Give me a minute." Carson's thoughts asked, **"Why is the giant looking for me?"**

A few minute later he walked out. "You're that guy."

Ohen nodded. "Will was my guard when I was first captured."

Carson caught a glimpse of the loosely stitched black patch. "What happened?"

Ohen gestured to the direction of the Common House, "You know I work with the officers? Well, sometimes I hear things before most people."

Carson felt his dread increase. "Did Will …?"

Ohen nodded. "They won the battle, but Will didn't make it."

Carson nodded. "You know he's my cousin?"

"Will was very proud of his family here in Chia. While we were still together, he bragged about them quite a bit."

They sat down at a table and ordered fried vegetable chips and a bottle.

Carson looked at his patch. "I didn't realize you two were friends. He griped about you a lot." He poured two cups.

Ohen chuckled. "I got him in trouble too often, I guess. Yeah, maybe he didn't think of us as friends, but really I had no one else. I've always thought of him kindly."

Carson drank his cup down. "I wish I had time to know him better. Our families have been apart for twenty years or so."

Ohen tasted his drink, but didn't want or need the intoxication. He could knock himself out quite easily through other means. He really just needed to do his part.

A couple of drinks down, Carson said, "I guess I'll need a black patch myself on my right side, since he's family." He shook his head. "You haven't sewed that very good."

"I'll fix it later."

Carson shook his head. "No, take off the jacket. I'll do it."

And there in the middle of the crowd, no one really had any questions about one soldier helping another sew on a black patch.

...

It was several weeks later that Kobb came hunting for him.

Ohen looked up, sensing the conflict in the man's mind. "What's new?"

Kobb sighed, "You've done too good a job. The word got to the capital. The Royal Council has asked to see you."

"Is that good, or bad?"

"Bad for me. I've appreciated your insights. As for you, well, the court is a tough place. You won't have anyone to back you up."

Ohen sighed. "I thought things were going too well. Nobody has tried to kill me recently."

Kobb said, "Come with me, and bring a notepad."

They walked over through a causeway to a small building nearby. Ohen had heard of this place, but had never been permitted to enter.

There were three of the computers on a table with junior officers typing at two of them.

Ohen said, "You've got three computers. I thought they were rare."

"One is dedicated to communication with the capital. We use this other one to communicate with remote cities. The other is out of duty."

"Why?"

Kobb shrugged. Field Officer Dehghan said, "Two years ago, the computer reported that it was low on power. We're keeping it silent to use in case of emergency."

Kobb said, "I want you to set up a personal account on the computer system, so that I can communicate with you when off at the capital. Dehghan will help you with that. But, I've got to go for now. I'll need your public code before you leave."

"Thank you."

After Kobb left, Ohen waited until the officer was between tasks, before asking. "I've seen one of these before back in Dumont. If possible, I'd like to set up my account myself."

Dehghan frowned. "Do you know how to use a keyboard?"

"Oh, yes. I've seen it in action." The officer was doubtful, but moved aside so Ohen could sit at the computer.

Rather than speak to it, Ohen typed away.

"Computer is it possible for me to set up a public identity for communication."

A list of options appeared. Dehghan quickly lost interest as it appeared the giant knew what he was doing.

Ohen quickly identified himself using his previous code attached to the name "Ohen bar Clay" and chose to set up an alias, "Owen Barclay." He'd totally given up trying to get people to use his correct name.

Quickly he had the necessary public code and alias written down.

He asked the computer to give him a tutorial on how to send and receive messages. It wasn't difficult and no strain on his memory to remember everything.

He was sorely tempted to ask some of the questions nagging at him since he arrived on Mars, but now wasn't the time. Kobb just might question the officer on what Barclay had done.

...

The trip to the capital was an entirely different experience than the trip to Chia. He was assigned the task of taking care of three large crates filled with documents. They had nearly instantaneous communication over the computers, but routine paperwork and historical records were too extensive to turn over to a person to keyboard into the system. And at the receiving end, there wasn't anything like a printer to make a permanent record of what was received. All that was done by a communications officer as well, copying text from the display by hand.

In a dark brown satchel, Ohen also carried his personal records and a letter of introduction to a General Jonah. His uniform jacket had a new pin, marking him as a civilian asset.

Ohen wasn't entirely sure he had escaped the "suspected spy" category, but he could at least pretend he was respectable.

He had chosen to avoid saying goodbye to anyone other than his coworkers. How many of them were heading back into danger? He couldn't avoid his feeling of guilt every time he recommended an attack, knowing they had to face the sharp blades and flying bullets.

Analyzing the movement of opposing forces was very much engineering—something he was good at. It was altogether different that he was working with human lives rather than electrons.

Out the window, the lands east of Chia were more rugged and pockmarked with old crater valleys than the flatter lands to the west. The road took many twists and turns, adding many more miles on the trip to Orson, the capital. *I really ought to start thinking in kloms, rather than miles.* It was just easier to convert what he had to say.

The capital city was in another valley, likely originally a crater. Then, long before the terraforming, back when Mars had its own rivers and seas, the crater had been carved into a valley by a river flowing north to the ocean.

On the oldest maps, it had been named Orson Welles, spelled "Welles" rather than "Wells". Since there were really no wells in the area, people just shortened the name to Orson.

The city was central to the Xanthe region and had a navigable waterway to the ocean via the Shalbatana River. The road overland to the Central Waterway was smooth and well traveled.

Ohen hadn't been able to find a good history of the region's settlement days. Post-Plague was a time of conflicting legends. Every community of survivors had their own story with their local great heroes and evil villains from neighboring lands. Xanthe's official history told of the days when the Shalbatana, the Dorsa, the Ganges and the Tuskegee tribes were conquered and combined into one kingdom.

And at least in the central regions, it was a prosperous and relatively peaceful land.

They stopped for the night in a farming town that hosted a military way station. Horses were swapped out for rested ones and officers could sleep in real beds. Ohen grabbed a blanket and found a makeshift bed of hay where he could rest the night.

The sky was clear and the stars were out. He made out the constellations and it was certainly a different experience than it had been on the boat in the vacuum. There were several hundred stars visible, much fewer than it had been in space. Some of the constellations like Leo were very plainly visible. Others were less so, as their fainter stars were hard to see.

He wondered if the terraformers had moved lions to Mars. Certainly there had to be some predators to keep the ecology in balance. He'd never seen a lion other than the sketch Abe had made. It ought to be a fascinating beast.

Sampling the thoughts of the nearby farmers made him wish he'd landed in this region instead. They were worried about crops and pests getting into their grain stores. Thoughts of the war were rare and more concerned with Geason's son Tim, who had been conscripted into service, than with any immediate threat of danger to themselves.

Ohen woke before dawn, and was pleased to see the doublet morning star, Earth and the tiny Luna beside it. He wished for his telescopic camera, but he didn't even have one of the field glasses some of the officers used.

He cleared his thoughts and reached out to sense thoughts in the far distance, but other than just a hint, which could have been from distant people on Mars, he couldn't be sure there were people on Earth.

He'd dearly love to understand the legend of Earth. Why was it blocked off?

Perhaps if he survived Mars, he'd chase that goal.

Orson

Access to Orson, the city, was relatively easy. Their military wagon train barely stopped on the main road at the guard station. But there were levels to pass—the city, then the military base called Fort Dell. And then, off against the ancient crater wall was an impressive tower made of metal and glass. It looked like something more at home on Ha than on Mars. It had to have been built in pre-Plague times.

There were a few other glass-and-metal buildings in one region of the city, but none were as impressive as the Xanthe Tower.

Their wagons stopped just outside the tall gray stone wall that circled the tower. Ohen eyed the barricade. *I've got to start thinking in local measurements.*

He eyed the wall carefully and nodded. Ten meters high, giving the tower a fifty-meter protected area. Entrance any closer was restricted to foot traffic and push carts.

And a careful look at the tower showed why the barricade was built. The glass walls had been replaced on the floor level, probably scavenged from some other glass-and-metal building. There had been battles here, and the tower was impressive, but couldn't stand up to bullets and battering rams.

Some of the officers went inside, but it was nearly two hours later when someone came back out and ordered Ohen to pack his document crates onto a cart and bring them in.

Ohen packed all three of his crates on the provided cart and had no trouble pushing the cart over the smooth walkway into the building. Even the slight ramp at the entrance didn't slow him down much.

A soldier in an ornate uniform, brown with lacy, gold-colored trim, looked at his orders and then pointed him to a large, marked square in the floor. "Center yourself and your cart there."

It took him a moment to realize what was going on. As he moved into the square, a circle with a dial changed its reading, giving the weight of Ohen and his cargo. Once the soldier noted down the value in his log, he handed Ohen a card with a number.

"Wait over there until your number is called."

It was a long wait before it was his turn on the elevator. Ohen had plenty of time to watch how it worked.

He was familiar with elevators, but this one was servicing a twenty-story building in a world with no electricity. At least, he'd never seen electricity used for anything but the computers, and those all worked on an internal battery of some kind.

They had electricity when the building was built. The elevators had been electric originally, but they had to find an alternative, or make everyone walk up the stairs.

Someone had decided the tower was too impressive and useful to abandon. They had reengineered the elevators. Instead of electric motors, there was a simple pulley system, where one car went down as the other went up. The weight in the down car pulled the other one up.

Every time one of the cars arrived at the ground floor, a brake lever was pulled and then the people, cargo and ballast stones were unloaded and people waiting to go up loaded on board.

Ohen asked, "Do you sent ballast stones up over night?"

The soldier frowned at him. "Yes." He pointed at a large pipe. "That cable goes to a team of horses behind the tower."

Ohen nodded. "Nice. Elegant."

There was a nod, but inside the man's head he thought, **"When it works."**

The elevator crew were kept busy, juggling the weight requirements and the floors where people got on or off. There was a speaking tube beside the elevator where requests from the upper floors were relayed down. With the wait time, many people just took the stairs if they didn't have anything to carry.

Finally, it was Ohen's turn and he pushed his load inside. He was the only one. There was a slight jerk when the elevator lifted and there was a stop, probably for the down car as someone got on or off and then he was delivered to the archives on the 12th floor.

He turned over his orders and the archivists got to work processing the documents in the crates.

"I'm new here. Do I take the cart back down to the ground floor?"

One of the archivists, the first women he'd seen in uniform, laughed. "Oh, no! We never move anything on the elevator until it's needed. We'll keep it here on the 12th floor until someone else needs a cart."

The trim, gray-haired lady looked at his orders. "Besides, it says here that you're supposed to report to the Western Reaches Department on the 7th floor when you're done here."

He nodded. "I can take the stairs?"

"We all do, unless you've got time to kill."

...

There was a surprising amount of traffic on the stairs as he went down. It would have been so tempting to leap a dozen steps at a time, but he contented himself with two at a time to keep from bumping into anyone.

It was interesting that the stair height was taller than what he'd seen on Ha and other U'tanse settlements. These stairs had been constructed with the Martian gravity in mind. He wondered what the formula was. Steps needed to consider both the normal dimensions of the human body and the effort it took to step up and down, but were these measurements arrived at empirically or mathematically? Ohen shook his head. It was all done pre-Plague. He doubted anyone knew the answer now.

The 7th floor had a desk with a solemn-faced soldier who checked his documents. **"Ah, the giant. Jonah has been waiting for him."**

"Go to room 722, down that hallway." He handed back Ohen's documents.

On the doorway, there was a lettered plaque—General T. Jonah, Operations.

There were two men inside, and Ohen could tell that this was just the outer office. These two were assistants. Ohen introduced himself.

"Ah, Barclay. The general will see you soon. Sit there."

Ohen was well aware that "soon" was a very imprecise term. He was just one item of many that had been added to the general's list when the wagons had arrived. The chair was reasonably comfortable, but designed for smaller people. He settled in as well as he was able.

He closed his eyes and listened to the thoughts around him.

The Xanthe Tower was quite a beehive of activity. For the first time, Ohen got the sense that having the central government all in this one building was done for more than just prestige. The twenty stories, all stacked one on top of the other, gave them lots of storage in a very compact place. The archives in the higher floors were preserved and indexed. The military leaders were just a couple of floors away from each other at worst and they had large conference rooms where they could meet. The king and his family occupied the top three floors and the windows there gave them a great view of the city. It worked the other way as well. People in the city could see when various rooms on the tower were lit up at night and knew that the king and his government were busy.

...

General Jonah looked over his papers, although Ohen was aware he'd reviewed them just a few minutes earlier.

"It says here you came from Chase-on-Ha. Where exactly is that?"

The general had copies of all the interviews, even the ones from Marion when he was barely coherent. It would do no good to give him a new story.

"Ha is the moon where I grew up. It is very far away—not some place on your map."

Surprisingly, Jonah didn't immediately think he was crazy. There were flickers of thoughts—**"Phobos, Deimos? Luna? Atmosphere there. Spaceship? Barsoom?"**

But then the general moved on, not really caring where he came from.

"You're supposed to be some kind of strategic genius. Have you fought in wars before you came here?"

"No, sir. I can't really fight. I just look at the maps and suggest possibilities."

The man picked through the papers and asked, "When you suggested to Baron Rusher that Candorians might be at Foster's Pass, you explained that since the Candorians came from the south that they could block the road at any point. Your story at the first was that you had dropped in from the sky and knew nothing about local issues. How did you know that Candorians were attacking from the south?"

Ohen appreciated the precision of the general's thoughts. He needed to be precise as well.

"Being locked up with nothing to do, I listened to what people were saying around me."

"You were being held in a cell, with a guard ordered to avoid talking to you."

"There were other opportunities. As I was being loaded onto the wagon during the evacuation, I overhead an officer who I believe was named Wallace speak to Baron Rusher about the approaching Candorians, who were then three hours away to the south. It was obvious that these Candorians were the invading force that had a chance to take Dumont. If they were that powerful, then likely they had multiple forces in play. I had to keep my eyes open."

The next question was more detailed, concerning a couple of recommendations he'd given at Chia. Ohen replied in detail, stepping through all his thought processes, only hiding his psychic insights.

General Jonah wasn't satisfied.

"Barclay, do you have a perfect memory?"

Ohen nodded. "I don't brag about it, but I don't forget like most people."

"Then why have you forgotten how you arrived at the village of Marion?"

"I never forgot. People just couldn't believe me and made up their own explanation. It just got easier to go along with it when they claimed the blow on my head cost me my memories. I was always on the verge of being killed just for being a stranger. I didn't put up much of a fight."

Jonah leaned forward a bit. "Then tell me. Don't worry about what I believe or not. Just tell me the truth."

Ohen hesitated. It was a risk. He just had to go with his instincts and the general's thoughts.

"My people are the U'tanse. My ancestors lived on Earth, but were captured by people that weren't human back at the time of the Star."

"Demons?" came the man's thoughts.

Ohen tried not to let it show what he'd sensed.

"These captors were powerful, with machines that let them travel from star to star. They were also strong and beast-like, but in spite of all that, they were just people. They took my ancestors from a place on Earth called Texas and although my people were overpowered, the beasts could still bleed and be killed like anybody else. We were taken to their planet and made to serve as slaves for generations.

"Eventually, the U'tanse got the edge and took over all their machines. We left them as beasts hunting their favorite prey on their ancestral plains. Instead, we moved to their moon with all their machines.

"But among all the stars in the sky, we knew that Earth still existed and we hunted for it. I was among the crew of a star ship that finally found our home star. When I saw the cities and farmlands of Mars, I decided to visit here first.

"If it hadn't been for that bull and my head injury, I might have gone on to hunt for Earth."

The general sighed. "That's a story. So you say you're something like an ambassador for this lost branch of humanity?"

"More like a scout. I was just going to take a peek at the Mars people, just to see if the real ambassadors should land here."

Jonah shook his head. "Not in the middle of a war. Not here. Are you going to be rescued?"

"Not any time soon. I'm on my own, to survive or not. I was dropped into this war and I had to choose a side and be useful. There's no place for an outsider here."

"How soon do you expect your people to return for you?"

Ohen sighed. "A voyage to another star is very expensive and we only have a few ships. Years, if they ever arrive."

It was interesting that the general didn't consider whether Ohen's story was true or not. He was concerned with a more immediate point.

"Barclay, your work at Chia was considered valuable. What can you do for us here at Orson?"

Ohen could already tell that the man was planning to ease him into an advisory position much like he'd had at Chia. But now that he'd given his story, there was something more he could ask for.

"General, I could continue to look at maps and make suggestions, but there is something I've been hesitant to mention before."

"Go ahead."

"You see, my people, the U'tanse, are not as technologically advanced as your ancestors who put a breathable atmosphere on airless worlds, but we are more advanced than the current engineers who serve the Kingdom of Xanthe. It occurs to me that the main cord that holds the kingdom together is the communication supplied by the computers. And yet, one by one, they are dying and no one seems to be able to bring them back to life.

"I would like a take a good look at one and see if there was anything I could do about that."

Broken Computers

It took four days before he was granted access to the warehouse where expired computers were kept. General Jonah made it clear that his main job was to show up on the tenth floor where the map archives were kept and assist the officers who made use of them.

At first, it was to be a clerk's job, but he was allowed to speak when he had ideas. Ohen wasn't in any hurry to suggest military operations, not until he had gotten a lot more familiar with the bigger picture.

But then the clearance to visit the warehouse came through. The tired guard at the entrance looked over his papers, and Ohen could tell that with his eyesight failing, he was having trouble reading the smaller print.

"General Jonah wants me to look over the condition of the expired computers."

"I see that!" the gray-haired guard snapped, although he hadn't actually read those lines.

He was waved in. "The computers are stored in the back rooms."

Ohen nodded, "Thank you."

With his clairvoyance, he really didn't need a guide and Tom, the guard, was just as happy to stay in his office.

There were many different types. Ohen was glad that an attempt had been made to store them by class. One room had many smaller units that he'd never seen before—small ones like cylindrical food canisters in all colors. He'd heard that in the ancient times, back before this plague that had caused the collapse of civilization, that every home had one or more computers. Probably these little ones were from that time. They certainly had enough dust covering them that he could believe it. They only had a speaker grill, no keyboard, no screen.

There were others that looked portable, things people could carry in a bag or even a large pocket. He couldn't tell how people interacted with them. Certainly he couldn't put one of the U'tanse computers in such a tiny package. But they were all labeled as computers with the date they were archived, hundreds of years ago. These smaller ones had run out of power first, before the others.

Many of the gadgets weren't even computers. There were electric stoves, lamps, and other electrical devices that Ohen couldn't decipher at a glance.

Then he found where the bigger computers were stored. Some were elegant, with displays and keyboards that folded out of the case. More were like the one's he'd seen before, with a detachable case to protect the built-in keyboard and screen.

And other people had been there before him with the same goal.

Piled separately were the failed attempts to revive computers.

One had holes drilled in it and it appeared like it had been drenched in lubricating oil. He could still smell the residue—probably oil harvested from some animal, but now long dried out.

Another had feathers arranged in patterns, perhaps some kind of magic spell.

Three showed severe case damage, as if someone had opened them with a pry bar.

Ohen was overjoyed to see the insides exposed. It was clear someone had tried to revive a computer by swapping out parts from one computer to another. The attempt had been competently done. The case damage was the worst of it. Inside, many of the parts were modular and could be clamped in place with the electrical connections looking like engravings on the structural supports.

Ohen's clairvoyance allowed him to trace many of the connections, even when they weren't clearly visible. The keyboard and display connections were simple wires. The heart of the computer was a dense three-dimensional maze that was far beyond his ability to comprehend.

Back on Ha, he'd built computers by hand. He knew all the details of how transistors and large scale fabrication circuits worked. This computer was an entirely different class altogether. It would take him years just to map it out, if he could.

But that wasn't even the biggest mystery.

The whole unit was powered by something very familiar—a Delense-technology power cell, just like the ones in B3, his boat still hopefully hidden in the woods near the village of Marion. It was the same kind of power cell that powered all of the U'tanse technology.

This tiny power cell was obviously made with different materials and in different factories than the U'tanse used, but the components were all the same. The ancient humans had somehow acquired the tractor/pressor technology.

Could they have independently invented it? Somehow he doubted it.

The history of the extinct Delense was only partially documented. The U'tanse were sure that the Delense had made some trade to acquire the starships from some other race. There was a strong argument to be made that the tractor/pressor technology was also purchased. Every type of TP generator, from the tiny ones that gave his boat floor gravity to the large ones that stored massive quantities of energy to power the faster-than-light starship leaps, were all based around a crystalline matrix that could be grown, but no one had ever been able to create from scratch.

All the new units made in U'tanse factories were grown from previous starter crystals that could be traced back to the originals owned by the Delense. And the Delense factories discovered on the airless moon Ha were also designed to grow TP crystals from previous starter materials.

A reasonable theory was that the Delense somehow managed to make contact with other races while still just slaves to the Cerik, and had traded for both the TP technology and the starships. They just hadn't documented it. The Delense written language was nearly exclusively for technical use, never for stories or history. And now the whole species was extinct.

Ohen sat on one of the dusty piles of expired computers to think through what had happened in the past.

The Cerik had attempted an invasion of Earth, back during the supernova when civilization was collapsing. Abe's story in the Book told of Cerik boats that had been destroyed and contributed to the failure of the invasion. Abe had discovered a tractor/pressor generator that he had used in his own battle with the Cerik. Had it been rediscovered after they all left in the starship? Had Earth-based humanity built their own TP devices with Delense crystals as the starter?

It changed his whole view of what human civilization might have been like after the Star. Basic humanity and the U'tanse had both built their technology with the help of TP and the power cells. Obviously the original humans had gone far beyond the U'tanse if they'd used it to terraform Mars and Luna.

It was now obvious how Earth had acquired two more moons, but he was in awe of just how powerful the TP beams must have been to move those large bodies.

He shook his head. None of that history had any impact on what he needed to do here. What was important was that he knew that the output of a TP power cell was a direct current voltage—simple electricity. All he needed was to discover what the operating voltage for the computer was and then duplicate it. He didn't need to recharge the TP power cells. Batteries would do, or a hand-crank generator if it came to that. He just needed electricity.

The old computers could come back to life, and that would give this kingdom an edge over all their neighbors.

...

Lieutenant Pascal frowned. "You've never heard of concrete?"

Ohen shrugged. "I've heard of it. I've just never seen it before."

The Book mentioned concrete and back when the U'tanse were just slaves living in underground burrows, they had used that building material. Once the U'tanse moved to the airless moon of Ha, all building was done with metal and Delense technology ceramics. He wasn't even sure how concrete was made.

Pascal tapped the dense, rock-like wall. "We don't use it much, especially now that shipping from Isidis has fallen off—that's the region where most of the carbonates are mined. Most of the concrete construction you see around here happened over a hundred years ago."

Ohen nodded. "Isidis pretty far away."

"Yes, on the other side of the ocean, really." Pascal grinned, "You don't happen to have heard of any other limestone mines in your travels, have you?"

"Sorry, no."

Pascal said, "With the limited supplies we have around here, most carbonates go into making mortar for stone construction rather than big concrete slabs like this one."

Ohen resolved to take a closer look at the Isidis region when he got back to the map room. Some things puzzled him, and not just the chemistry of concrete, which he'd never studied.

Pascal led him on to the ironworks, a much smaller operation than Ohen had expected in the capital city. Likely, it was just one of many. The lieutenant left him to his research and headed back to the tower. Ohen had been grateful for the assistance. Finding his way around the city was still a trial for him. Going to work from the dorm building in the shadow of the tower was about all he'd managed thus far.

A middle-aged man in a leather apron holding a hammer looked up when Ohen walked into the noisy, smelly barn-like building. "Who are you?" he asked.

Ohen handed him the letter written by General Jonah.

"This doesn't make any sense," the blacksmith said. "There's no description of what you want done."

Ohen nodded. "That's my fault. I'm Owen Barclay, a civilian assistant to the general. I'm a foreigner, and I know a little bit about electrical work."

"Electrical? I'm no help there. I can make pipe fittings, pulleys, even a few custom guns, but nobody here knows electricity."

Ohen nodded. "But I do. I know how it works and I could even make a few things on my own, but I don't know where to get the materials or how to make something professional grade. I know less than your apprentices about how to make things well. I need your help."

After the blacksmith read the letter again, he sighed. "I'm Carl Meti, and I don't really have a lot of time to babysit something like this."

"I understand. Is there someone I could talk with? All I need is help from someone familiar with this place."

Meti nodded and bellowed, "Raymond! Come out here!"

Raymond Wills, the apprentice, looked in his late teens, and well on his way to developing muscles like Meti and Ohen himself.

Ohen had to be content with the boy, and that was reasonable. The military had regular jobs with the blacksmith and the letter from Jonah was clear that this was just a favor that the general would appreciate, rather than an urgent job.

Raymond asked, once Meti went back to work, "What can I help you with?"

"What kinds of metals do you use here?"

It turned out that in addition to iron, they used copper, zinc, tin, and lead, as well as a limited amount of gold and silver for some special projects.

"Copper? Do you have copper wire?"

Raymond chuckled. "Oh, yes. That's our starting material. All the old buildings had copper wire running through their walls. Every time one of those places had to be torn down or repaired, the workers stripped out the wire and sold it. It's not terribly expensive.

"One of my jobs is to remove the insulation and melt the copper down into ingots for other uses."

Ohen got a tour of the place. The iron stock was in the form of pipes of various diameter. Xanthe had a regular trade with Tempe where there was an iron smelter dating back to the historical Plague. Raymond didn't know much about how it worked, only that they could order iron pipes and get new stock within about three months. One of his jobs was to monitor their stock and get Meti to order replacements when it got low.

Sadly, Raymond knew nothing about magnetism. Ohen did some sample testing, and nothing showed any evidence of magnetic attraction.

Raymond watched his antics as he tapped pieces of iron against each other. "What are you trying to do?"

"We can make electricity by moving metal through a magnetic field. I just wanted to see if any of these pipes had magnetism."

Raymond frowned, "This isn't magic, is it? That's prohibited around here."

Ohen chuckled. "No. It's no more magic than starting a fire. And that's that we've got to do to regain the ability to make electricity—kindle electricity in some copper wires."

Coils

Ohen put his hand on the meter-wide globe of the planet Mars. Gloves were required, although he'd seen senior officers touch the maps with bare hands on occasion. He certainly couldn't afford to take such liberties. He wasn't even surprised when his gloves cost nearly twice what the normal sizes cost. It was one of the perils of his size.

Isidis was a large gulf on the opposite side of the globe, still part of the great northern ocean. Using the globe helped him locate it with his secret senses.

His clairvoyance had its limits. Alone at night, he could sense his boat, still apparently hidden in the woods far away in enemy-held lands. The Isidis Gulf was over five thousand kloms distant overland—even more taking the sea route. He couldn't sense much more than the presence of the gulf itself, and telepathically, the cities on its shores.

He certainly couldn't get any clue why shipping from there was less than it had been in the past. There was no hint that the weather had changed or that the place had been depopulated. It was likely something political.

Lieutenant Pascal said, "Are you asleep on your feet?"

Ohen blinked. "No, I was just thinking about what you said the other day. I'm puzzled why shipping from Isidis dropped off."

"Ask some of the old guys. That happened long before I came on board."

Ohen nodded. He might just do that eventually, but only after a quiet psychic probe at night when his dorm was quiet and it was daytime over the Isidis Gulf.

Most of the day was routine. He reviewed dispatches from all over Xanthe, including updates from the battles with the Candorians as well as reports on their other neighbors as well.

He marked the paper reports, underlining phrases or sentences to highlight points that he thought important. It was important that he had excuses for any of his opinions, because his notes were occasionally challenged. It was great if people acted on his insights on Candorian battle strategy or the piracy in the central straits, but he could never rely on his "hunches" alone.

At the end of his shift, he hurried over to the iron works.

"Hey, Raymond! What do you have for me?"

The apprentice waved him to silence. Ohen nodded. The boss must be irritated at this "electric nonsense" again. Meti couldn't really turn down the military's request, but he still objected to the time and materials Raymond was using up. They hurried over to the shed Raymond was using for the effort.

Ohen could just soak up the boy's pride in what he'd accomplished.

"Wow!" Ohen was honestly impressed at the second version of their battery. Ohen had sketched it out, but Raymond had made it real.

There were four hundred cells, twenty by twenty. Each was a thin plate of copper separated by cotton cloth from a similar plate of zinc. Each cell was contained in its own wooden box. The plates were wired together with copper wires as a series/parallel array.

"Have you tried it?"

Raymond shook his head. "I wanted you to check it out first."

Ohen felt his uneasiness. The boy had almost jumped out of his skin the first time with the original battery array, only four by four had been connected to a little hand-wound electromagnet and the current it produced had caused an iron nail to roll close enough to snap to the coil.

Ohen would have paid its weight in gold for a real voltmeter, but he was having to make do with what he could construct himself. Or rather, what he could get Raymond to construct for him.

Today's version was a small bobbin of wire connected with a hinge to an iron plate with a spring. By twisting the tension on the spring, he could theoretically test relative voltages.

Step one, they soaked the cotton with lemon juice. Next they connected the voltmeter to the battery.

SNAP! Raymond flinched. Ohen opened the connection. The spring flipped the plate back up.

He was all smiles. "That sounded like a decent voltage."

Raymond nodded. "That's electricity from my battery?"

"Of course. The electricity made the magnetism, which moved the metal plate."

The apprentice said, "Electricity can move things. What else can it do?"

"Once we make it reliable, electricity can light up buildings at night. It could also heat places. But the most important thing I hope to accomplish is to make the obsolete computers work again."

"Heat and light, I can understand that. But why not just use fire."

Ohen said, "You talked about all the copper wires in the old buildings. They were all there for a purpose. Electricity could be made in one place and wires could run to all those buildings. Instead of hundreds and thousands of fires to be started, maintained, and cared for, people could touch a switch and turn heat or light on at will. The same wires could run their computers or pump water or haul people or goods uphill. It could keep the bellows running for your furnace. Believe me, once you get used to electricity, you'll never want to be without it."

Raymond shook his head. "That's a lot of batteries."

"Oh, we won't use batteries, not like this one."

"Why not?"

"They don't last. You know how iron rusts?"

He nodded.

Ohen said, "Well the zinc and copper plates of the battery corrode like that as well. The more electricity you use, the more corrosion. Very quickly this battery will give up all its electricity and be useless. We're going to use this chemical electricity to make permanent magnets and with those, we'll make generators that don't corrode or run out. That's the goal."

...

It took a week's worth of experiments to find the best type of iron to make permanent magnets. Raymond was constantly puzzled at the techniques Ohen used, what with the different coils of wire he used and the physical strikes on the iron as the electricity was being used.

"Honestly," Ohen confessed, "this is the first time I've tried to make permanent magnets and this is all just trial and error. We'll make a dozen magnets and see which ones are strongest. Find a good recipe and repeat it. Back in my home city, I'd just buy strong magnets and never think about how they were made."

But the collection of reasonably strong magnets increased. None were as strong as the ones he'd used back on Ha, but those all used special alloys, not simple iron like he had here.

He was also working on the generator design. He knew the basics—spin a coil of wire in the magnetic field (or spin the magnet, whichever worked best) and then, for a DC generator, use a split-ring on the shaft to switch the electricity back and forth so that the negative output always came out the same wire and the positive came out the other.

Ohen drew the diagrams and explained them to Raymond. His assistant did the hard work of actually building a working model.

...

Ohen smiled at the surly warehouse guard. "I'm back again." He handed the new authorization sheet over. Since he knew the guard wouldn't even read it, he explained.

"This is an authorization to remove up to five devices of my choice from the warehouse. I'll go pick them out. You'll need to sign at the bottom when I've packed them up."

He wheeled the cart into the passageway. He picked out his choices; two full quality computers, two decorative lamps, and one table-top kitchen stove. The guard barely looked at his cart and scratched his signature on the sheet.

...

"Six weeks you've been coming here and treating my apprentice like your personal slave. His regular work has fallen off and you tell me you want him to start working on your project full time?" Meti crossed his arms and frowned. "You'd better have a good explanation for this."

Ohen nodded. "I do." He nodded to Raymond. The fifth version of their generator had a big flywheel. Raymond's muscles worked the crank, getting it slowly up to speed. The lamp on the table started glowing dimly at first, and then blossomed to full brightness. Meti put his hand up before his eyes as he adjusted to the light.

"That's bright."

Ohen nodded. "Touch it."

"What?"

"It's okay. Reach out and touch the light."

Meti looked suspicious, but hesitantly reached out. "It's cold. Well, not cold, but certainly not hot."

Ohen nodded. "There's a warehouse over by the river where there's dozens of those lamps. Just imagine a larger version of this generator, powered by oxen instead of Raymond. Don't you think the Xanthe Tower would just love lighting up the place with electricity. I do. I've seen the cleaning crew working every day to clean off the soot that collects on the inside of those windows. They'd love clean, bright electric lamps to work by rather than flickering candles and oil-burning lamps."

Meti asked, "You can work several lamps from one generator?"

Ohen flipped a switch and a second lamp lit up across the room. "All it needs is copper wires leading from the generator to the lamp, and the tower still has all its wiring in place."

He tapped the little stove. "This gadget is a stove to cook food. Sadly, Raymond isn't strong enough to get that working, but the larger generator would handle it."

Ohen waved his finger. "But lights and stoves are just the first step. If you really want the Xanthe royalty to shell out the gold for the generators that only you and Raymond can make, then imagine making generators that can run a computer. That's my real goal—bring the dead computers back to life."

Meti was struggling. "How much electricity does it take to make a computer run?"

Ohen shrugged. "That's my next project. I expect two to five times the power it takes to run that lamp."

Raymond gave a sigh and let the generator run down. "Sorry, but my arm was giving out."

Ohen gestured at the generator. "That's why I need Raymond full time. We need to make a generator that a troop of soldiers could take with them that would run a computer. Whether powered by soldiers or their animals, it needs to be something they can haul with them and set up quickly."

"But will it work? I've always been told that once a computer runs out of power, then it was dead forever."

Ohen smiled, "We'll just have to test that statement, won't we?"

Meti sighed. "So how much?"

Ohen could read his thoughts. The blacksmith was sold on the idea that electricity was real, and that he could make a great deal of money by being the only person who could build generators for the government. He was dreading how much Ohen would charge him for the privilege.

He held up one finger. "I'm working for General Jonah and I can't make those kinds of decisions." He held up a second. "I couldn't have gotten this far without Raymond."

He shrugged. "You're going to make some money. I'm going to get recognition for my work. If I need more money, I'll ask the general for it."

Meti nodded. "I'll need to hire some more people."

"Get ones like Raymond."

...

As much as he praised the apprentice, there were some tasks that Ohen couldn't trust to anyone but himself.

When Raymond was busy on the other side of the room altering the generator to work with foot-powered pedals, Ohen concentrated his clairvoyance on the interior of a computer.

Rather than pry the case off it like the one he'd seen at the warehouse, he wanted to make a very careful alteration to allow it to work with external power.

He marked two dots on the case, one above the main positive power cable and another over the negative line. With a small drill, he carefully cut the two small holes. With a tree sap resin to insulate them from the case, he carefully inserted threaded bolts into the hole just deep enough to make electrical contact with the power lines in the dark interior. With a little heat to seal the hole with the resin, he had two external contacts he could use to apply power.

The next step is going to be nerve wracking. Just what voltage needs to be applied to make the computer work? I'd hate to fry it. It really would be dead forever then.

Alive Again

Ohen knocked on General Jonah's door.

His assistant looked up. "Barclay. I'll tell him you're here."

The general was, as usual, behind a stack of papers. "Did you find what you were looking for in the naval archives?" He gestured to the chair. On an earlier visit, Jonah complained that speaking to his giant assistant gave him a neck ache.

Ohen sat. "I believe so. As I told you before, I was interested in the lack of shipping from the limestone mines in Isidis. I believe I have evidence that the trade was deliberately restricted some decades back, possibly by piracy."

"Your evidence?"

"Shipping records in the past showed a yearly fluctuation. Northern ice extended in the winter months all the way to the Arabian shore, sometimes closing off the passage altogether. There were increasing reports of piracy as well, when there was a sister ship close enough to observe the attack.

"The insurance rates on ships heading east climbed significantly during that time. Quite possibly shipping ended just because the ship owners didn't consider the trade profitable anymore. Even in the warmer months, ships try to stay within sight of land, rather than risk getting lost."

Ohen had much more evidence than he was saying, but he wasn't about to mention the few telepathic thoughts he'd collected from an island nation off the northern Arabian shore. From the few isolated thoughts, there was a hereditary ruler, the "Pirate King", who controlled all shipping for a thousand kloms in either direction. There was apparently a thriving economy in Isidis and points east that was the pirates' main hunting grounds.

He also knew that none of the ships, traders nor pirates, used computer communication. The devices were just too rare to risk on the ocean.

Just two days ago, he got his own computer up and running where he could pedal the generator and type at the same time. When he had a few hours alone after Raymond had given up for the night, he'd asked the computer a few questions.

Once he revealed to the military that he had a functioning way to power the computers, they would want every one of them. He doubted he'd be able to keep one for his personal use.

He was surprised that no communication could be read by a third party. Everything was encrypted, totally inaccessible without the proper private code. The concept was a little strange to the U'tanse. He understood encryption, but in a civilization of clairvoyants and telepaths, the very idea of secrecy was a little odd. You could keep your own thoughts secret, by constantly practicing a solid ineda, but sending a secret message? That was crazy. His whole new life on Mars had been learning how to keep his own secrets, and it wasn't comfortable.

Secrets were the realm of physics and history—puzzles to be solved. Secrets between people were unnatural.

Jonah looked at him, wondering if there was more that his strange new assistant was hiding.

Ohen caught the thought and decided it was time.

"General, in addition to this little historical puzzle, I had hoped to have some of your time to show you the results of my electrical work."

"Oh? I would be very interested in that."

...

Raymond was a little awed by the metal sparkles on Jonah's uniform. The general looked out of place in the blacksmith's work room.

Ohen said, "Raymond, could you show the general how the generator works?"

The boy hesitated. "Um, sir. This is an electric generator, just like the ancients used."

General Jonah nodded slowly. "Okay, but what can it do?"

"Um, let me show you!" He sat down in front of the pedals and started things moving.

"Well?" asked the general.

"Sir, if you would move that little paddle to the side, please."

"This one?"

"Yes, sir."

The lamp lit up. Raymond beamed. "The energy of my leg muscles is converted by this generator into electricity, which makes that ancient lamp glow brightly. Flip the paddle next to the first one."

The second lamp lit up.

The general frowned. "This isn't magic, is it?"

Ohen was ready to explain, but Raymond beat him to it.

"No, sir. This is just simple Pre-Plague science. There is electricity and magnetism, and they're like cousins. If you move a metal wire through a magnetic field, then it makes electricity move. It works the other way, too. Move electricity near magnetism and it'll make objects move. It's really simple, when you think about it. No magic at all."

When he stopped the pedaling, the flywheel slowed down and the lamps dimmed.

Jonah looked at Ohen. "If it's all that simple, then why did we ever lose the skill?"

Ohen shrugged. "As I understand it, when the Plague happened, everything collapsed. Spaceflight, of course, but everything that depended on spaceflight as well.

"There are many ways to make electricity. You can put two different metals in an acid solution and they'll make a little electricity. There's this generator Raymond and I have spend several weeks making. There's a lost skill of making electricity from sunlight as well.

"But the most powerful way uses the motion of the planets and the moons to make enormous quantities of electricity, and that can only be done in space. As far as I can tell, all of Mars was powered by that space electricity and when it was cut off, the survivors of the Plague just used the stored up energy they had left until it ran out. Nobody was really skilled in making generators like this one."

The general nodded. "And one by one, the computers ran out of their stored electricity. You say this all came from space?"

"Yes. My people were familiar with it as well. But we had records of the other methods as well. That's why I knew we could make this generator."

Jonah asked, "But is there any way to use this generator electricity to power a computer?"

Ohen nodded. "That's my goal. Let me show you something."

He lifted a modified computer from its storage box. He tapped the two bolts on the side. "This computer was pulled from the warehouse. I dusted it off and made connections to the electric power wires inside."

He pulled a cable that was connected to the generator and clamped the jaw-like connector onto the two bolts, making sure the black and white markings matched.

He gestured to the general. "Have a seat."

Jonah tapped on the computer. "It's dead."

"Raymond, start pedaling. Make sure you watch the limiter."

"Right." He began pedaling and the lamps began to glow again.

Ohen said to the general. "Try again."

There was a keyboard tap and the screen lit up. Jonah chuckled. "It's really working. Can I send a message with this?"

"Try it."

The general typed in his code and then sent a message to the officer on duty at the Xanthe Tower. A moment later, there was a reply.

General Jonah asked, "I'll buy this generator right now. How much?"

Meti, who had been lurking in the shadows, just watching the demonstration, took a few steps into the light.

Ohen said, "You'll have to discuss price with the head blacksmith here. However, there are two more things you should know.

"One, is that we're not finished with the design of this generator. It works fine here in the blacksmith shop, but you really want something that works on a wagon that can be pulled along with the other supplies supporting a cavalry troop. We don't have all the details worked out for that.

"Second, you don't want one of these generators and modified computers to fall into the hands of the Candorians or any other neighboring nation. Perhaps we can find a way to instantly destroy it or hide it in case a battle goes the wrong way."

Jonah nodded. "Yes, yes. I understand all that. But how soon? The quicker I can deploy another computer, the more lives we can save."

They had to discuss it. Over the next week Jonah made arrangements with the logistic officers so that they could understand the design needs of a wagon-portable generator. There would also be training needed. It wasn't as if you could point to the nearest soldier with good leg muscles and turn him loose to pedal the generator. Ohen had struggled to come up with a limiter that prevented the voltage from going too high if the pedaling became too energetic. It was basically a relay that switched in resistive wire when the voltage exceeded the desired level. The operator had to be listening for the click of the relay to avoid wasting effort.

In all, there were more weeks worth of design before the first of the military generators wagons was ready to be turned loose. Still, Ohen requisitioned more of the obsolete computers. He had to get started modifying them for external power, and he had his own motive as well. He wanted one for his own private use and the best way to make that happen was to take advantage of that warehouse guard who couldn't be bothered to double-check his numbers.

He'd learned quite a bit from late night conversations with the computer.

For one, although it was impossible to read anyone's messages without the proper code, he could ask certain questions that might have military consequences. One thing he learned was that there were only thirty-seven computers still active on the planet Mars, not counting the two he'd brought back to life. Comparing that with the eleven active in the Xanthe government, it seemed that most of the nations on the globe had only a handful at best.

Ohen had questioned his computer about the locations of the others but it refused to give him that information. There was some kind of built-in privacy rule. He was sure that the communications system itself had location data, if only to schedule messages at the right time when Phobos was in the sky. There appeared to be system data and public data and they had different rules.

If this had been one of the U'tanse computers, he'd have been able to change its programming to get access to that system data. Not with these. They were much more sophisticated than what he was familiar with.

In contrast, there were other details he was happy to get. The computer was open with the fact that its internal circuitry ran on eight volts. It would also give him the exact voltage he was supplying from his generator. That allowed him to calibrate his limiter relays and make a more accurate voltmeter.

He was disappointed that there was no way he could charge the internal power cell from his generator, but he hadn't expected that anyway.

The power cells, even on his hidden boat, were generally designed only to provide power. Setting up a charging beam was more complex, requiring more general purpose beam equipment.

I could probably get permission from the general to keep using one of these computers for my generator testing, but if field conditions changed, even that wouldn't last long. He's desperate to get more communication links to the remote forces.

The only way Ohen could see to keep a computer was to get one now by subterfuge and keep it hidden. It would be bad if he were caught at it, but as a pure information resource, it was just too valuable to give up.

When he picked up the newly requisitioned computers from the warehouse, he added several other items, like lamps, a couple of the voice-only computers, and several devices which were only marked as unknown-purpose devices. His primary purpose was mixing up the numbers so he could hide another computer for his own use. His excuse was that he wanted to reverse-engineer the house and building electrical wiring that had been in use before the Plague.

He managed a room for his own use at the ironworks, a place where he could close the door and work without being interrupted by anyone but Raymond. Even then, he had a good feel for Raymond's thought patterns, so he was never likely to be surprised.

He had a lot of questions to ask of the computer.

King's Demo

General Jonah was frustrated at the delay in getting the new computers into the field—so much so that he confiscated the two prototypes Ohen was using, putting them into service at the tower. The general sent the old ones off to the battlefront. There was a regular flow of officers who came by to see the generator in action. The communications staff complained about the generator noise and the periodic delays when the soldiers with strong legs had to swap out, but the general's word was law.

Ohen insisted on having a second generator on hand and wired up, just in case the first one failed for any reason. He was too much an engineer to believe that equipment lasted forever.

Raymond and the blacksmith staff took over all the generator work. Ohen only showed up periodically to review the design changes and give his blessing. Raymond was becoming even more skilled at generator design that Ohen was. He had a good feel for how this part of electro-magnetic interaction worked.

Raymond even took over the task of drilling the charging ports in the old computers, based on exacting templates Ohen had created. Only when Raymond had successfully installed the bolts three times did Ohen relax about walking away from the process. The craftsman really did good work, even if he couldn't see the insides of the boxes like a clairvoyant. Imagination and a sensitive feel for the pressure on his tools gave Raymond nearly as good an image in his mind as if he could see the real thing.

Ohen spend most of his days in the map room.

Lieutenant Pascal asked, "With all the pressure on the southern front, why do you spend so much time looking at the naval maps? We aren't fighting the Candorians on the sea."

Ohen shrugged. "Maybe we should."

"What do you mean by that?"

"Oh, I'm just trying to get the big picture here. If the Candorians suddenly made peace and retreated back to their valleys, where would the next dangers arise?"

Pascal frowned, looking over the maps. "It's hard to tell. We've had conflicts with Margareta and Echus in the past. And of course, there's always the problem of the pirates. And since we're sending most of our troops to the southwest, the Tempe in the north are taking advantage of our weakness there."

Ohen nodded. "At first glance, all the nations are the same. Their farmers feed the population and the soldiers keep the borders safe. They trade with their neighbors, when they're not fighting over the border lands.

"Xanthe Kingdom has gotten so large and powerful because of two things; the Old Road and the computers. The computers keep the king in touch with the remote districts and the road allows troops to move quickly to where they're needed."

Ohen looked at Pascal. "Don't you think that the kingdom would be much more secure if there were more computers and much improved roads to the districts that are distant from the Old Road?"

"Well, yes, probably. That's something to do, but after the southern conflict is resolved. We can't afford to send people to build roads when they need to be fighting."

Ohen shrugged. "Maybe. But you can never count on an extended period of peace. Like you say, there are always neighbors waiting for weakness."

He sensed the general listening in. He stood and bowed his head.

General Jonah waved a dismissal. "Barclay, I need to speak to you."

They walked out and headed to his office.

Ohen had noticed that the general had a rudimentary ineda, although he was sure the military man had no idea that he had a telepathic block. It came and went, depending on what the man was thinking about.

Ohen could usually follow anyone's thoughts, but Jonah's drifted in and out, depending on the topic and how sensitive the issue was. Ohen was sure he'd never had any training at it, because it wasn't reliable at all. But it was fascinating that ineda was something that could appear spontaneously in humans. Real ineda training among the U'tanse was handed down from concepts learned from the Cerik. The name "ineda" itself was Cerik.

He shrugged. If telepathy was common across species, then it wasn't too surprising that ineda, the telepathic block, could be as well.

The general waved at the guest seat. He sat at his desk.

"Barclay, the king has noticed the generators. He's been briefed, but he wants to see it in action. You'll need to do another demonstration."

Ohen frowned. He didn't want to be too public.

"Do I need to give the demonstration?"

"Yes." The general was certain.

Ohen sighed. "Okay, how much time do I have to prepare? I assume here in the Tower?"

"Yes, that would be best. And today or tomorrow."

Ohen stared up at the ceiling. "Okay. I'd better make preparations."

. . .

"Raymond!" Ohen called as he jogged up to the ironworks.
"Raymond!"

Several workers looked up. One pointed to one of the work sheds.

Raymond looked up as he came in. "What is it?"

Ohen was breathing a little heavy. He'd run nearly the whole way from the Tower.

"Did you ever finish that spring-wound thing you were playing with?"

"Um. Nearly. Do you need it?"

Ohen nodded. "Yes, before tomorrow." He explained his urgency.

Raymond's eyes went wide. "For the king?"

. . .

I hope I don't look like I've been up all night.

Ohen looked at Raymond. Other than looking like he was dressed in borrowed clothes rather than his stained work apron, he looked a little nervous. It had taken a special request from the general to allow the blacksmith apprentice into the restricted areas of the Tower. Raymond tried to keep his eyes on his equipment rather than make eye contact with any of the people in fancy uniforms.

They were set up in a conference room just a few doors down from the computer room. The Tower had four computers in use nearly all the time. Two had been replaced with his prototypes and Ohen had heard the noise from the generator when they'd arrived. It wasn't too bad, but it was different from the normally silent workrooms in the Tower.

Ohen was unhappy with the number of people in the conference room. He had planned for a more personal demonstration for the king. This wasn't like a U'tanse conference room with a large display where he could show off the details. His demonstration was more designed to be hands-on with the king or perhaps an assistant. It would be difficult for showing a dozen people at a time.

He could tell that Raymond felt he was out of his depth. Ohen hoped that he wouldn't freeze up.

A superficial telepathic survey of the spectators showed some were just curious, some wanted to be in any meeting where the King Harmon was present, and a couple were actively hostile. Perhaps it was because he was an unknown foreigner coming in and making changes to the computer system.

Everyone rose from their chairs and bowed as the king and his two assistants entered. General Jonah greeted him and introduced Owen Barclay.

The king was a little distracted, worrying about the news from a previous meeting. Cotton imports had been cut by the nation of Margareta across the Central Waterway with no explanation. All the merchants were reporting the same thing and he was worried that there was some conflict in the making, but there was no clue as to the cause.

Still, the king had been impressed by the general's excitement about the computers, and he really needed to know whether this was just a minor improvement, or something significant.

Ohen met the king's gaze and smiled.

His majesty nodded and asked, "What's this new thing I hear about?"

Questions from the beginning. Ohen was pleased. He could work with that.

"Your majesty is aware that everything must be fed." He gestured to the room. "Soldiers must be fed. There is grain and hay for the livestock. Even the ships at sea must have good winds to sail.

"Everything it seems, but the computers that provide rapid communication with all parts of your kingdom. But you see, they need their fuel as well, and it's called electricity. The computers have lasted so long because they have contained a store of electricity left over from Pre-Plague times. And as I'm sure you know, one by one, the computers have starved to death as their store of electricity has been exhausted.

"In the whole world, there are only three dozen computers still working, and many are on their last legs. The rapid communication that can be the lifeblood of the kingdom has been dwindling away, year by year.

"Until today."

Ohen began a repeat of the explanation he gave the general, explaining why Mars lost access to space-generated power and why other ways of power were never applied.

He had to pick up the pace, because many of the audience had been distracted by the news that there were only three dozen computers left. That hadn't been public knowledge. Many thought that there was always a new supply of undiscovered computers to fill the gap, just waiting to be found.

"As you're aware, I wasn't born here. My people have been aware of other ways of generating electricity, and with the help of the excellent people at Meti Ironworks, we have been able to recreate the mechanical generators that were used by the human race back before space-generated electricity took over the market.

"Raymond. Bring out prototype three."

It was a small, hand-cranked generator, already wired up to one of the lamps.

Raymond had been coached, starting slow and cranking unevenly, so that the audience could easily see the light brightening and dimming in sync with his efforts.

Then the king asked the usual question. "This isn't magic, is it?"

Raymond spoke, "No! It's just …." It was an automatic thing with him, since so many people asked that question. And then he realized he'd spoken out of turn, to the king, no less! His face showed his panic.

Ohen said, "Go ahead Raymond, you explain this better than I do."

To the king he said, "Your majesty, Raymond Wills is an employee of Meti Ironworks and has proven to be an excellent designer of electrical generators."

The king nodded. "Proceed."

Raymond stuttered a little, then began his explanation of how electricity and magnetism were cousins and worked together. It was plain to everyone in the audience that Wills was uneducated and spoke with a workman's accent. His explanation was simple and easy to follow, even if half the audience never quite understood the physics of it all. He sounded like a blacksmith explaining how to hammer out a horseshoe, not at all like someone using a magic spell, and that was all Ohen had hoped for.

When Raymond stalled out, Ohen picked up the explanation.

"This hand-cranked generator is just an early effort. The one in the computer room is worked with the strong leg muscles of healthy soldiers, and even that is just temporary. You're aware of the oxen that lift the elevator stones during the night. Soon, there might be another ox circle where their efforts could power a larger generator day and night. Not only could this electricity power keep the computers running, but also light the whole Tower with these electric lights.

"You might come to miss the scent of oil lamps eventually."

There was a chuckle from the audience.

Ohen skipped over his grand plan to build a water-powered generator and provide electricity for more than just the Tower. He had to keep the king's interest. The man had other problems on his mind.

"And now, Raymond and I have made a gift for your majesty."

Raymond lifted the wooden box with the small gold-colored canister in its center. There was a crank on the side.

The Gift

King Harmon asked, "What is it?"

Ohen said, "When I was searching the warehouse, looking for computers to bring back to life, I discovered some that look like this—a simple canister. This is a computer, but one that isn't really useful for the military. It has no keyboard and no display screen.

"However, once the owner of the device registers their identification number by speaking it in private, this computer will recognize the owner's voice and perform many of the standard functions."

He nodded to Raymond. The assistant cranked the handle on the box several times and then pressed a button.

"Just to demonstrate, I've already registered my number before coming here. Let me show you.

"Computer, does General Jonah of Xanthe have a public communication identity?"

The voice, slightly different from the ones used by the computers down the hallway, spoke, "Yes."

"Please send the following message to General Jonah, 'Urgent: Owen Barclay requests a steak dinner at your earliest convenience.'"

The computer said, "Message sent."

Ohen smiled and said to the audience, "I apologize for that. I've got a really big appetite."

There was a polite chuckle from the group. But barely had people reacted when running footsteps could be heard. A messenger requested entrance and a slip of paper was handed to the general.

Jonah read from the paper. "Owen Barclay requests a steak dinner at your earliest convenience."

Ohen nodded. "So, after the king takes possession of this ... personal computer, and in the privacy of the top floor, enters his secret number, his majesty can send and receive messages to anyone who uses the computer system for communication."

He looked directly at the king. "Your majesty, in the privacy of your residence, you will now be able to directly contact anyone in your kingdom. Or even farther."

The king frowned in puzzlement. Ohen pushed on.

"For example, there are other nations who use computers. It might be possible, just for example, to request a private dialog with the leader of ... Margareta, perhaps, or Tempe or Cydonia. I honestly don't know which nations still have computers, but just as I requested to see if General Jonah had a public identity, the computer knows these things and can be asked. The computer keeps all communications private, but it will tell you if they can be contacted.

"There are many other things that can be asked as well."

He turned to the computer. "Computer, how far is it to Olympus Mons? What is the weather over the Central Waterway? If a ship can make three kloms per hour, how long would it take to sail from Da Vinci to Mclaughlin? What is the price of wheat in Tempe? Where is the best place to buy horses?"

The computer began speaking its answers, but just after it said it didn't know the price of wheat, it said, "Power dropping."

Ohen reached for the crank. "Raymond Wills created this special generator. It has just the right power for one of these canister computers and the crank winds a spring that keeps the generator running for five or six minutes." He quickly wound the spring and pressed the button.

The computer came back up and listed three different horse markets.

In the audience, one of the people was thinking, **This guy is dangerous. I need to report him quickly.**

Ohen couldn't immediately identify who that person was. He couldn't be distracted. He had to continue with his demonstration for the king.

King Harmon stroked his beard. "And this computer will do these things for me?"

"Yes, after I tell it to forget my voice and it registers yours. That has to be done in private."

The king nodded. He'd been keeping his personal code private since a child, even though he'd never had much of a chance to use a computer himself. They were all dedicated to the military.

After Ohen reviewed what materials were needed to make a generator, the group moved to the computer room to watch generator-run computers in action from the doorway.

"Electricity can run for long distances over copper wires, and the Tower has been wired for that since it was built before the Plague. Eventually the generator will be moved elsewhere, if for no other reason than the distracting noise. And if the generator is large enough, it could run lights and other things in addition to the computers."

As the meeting broke up, King Harmon said, "Barclay, come with me to the residence to make sure I set up the computer properly."

Ohen retrieved the canister computer from Raymond. "Don't wander. I'll come back for you. You'll have to be escorted out of the Tower."

Raymond nodded, grateful to take the rest of his gear, find a chair and be out of sight of all the important people.

Ohen picked up the gift computer and carried it easily, following the king and his bodyguard.

The bodyguard's thoughts were clear. This Barclay person was an admitted foreigner, also large and strong. The guard was on edge, ready to move the instant the stranger made any hostile action.

Ohen kept his distance, passively holding on to the box.

The elevator operators had been warned that the king was approaching. The elevator was empty and waiting for him.

The three of them walked in. A moment after the guard closed the door, it began climbing. The king said, "Are there more of these small computers?"

"Yes, your majesty, covered in dust, but many are still usable if paired with a generator."

The king nodded. He didn't say more, but Ohen could read his thoughts. There were Xanthe ambassadors in many of the neighboring kingdoms. If they could send reports back to the king at computer speed, it could be a game-changer in international politics. The trick would be disguising the computers so that no one knew what they were.

With Ohen's thoughts turned to the topic of spying on enemies, he wondered if the person who thought he was dangerous was some kind of spy in the king's court. How could he tell? It might just be someone afraid of magic who didn't believe Raymond's explanation.

He'd need to keep listening for similar thoughts.

When they reached the residence, the king led the way to a private office. Ohen was a little shocked by the appearance of the place. He'd sampled many people's imaginations when thinking of the king's residence floors. People had imagined gold everywhere.

Reality wasn't like that. Soft, comfortable-looking fabrics were in evidence everywhere. There were paintings on the interior walls. The lanterns were hardly visible in the daylight when the windows gave plenty of illumination.

"Put it here." The king moved a vase from a small table next to the wall.

Ohen positioned the computer where the king, who was right-handed, could easily turn the crank. Ohen himself wound the spring until he felt it tighten and then pressed the button that started the generator.

"Computer, release my personal identification and prepare for a new user."

"Previous identity removed. New user please state your private identity code."

The king waved Ohen and the guard out of the room.

The guard watched Ohen closely as they closed the door behind them. Ohen was listening to the king's thoughts as he went through the process of registering his identity. Ohen had no intention of ever using the king's private code to listen in on the king's communications, but the code was now in his memory, for better or worse.

The king then immediately sent a message to a cousin at his estate in Chamicel. There was a military outpost near there and he had to address the message to that location. He was confident a messenger would take the letter the rest of the way.

Most of the message didn't make sense to Ohen, concerned as it was with other family members, but he knew that the king was just testing the system.

He played with getting questions from the computer until the spring wound down. He wound it up and was pleased to get the acknowledgement from the military outpost that his message had been received.

When the door opened a few minutes later, the king was beaming.

"Barclay, why doesn't the computer know the price of wheat?"

Ohen bowed. "I haven't asked the computer directly, however I suppose that nobody has told any of the computers that information. If a person sent a private message that contained the price of wheat, then that message would still be private and the computer couldn't disclose it."

"But it knows the weather."

"Likely, there is a computer on the moon Phobos with eyes that can see the clouds on the planet below. I don't know how sharp those eyes are, but it might be interesting to ask."

The king nodded. "Yes, indeed it would. I thank you for this gift. Expect that I may order more like it in the future."

Ohen bowed. "I'll make sure that Meti Ironworks will be working on more of those spring-wound generators then."

He was dismissed and Ohen chose to take the stairway down rather than wait for the elevator. He had to pass several frowning guards on the way down.

He spoke to Raymond on the way out.

"The king really was impressed by the little computer. You'd better be planning on making more of those generators. He'll order more."

Raymond nodded. "I'm just glad to be gone from the Tower. There were so many soldiers, and they all were suspicious of me."

Ohen chuckled. "It's the uniforms. You were wearing the wrong colored clothes. With me, it's my size. I stand out as well."

The both of them went back to the ironworks. Meti was updated on how well the king's demonstration went and looked thoughtful when he considered that he'd need to add producing another kind of generator to his already full work schedule.

Ohen retired to the little workshop he used when he wanted to experiment with the computer. Once the door was closed, he sat in the chair and began slowly pedaling.

"Computer, can you display your most recent image of Orson Welles crater as imaged from Phobos?"

"Yes, at what resolution?"

"Showing the smallest ground features."

The screen, which normally only displayed lines of text, cleared and the image appeared. The crater with the river flowing through was easily identifiable. It was obviously taken at an oblique angle. He wondered if this was just part of some larger image.

"When was this taken?"

"Four hundred and thirty-seven years ago. It is the only image in local memory."

"Are images still being taken from Phobos?"

"Yes."

"When will Phobos be in position to take more photos in this local area?"

He'd just missed the window, so it would be several hours before Phobos would be overhead again. He'd have to wait.

Should I do this alone, or share this with the general?

Mapping Thoughts

General Jonah walked into the map room.

"Barclay, what are you doing here this late? Don't you eat? Sleep?"

Ohen chuckled. "Sorry. I was just getting a real good look at this detail map while the place was relatively empty."

The general moved up beside him. They leaned over the glass. "What do you see?"

Ohen ran his finger over the glass, tracing the bay and the port city of Simud. "How old is this map?"

Jonah shook his head. "Pretty old. I think I read that the glass protection sheets were added about three hundred years ago. It was a major effort, getting those large glass planes into this room. They had to dismount some external windows and haul them up the outside of the tower."

Ohen shook his head. "Older than that, probably. Probably Pre-Plague."

"Your reasoning?"

Ohen scratched his face. He hadn't shaved in a few days and it was getting rough. "Well, I guess two lines of thought. One is that the current map of Port Simud is a much larger city than is shown here. The detail is remarkable on this one, but the city looks new, with more glass buildings and much fewer stone ones."

"You can tell that?"

Ohen pointed, "Yes, see, there are bright dots here and here. Glass buildings could catch the sunlight and reflect it up like that. Stonework and wooden buildings don't do that."

Jonah peered closely at the map just under the glass. "I can barely make out the buildings, but I see what you mean."

"Another thing is that I don't see any ships. For a port city, on a clear day like this one, there should be at least some ships with their sails unfurled. That should appear as white dots here in the bay, but I don't see a single one. There might have been boats Pre-Plague, but they might just have been electrically powered, since power was so plentiful back then. Nobody had gotten around to building sailing ships."

Ohen straightened up a little. "And the other line of reasoning is that this is obviously a photograph, taken with a camera from space, or possibly from a flying craft of some kind. I suspect it's from space because of the slightly hazy quality of the image.

"And when I asked for the weather over the Central Waterway during the king's demonstration, the computer was able to answer. The only way it could have known about that storm was that the relay computer on Phobos could see it."

The general frowned. Ohen could tell that he was a little amused.

"Barclay, for all your amazing ability to think through things, you have one bad flaw."

"Oh?"

"Yes, you can't lie very well. Showing me this map information was some kind of ploy to get me sucked into some scheme of yours, isn't it? What do you really want to tell me about?"

Ohen sighed and shook his head. "Okay. I'll get to the point. Phobos has a camera. What do you know about cameras?"

"Not much. They're well known, historically." The general gestured to the room. "We know these maps were made with some kind of camera, but it's a lost technology. About a hundred years ago ... no, less than that, maybe eighty, there was some genius in Tempe, some artist. He experimented with camera work. He made some court portraits that looked like fuzzy engravings on metal plates. It was remarkable, according to what I've read, but nothing at all like the colorful details we have with these maps."

"Has there been any work on photography since then?"

"No. The artist died and his work was lost."

Ohen frowned. "That's sad. Someone else should have kept working on it."

"Barclay, that's not how things work in the real world. You think Meti will happily turn the plans of his generators over to other blacksmiths so that they can compete with him? No, he'll keep the secret locked up as long as he can."

Ohen said, "Maybe I should have a talk with him."

The general chuckled. "No, we *want* the generator design to remain secret. I certainly don't want the Candorians to coordinate their troops using computers like I'm trying to do."

"I see that, it's just that I'm thinking long-term. One genius invented some kind of camera, but when he died, that gain was lost. If over the past eighty years, a dozen, or perhaps a hundred people had been working off of that same discovery, then maybe your troops could have been able to take detailed photos of enemy positions and learn much more about them than can just be learned in a quick encounter and written down later. Better photography could change a lot of things."

Jonah looked down at the map. "Maybe."

Ohen said, "It's certain. The more people that work on the puzzle, the faster it'll get solved. I had the knowledge of how generators worked, but Raymond Wills knew how to make actual machines better than I ever could. Meti knows how to coordinate the whole ironworks so that the right people and the right raw materials come together to get things done. One soldier can't win a battle."

"I still don't want the secret of the generators to get out."

"It may be too late for that. Who were all those people at the king's demonstration? Can you guarantee that all of them are perfectly loyal to Xanthe? Then, there are the common workers at Meti's ironworks. How many of them know enough of the workings that they could walk away, take a trip to Tempe or elsewhere, and set up shop for themselves?"

The general grumbled. "That's a problem."

"Perhaps. You're still in a position of power. You've got the money and you've got me. I'm the one who brought the idea to Meti and he's always expected to have to pay for the privilege of using my invention. You can demand that the designs for every generator version has to be turned over to you. He can make improvements, but as long as you're paying for everything, he has to document them well enough so that you could turn to some other blacksmith and get the same generator from them.

"Make it very clear to Meti that the gold will only keep flowing his way if he keeps producing good product, and that it could all stop if the secret gets out. Make sure he knows that he has to keep his workers loyal. Some of that gold has to go to them."

Jonah sighed. "You seem to think I have an infinite supply of money."

"The budgets for Xanthe's military and Meti's blacksmith shop are not even close to the same. I'm sure you have an officer somewhere who is very good at making merchants happy on a minimum of gold."

"Probably. Just more to keep me working late. But, we've gotten off track I think. What is Barclay's latest scheme?"

"Can we get some time on one of the computers privately, just you and me? We don't want things to be overheard."

The general pulled a timepiece from his pocket. "Yes, probably. Now?"

"Yes, that would be ideal."

They went into the computer room, still the only room illuminated with electric lights. There were two people—a middle-aged man at the keyboard of a computer, and the soldier slowly pedaling the generator.

They chose the computer on the left that was as far as possible from the other people. They pulled up two chairs and Ohen signed in. He typed, "Display the photo I requested yesterday."

The general gasped when the screen blanked and the image appeared. He whispered, "Is that a map? I didn't know computers could do this."

Ohen nodded, then typed, "Center the image on the port city at Melas."

The image zoomed in on the central bay of Candor and a crater at the edge of the waterway covered the central third of the image. On the land, the buildings of the city could be made out.

Ohen tapped his finger on the screen and looked at Jonah.

The general frowned, then whispered, "All of those white dots are ships?"

Ohen said, "I'm only guessing, but I see a dozen ships in that bay. If their sails are furled, then we might not see them at all. And I can only guess what they're doing there."

"Where are they from?"

"This is just a snapshot in time, taken from Phobos yesterday afternoon. We'll have to take more if we want to track the ships. However...."

Ohen typed on the keyboard and the image shifted eastward. There were two more white dots making their way in the channel that filled the Mariner Valley. He repeated the process several times, noting other ships.

He whispered, "If all of these ships are part of the same trade with Candor, then it appears that they are ending up at the Margareta port of Conches."

Jonah gave a heavy sigh. "Margareta. They've been acting strangely lately. Could they and Candor have made some kind of pact?"

"You're the general. I have no idea why Margareta would want to be involved in this."

Jonah grumbled. "I can imagine several reasons. But if Candor is getting dozens of ships worth of supplies from the outside, then maybe that's why they've been pressing the battle for so long."

He looked at Barclay, "How long has this been going on?"

Ohen shook his head. "I can't look into the past. Phobos only takes these kinds of photos when requested or for its own reasons. I don't think there is any historical archive that we can look through."

"But the computer took this map at your request?"

"Yes, but I get the impression that there's a limit of how many it can take, and it can only be done when Phobos is overhead during daylight hours."

The general's thoughts were racing. Ohen couldn't follow all of it, the man had decades of experience and his own internal thoughts were an opaque flicker of shortcuts and partial concepts. And then as if he tightened up, the general's thoughts vanished as Jonah's own version of ineda made it a useless effort to guess what he was considering.

"Barclay, we can do this again?"

"Yes, but there can be no hint of this. If Tempe or Margareta has a computer and wants Phobos to take a picture of Xanthe, there's nothing we can do to stop the computers from complying with them."

Jonah nodded, his eyes like a thunderstorm. "I'll need a separate room for this with its own computer and generator, I guess. Can we see troop locations on the ground with this?"

"We can barely see a full sized ship at sail. We can't see people, but maybe supply wagon trains or clouds of dust. I just don't know. I've never tried."

The general nodded. "I need a trusted officer with really good eyesight. I think I know the man. How soon can we get another computer?"

Ohen sighed. "I'll have to check with Raymond."

Chimbote Siblings

Adding a new project to his plate, a very secretive one at that, meant that none of Ohen's regular duties went away. Ten-hour work days crept up to twelve, and beyond as necessary.

He was surprised when Lieutenant Pascal popped into the map room a little after sunset and waved.

"What's up?" Ohen asked.

"A steak dinner, with all the extras. You just have to quit work in the next thirty minutes, or the opportunity is gone."

Ohen put his hand on his stomach. "You're buying?"

"Well, let's say you won't be. Are you coming?"

Ohen waved at his papers. "Fifteen minutes. I'll meet you at the stairway."

Pascal's mind was easy to read, but Ohen just gave it a light scan. This was supposed to be a surprise and it would be easier to play the role with no preconceptions. Someone wanted to meet Owen Barclay and was using his friend Pascal to get closer. That's all Ohen really needed to know.

He was honestly surprised when they walked up to the gate of a very nice stonework mansion with gold-tinted windows.

Pascal gestured as the door opened. "Owen Barclay, may I introduce you to Lord Casey from Chimbote."

Ohen knew enough of the local etiquette to make his bow and shake the hand of the well-dressed young gentleman who obviously was his host.

"Come on in. I'm very glad to meet you, Barclay. Pascal has told me so much about you."

A female voice called out, "Is he here?" A dark haired, lovely woman, obviously Lord Casey's sister, hurried into the room. Lady Luthe smiled widely and beamed a smile his way.

Superficially, it was a brother and sister, rich nobles, who wanted to meet the giant. They were very friendly, and about the same age as Pascal and Ohen. Telepathically, Ohen was picking up much more than that.

Ohen's reputation as a big eater was well known, and they went straight to the dining room where servants were bringing in the dishes. Ohen's stomach rumbled, loud enough to attract some chuckles.

The food was most welcome. Even with a bigger personal budget to spend at eating with the other soldiers, his options were limited.

The lady had all the usual questions: How did you grow so big? Where did you come from? How did you get to be a favorite among the top level officers?

Ohen had all the usual answers. He even told them of living on Ha, even if they really didn't understand the idea of living on a moon with no atmosphere.

It was their thoughts that were interesting.

Lord Casey was mentally taking notes. He had to report all of this to Duke Paul of Da Vinci.

Ohen was aware of the duke. He was probably the second-most powerful person in Xanthe, behind King Harmon. It was an uneasy relationship, with the duke supplying many of the resources required to pursue the war. Decades past, there had been armed conflict between the cousins. Only the danger from outside had brought them together.

Lord Casey wasn't passionate about his role as a spy, but not reluctant either, since his family at Chimbote was very dependent on their much more powerful neighbor just over a hundred kloms to the north of their lands. Casey was also a third son, hardly in line to inherit Chimbote when the time came. He knew he had to trade on his family name to secure some kind of position in the world.

When Duke Paul had suggested this role of learning everything he could about this new player in the court, this strange outsider who had much more influence than he ought, Casey was eager to leave for the court life in Orson and do his part. Still this was just a means to better his position in the world.

Lady Luthe's thoughts were more intriguing. **At least they know how to handle a fork.** She had little real interest in low-level military officers. Her own position in the future was less secure than her brother's. All she had was her name and her charm. She'd insisted on accompanying her brother to the court at Orson, where she had some possibility of meeting some noble with money or position that needed a wife.

She was throwing her all into being a charming hostess tonight, since the meal was not that expensive compared to the other parties that she hoped to attend. She had very few contacts as yet, so she needed to meet everyone she could.

The giant is pleasant enough. If we can invite him back regularly, then I can invite others to attend to come see him as well.

She was only marginally aware of her brother's duties, but she would attach herself whenever it enabled her to widen her circle of connections.

Ohen, for his part, was happy to be in the company of such a beautiful young lady. Females in the military were quite rare. The U'tanse culture was quite different, with women in all specializations, and especially prized as healers. The skills for controlling details at the biological cellular level were bred into them. From the very beginning, U'tanse females had to have the skills to choose which sperm would be the lucky one. It was the only way the inbred subset of humans had managed to survive on their new world, ruthlessly culling out undesirable genetic traits.

He had the feeling that Lady Luthe had excellent managerial skills, but in her world, she'd need luck to weave herself into the position where she could use them. Reading her thoughts, it was plain she had been trained to the position from an early age. Whether her guest was another noble, a giant with a strange accent, or just a timid soldier out of his depth, she knew just what to say to put everyone at ease.

Beside him Lieutenant Pascal was hanging on her every word. He, too, was starved for female company and was overwhelmed by her charm.

Ohen hoped his friend wouldn't get too swept up by it all.

...

Meti's face was a thundercloud, but the general was like a stone wall.

"You will turn over all the designs for the generators," he said. "The invention came from my assistant. Certainly you didn't think it was all a gift did you?"

The blacksmith fumed. "I've never had to do anything like this before."

"And I've never had to pay such high prices for these gadgets before either! You're not supplying the computers, but that's what I'm paying for. Barclay is mine and I'm sure he could coach another blacksmith through the process if necessary. I'd rather just keep paying you, but the only way that'll happen is if you supply my requirements and you make dead sure that none of your workers get the idea of going into business for themselves."

Meti's eyes widened, as if he hadn't considered that problem before. He mumbled, "I'm sure we can work something out."

...

Pascal was watching him all through the meeting a week later as they discussed the latest troop reports from the western reaches. Ohen could tell he wasn't paying all that much attention to the battlefield details. As the meeting broke up, the lieutenant followed him out.

"Hmm, Barclay, did you get the new dinner invitation from Lord Casey?"

Ohen smiled. "Oh, I think I saw it."

"Are you going to attend?"

"I'm really busy."

Pascal sighed. "I just know that Lady Luthe hopes that you'll come."

Ohen paused and faced him. "And how important is that to you?"

The man glanced away. "Oh, well, she just hadn't heard from you and sent a message to me asking about you."

"And what does that mean to you?"

Pascal shook his head. "I'd hate for her to be disappointed."

Ohen could tell that his thoughts of Lady Luthe were tinted with a glow of perfection.

"Pascal, are you invited as well?"

The lieutenant shifted uneasily. "I'm not sure. I'm just a soldier. You're a—"

"An entertaining freak?"

"Oh, no! She said nothing like that."

Ohen chuckled. "Don't worry. I know I'm unusual. I've been the odd character all my life. I'll tell you what. Why don't you let Lady Luthe know that as a favor to my best friend Pascal, I'll attend with him, but that I'm usually very busy and have little time for social events."

Pascal was nodding his head, memorizing the lines. "I'll do that. I'll let you know when the date is confirmed." He hurried off.

Ohen wondered if he was doing his friend any favor in setting him up like that. Lady Luthe had her sights set on someone a lot more higher than a lieutenant.

. . .

It was two weeks after Ohen had first revealed the Phobos images that they held a secret meeting in the new computer room. Ohen did the honors of pedaling the generator while General Jonah and his new computer specialist briefed Admiral Falcone on the new information.

Jonah said, "Killingsworth, please show the Admiral the route you've plotted out."

The specialist had produced a heavily annotated hand-inked paper map showing all the traffic in the Central Waterway and up the Mariner Waterway between the ports Melas and Conches that he'd collected from a dozen overhead photos. He'd marked twenty-two ships that were part of the trade happening between Condor and Margareta and clocked their position and speed.

Admiral Falcone sniffed and shook his head. "They must really think we're stupid, running so many ships only a couple of hundred kloms from our port at Timbuktu."

Killingsworth noted, "They have been taking a southerly leg directly upon leaving Port Conches, probably to stay out of view."

The admiral nodded. "We have noticed the increase in Margareta ships over the past few months, but this—what is it 2,500 kloms?—of shipping supplies to our enemy. It's more than I'd ever considered. I wonder what they're getting out of it?"

Jonah shook his head. "It might be just for the purpose of weakening Xanthe's power in the region."

Falcone tilted his head. "Perhaps, but I guess the best way to find out is to capture one or more of those ships. Either the cargo or the officers would tell us a lot."

He picked up the chart again. "This could give us a hunting ground where we could expect to find a Margareta ship."

Ohen had kept quiet for most of the discussion, but he said, "Well, that's one way."

The admiral looked at him. "The general says you're the inventor of these generators?"

"Yes, sir. It occurs to me that if you had a computer like this one and a generator to go with it, that you could follow a ship day by day and never have to hunt for it. You could position your ships directly in its path and let it come to you."

"A computer on a ship? That's never been permitted."

"Only because they were rare and irreplaceable. That is changing."

The admiral looked at Jonah. "Is that true?"

The general frowned. "I'd rather not put any computer in harm's way, but if the need was great enough, I'd consider it."

Ohen stroked his scalp. "There are various types of computers and some are less valuable to ground troops than others. Admiral Falcone, could you enlighten me about how a collection of ships at sea are coordinated?"

The admiral explained the flags used at day and the signal lights used at night. "Of course, once battle starts, every ship's captain is on his own."

"So...," Ohen began, "ships have to sail within sight of each other to read the flags?"

"That's correct."

"Well, there are some computers in the warehouse that I've never attempted to fit with generators because they aren't as capable as these are. However, they could certainly keep ships' captains in close communication, even if they were over the horizon and out of sight of each other. A computer like this one that could see the ships on the water wouldn't even need to leave the admiral's office at port. All the ships at sea would need would be simple voice communication."

It was the admiral's time to frown. "The admiral of a battle group staying on land? I'm not sure I like the taste of that."

Ohen shrugged. "That's not my area of expertise. It's just that cheaper and disposable computers could change many things. For example, if a battle went the wrong way, a disposable computer could be tossed overboard just to keep its existence secret."

The meeting lasted several hours. Although the general and the admiral were very high ranked, some decisions like beginning to attack a presumably friendly nation's ships wasn't something that could be decided without royal approval.

After the admiral left, General Jonah said, "Barclay, I can't say I like the term 'disposable computer' that you used. We can't give the navy the impression that we have so many computers available that they can just be thrown away like that."

Ohen nodded. "That comment was aimed at you."

"Oh? Why?"

"We do have a variety of computers, some of which could be used as voice-only communicators with nothing more than a small hand-cranked generator. We need to be thinking of ways to use them in order to preserve the limited number of computers with the keyboard and screen that you're used to. In spite of the feeling that we have an unlimited number of computers gathering dust in the warehouse, that's not really the case. We could run out. I'm assuming the Orson warehouse just contains the computers that were gathered locally?"

Jonah frowned. "I suppose that's the case. Most ran out of power long before I came along."

Ohen nodded thoughtfully. "If there are other warehouses in other cities, then it might be wise to secretly transfer all those dead computers to a central place under military control. There are likely similar collections of dust-covered computers in other countries as well, although it might be difficult to acquire those without triggering a lot of questions."

Jonah sighed. "You seem to have grand plans. Or is this just to forestall any other country from gaining access to new computers?"

"Both, but I can see the need for a large number of computers. Every city, every town in Xanthe needs the ability to report troubles and request assistance from the crown. Your military units down to the patrols themselves could work more effectively if they could communicate directly.

"And the navy, well, they think in terms of ships, but according to what Admiral Falcone was saying, the navy just might have an additional ship, once they take their prize to port and change out the crew. As the navy fleet size grows, they will increase their ability to grow ever faster, and all of those ships will need to be in communication with the admiralty."

Jonah sighed. "Is there an end to this?"

"Possibly. The navy just might become powerful enough to control the Central Waterway. They could put down the pirates and extend their control into the northern ocean reaches where the pirate nation rules."

The admiral flinched. "What do you know that I don't?"

Ohen smiled and nodded toward the computer. "Why don't you give Killingsworth a break?"

Social Life

Lord Casey watched while Ohen drank his brandy. Ohen was amused at his thoughts.

Casey spoke what he'd been thinking.

"I would have thought that a man as big as you are wouldn't be timid about how much you drink."

Ohen shrugged. "It's true that I'd have to drink quite a bit more than normal for it to affect me, but part of it is cultural. None of these drinks are ones I'm familiar with. Back on Ha, the most common fermented drink was based on rice. There were a few others, but as a conscientious student, I never spent much of my time drinking with my fellows."

He shook his head. "I'm still getting used to the taste. I rarely drink for the alcohol."

The third man in the room, Thomas Angelus, the owner of a large Shalbatana River trading company headquartered in Orson, said, "Well, if you find a drink you like, let me know. I can point you to the best suppliers."

Ohen nodded. "I'll do that." It was an easy promise, not that he planned to follow up on it. He had nothing against the merchant, but he did not want to get any closer to the man's daughter.

Maria Angelus had been seated next to him at the table, and it had been very difficult to block out her thoughts. Never in his life had he been subjected to such close range lustful urges. Of course as a telepath, he'd been exposed to the thoughts of many lovers in the throes of passion, but at a distance, he could submerge those uncontrolled impulses in the noise of many other minds.

And in close social circumstances, no telepath would ever revel in such detailed imaginings without hiding behind their ineda.

Maria had no clue that her private thoughts were out there for him to read. And so close to him, and so focused as she had been on his body, it had been nearly impossible for him to concentrate on anything else.

There was enough overt body language that Casey and several others at the table could guess what the girl was thinking as well. Ohen was grateful for Casey's invitation to a men's-only after-dinner drink in the parlor.

Lord Casey had no telepathic skills, but he was trained enough to recognize Ohen's discomfort and the source. Maria Angelus had a reputation for sexual dalliance that no one but her father had been able to deny.

Although, Thomas had sensed something. "Barclay, have you give any thought to settling down after you travels? The capital city has lots of opportunities for someone who's been making a name for himself. That Lieutenant Pascal certainly seemed interested in finding a nice girl." He eyed their host.

Lord Casey sighed. "He's a nice guy, but I suspect my sister has her eyes on at least a title."

Ohen nodded. "I've suggested as much to him, but Pascal hasn't given up yet."

The men chuckled.

Ohen didn't want to give in to speculation. No matter how many nice girls there were in Orson, he still had hopes to visit Earth. It wasn't time to give any thought to his eventual destination.

But you know, I think I'd rather live in this star system rather than orbiting the home world of the Cerik. Mars alone is so much more alive than Ha.

And he certainly wasn't interested in Maria Angelus, in spite of what her fantasies had done to his hormones. His family had an interesting history, and he had no interest in a Delilah.

...

"Eleven generators, but I'm not sure Meti will be able to make them any faster than they are right now. In fact, unless they can increase their supplies of iron from Tempe, the production rate might drop off."

General Jonah frowned at Ohen's report. "We can't have that. Do you think we can confiscate materials from other ironwork companies?"

"It'll cost you. There will also be questions about why Meti needs more materials and why they're making so much money from the military. If you start to directly assist him, the gossip will get even worse."

Jonah grumbled, "Well, I need more computers in the field, and Admiral Falcone is complaining that the three he needs for his first computer-assisted ships haven't arrived yet."

Ohen sighed. "Well, we haven't shipped them yet. You took the one with the good display."

The general nodded. "And don't forget the two canister computers I promised the king."

"I know. Those should be ready within the week. Those generators aren't as big, but sometimes making smaller, clockwork gears can take longer than the big ones."

Jonah shook his head. "Barclay, it's your fault, telling us all the wonderful thing we can accomplish with more computers, and then not being able to produce them fast enough."

Ohen chuckled. "Probably correct. Ideas are fast and slippery. Real hardware takes time. Maybe I should just take a vacation and stop thinking."

"No, we can't have that."

Ohen wondered if it was the right time to bring up his latest worry.

Jonah saw something in his expression. "Okay, what is it?"

"Oh, nothing much. Have you heard that Lord Casey of Chimbote has invited me to Paladin Estate to look at horses?"

The general's mind grew quiet. "Oh, are you interested in horses?"

"Not too much, but at the last dinner, I told the story of the first time I'd gotten on a horse and there were a few jokes about long-suffering horses under oversized riders. Lord Casey said he knew of a breed of horses that were large and would probably be a better match for my size.

"What do you think, General, about that?"

"What, the horses?"

"No, about leaving the capital for a trip like that."

Jonah frowned. "Your meaning?"

Ohen sighed. "I've never been under the illusion that I'm a free man who can just wander off. You've made my situation here at the capital quite comfortable, but I'm still a foreigner under your direction. I don't think it's proper for me to go without your blessing. In fact, I've been under the impression that there is a man who has constantly been watching me when I went to Lord Casey's mansion for those dinner parties."

Jonah's face tightened. "Really, describe him."

Ohen was a little surprised that the spy wasn't under the general's command.

"Hmm. I'd say black hair, about 155 centimeters tall, perhaps 25 Martian years old. Wiry, but not terribly muscular."

Jonah chuckled, "'Martian years'? I guess you still think in your native years then?"

"Well, yes, but I try to convert everything."

"The description doesn't sound like anyone I know. There could be any number of people who would like to keep an eye out on your activities. Does he follow you to Meti's place?"

"Not that I've noticed. Are my visits there supposed to be secret?"

"I guess not. In any case, that information can't be made secret at this late date. You aren't talking about the computers at your dinner parties are you?"

Ohen sniffed. "Of course not. Both Lieutenant Pascal and I know that as far as civilians are concerned, we're just clerks in the Tower. Pascal gripes about it enough. He'd love to be able to impress the ladies he meets at these social events."

Jonah was quiet for a moment. Ohen caught a sense of what he was thinking. Finally, the general asked, "Barclay, is there any reason I should restrict your visits with Lord Casey?"

Ohen shook his head. "I suspect he has reasons for befriending me, perhaps because of his northern neighbor, but I have no reason to run off to Da Vinci, or some other country for that matter. I also doubt anyone is planning to kidnap me."

"Is there any other reason you might want to leave?"

Ohen waved his hand. "I still want to visit Earth, but until I figure out why it's off limits, I might as well stay here on Mars. And I've already made my decisions about which country needs my loyalty."

Jonah laughed. "You'd flap your wings and fly off then, if you could?"

Ohen chuckled. "Hardly that. My arms get tired enough with some of those generator cranks."

Jonah nodded. "Okay, then. Go visit your horse ranch, but keep your eyes open. You're not as immune to kidnapping as you might think."

...

Lord Casey was really enjoying the trip. The horse ranch was only about forty kloms from the city, but in spite of his task spying on Ohen in the capital, he was really more comfortable in more rural circumstances.

Casey pointed to a field as they stopped to water the horses. "That's corn."

"Yes, I know. We had corn as well."

"Really? On an airless moon?" He'd heard all of Ohen's stories.

"Yes, we still have to eat. My people are very practiced in building greenhouses, filled with air and electric lights to grow the crops we can eat."

"So corn? What else?"

Ohen shrugged. "I was never a farmer myself. But rice and potatoes were common."

"How did you get the seeds, on that hostile world?"

Ohen smiled, remembering all the stories in the Book. "Well, the Cerik were planning on attacking Earth and making a colony there. They looked at humans like animals to be hunted."

"Like a fox hunt?"

"Something like that, I guess. I've never seen a fox. But in any case, they were scouting the planet, waiting until the Star weakened humanity before their attack. On one of their scouting trips, they captured two large... wagons full of food supplies headed to a market. If it weren't for those supplies, and especially crops that we could grow ourselves under the right conditions, the U'tanse would probably have died out."

Ohen caught a whisper of thought from a man riding on the top of their wagon. Was it that spy? In any case, he was struggling to overhear what he was saying.

Once they were back on the road, and the spy couldn't hear, he asked, "Is this your wagon?"

Casey shook his head, embarrassed. "No, sad to say my budget can't handle more than just the town coach. I rented this one from Hessian's Travel."

"I'm sorry to have caused you this expense!"

"No, I'm happy to invite you along. It's rare that we get much time to talk. Luthe is always trying to make a big party out of every little thing."

Ohen nodded. The spy wasn't one of Casey's men. He wasn't one of the general's people. Who else was playing the game of spying on Owen Barclay?

...

"Computer, how long can you store these photos taken from space?"

Ohen was whispering, confident that none of the other workers at Meti's company could hear him. He'd come to the conclusion that he could talk to the computer much faster than he could type the questions. He hadn't yet adapted completely to the local's keyboard layout.

But the reply came as text on the screen. "There are other photos taken long ago that have never been accessed. Those will be purged first. Other data types are also saved based on their usage. In terms of a human lifespan, you can consider all those photos you requested as saved permanently."

As an engineer, Ohen could appreciate that the computer system on Phobos had likely been designed with a space-based civilization in mind. Probably it had much more capacity than people were using now.

He reviewed the photos he'd requested from a couple of days before.

Zooming in on the Paladin Estate, he hunted for the corrals where he'd been visiting at the time.

I can't see myself. Individual humans were much too small, even though he'd scheduled the photos for when Phobos was high in the sky. Still, he could see a blotch of pale white.

Those are the Creme Draft horses. I can see the herd, just not an individual horse.

He had ridden a couple of those pale white horses, and Casey was right. If he had to go for a long ride on horseback, those large horses were the right size for him.

Still, he'd rejected the idea of actually buying one of them. The only reason he might have to keep one was to make a dash back to B3 and escape the planet. But until that was more of an option, owning a horse would be a major drain on his budget.

Even riding on horseback, Jonah's computer-connected military would be able to track him down in short order. It would take a lot of luck and constant telepathic probes to avoid people hunting him down.

I may have made myself too valuable.

Another photo he'd taken for his own use was the Port of Timbuktu where he could see Admiral Falcone's ships heading out into the Central Waterway. Ohen wished he could follow them step by step as they captured one of the Margareta ships. He could only hope that it went smoothly.

The admiral's plan was to capture ships, one by one, without any hint as to why the Condor resupply vessel had vanished. He couldn't keep that up forever, but considering how many days it took to make the journey, he could likely take several ships before the first was reported missing.

The overhead photos were critical. They pinpointed the Margareta ship, gave the navy a good estimate of its course and travel speed, and made sure they didn't accidentally attack a convoy of ships that might allow one of them to escape.

Listening into the admiral's thoughts, they were planning to appear at dawn, approaching the target from all sides at once. Maybe if the cargo ship knew it had no hope, they would surrender without an extended battle.

That was Ohen's hope as well. He certainly wouldn't be linked to the sailors during the confrontation. It was too dangerous for him.

The last of the photos Ohen had requested were focused on the Isidis Gulf, giving him several sequential views of the area. He really wanted to see where ships were traveling in that area, and where the pirates were collected.

After an hour's worth of straining his eyes at the screen, he had come to the conclusion that he really needed to turn the task of analyzing the ship traffic to someone like Killingsworth who knew how ships and navies operated. It was just puzzling to him.

However, the photos of Isidis land showed large patches of white unlike what he'd seen elsewhere. Were these the quarries where carbonates were dug out?

And then, text appeared on the screen, "Message from King Harmon, King of Xanthe to Owen Barclay. Speak, display, or defer until later."

"Display the message."

Ohen frowned at the text. Why would the king want a secret private conference with him? He wasn't even supposed to tell General Jonah about it.

Hesitantly, he typed in his reply.

Interview with the King

"How did your tea party go?" Ohen asked.

Pascal nodded. "Better than I feared. It was more of a garden party than what I was expecting." He smiled. "I'm really grateful that Lord Casey took you off on that excursion. Lady Luthe explained that, apparently, the rules require an even number of men and women and with the two of you gone, she was happy to have me there."

"So, she's warming up to you?"

Pascal shook his head. "No, it's pretty clear she's concentrating on the peerage. We can talk, but if there's a real candidate in view, she's off in a flash."

Ohen chuckled. "So, were any of the other girls interested in a dazzling young officer?"

He sighed. "Hardly. Still, I'm grateful to be invited to these things. It never hurts to know people."

Ohen had to get through the workday without thinking too much about his upcoming visit with the king. He even arranged his work so that he was never in the same room as the general, using his clairvoyance to keep track of the man. Jonah was just too good at picking up on his uneasiness. He'd pester the truth out of him if they were together.

It was well after sunset by the time the map room cleared out. He put aside his work and went to the stairwell. It too was vacant, so he headed up. Sadly, the results of his high gravity training had faded too fast. He was still a lot stronger than the native Martians, but climbing floor after floor wasn't something he could ignore anymore. He was getting a little ache in his leg muscles.

Still, he reached the floor the king had designated. There was a guard there waiting for him. He recognized him by his height and waved him through into the corridor. This was two floors below the residence and he followed the directions he'd been given and opened the door on the second room on the left after the turn.

"Ah, there you are Barclay. Come have a seat so I don't have to strain my neck looking up at you." The king gestured to a seat next to a table covered in pastries.

"Your Majesty." He nodded and sat.

The king chuckled. "Go ahead and eat something. I've heard your reputation."

His stomach growled, and rather than apologize, he did as he was told.

"Barclay, I heard you went to look at horses."

"Yes, Your Majesty, Lord Casey of Chimbote knew of some larger horses that would be a better fit for me."

"Are you planning on leaving us?"

The king's thoughts were plain. He knew everything that Ohen had discussed with the general on this topic.

"Not any time soon. Still, travel by horse or carriage are the only options and I've always thought that I should be prepared for any eventuality."

King Harmon tilted his head. "You know of other travel possibilities? Other things you've seen on your travels?"

Ohen hesitated. "I'm sure your majesty has heard of other things in history."

"But you've seen them, right? On other worlds?"

He shook his head. "Nothing that could be of use here and now. I have traveled between worlds in a flying craft. On my home moon of Ha, there was a machine-powered craft that could travel the airless lands between cities, but it was no faster than a wagon."

The king shrugged. "I have to ask. General Jonah has complained that you reveal your marvels bit by bit, even though he suspects you have a much grander vision in mind. Do you? Do you have a grand scheme?"

Ohen sighed. This might be the main purpose of the interview. It was hardly the time for deception.

"I have spoken to the general about my people and that some day, perhaps many years in the future, others of my kind might want to settle on

Mars or Luna, or on the Earth. Just as I am unsuited to battle, so others like me are also unused to war."

The king was listening, and he believed what Ohen was saying. The history of this world had many tales of people living on other planets, so what he was saying wasn't too outlandish.

Ohen gestured, "Mars is a world with dozens of kingdoms, with every one at war with their neighbors. If not war today, then with plans for war in the future. If I had a grand scheme, it would be to put an end to war on Mars."

Harmon could not contain his dismissive laughter at such a thought. "Barclay, you deal in marvels, but isn't that just a bit too much to ask?"

Ohen nodded. "Possibly. And yet, and yet. I first landed near Marion, a little village settled by people different from those in Xanthe's city of Dumont. These were different people, and yet there was not the slightest thought of battle between them. Marion was no threat to Dumont, and from the villager's viewpoint, Dumont was so much more powerful than they that there was no suggestion that they attack their larger neighbor.

"When there was sufficient imbalance of power, then there was peace."

The king was listening, so he pushed on.

"My own history included some tales of Earth, before the time of the Star. It seems that in times past, there was nearly always some war. However, there were exceptions. When trade was profitable, then there was the incentive to avoid war. When there was some dominant nation who could enforce peace, sometimes there could be an extended time where there were more merchants than soldiers shaping the world.

"In the past, peace has happened. The puzzle is how to make it happen again, here on Mars. What if Xanthe was that dominant nation? What if you neighbors calculated the costs of war and just decided that peaceful trade was the better option?"

"You think that's possible?"

"Possible, yes. But certainty isn't ever realistic. Still, some strategies could greatly increase Xanthe's position of strength."

Harmon urged, "Then tell me."

"You already know it. Greatly expand the use of computers to allow instant communication throughout your kingdom's forces. And secondly, repair and build new roads, on par with the Old Road, so that anywhere you need to act, your forces can get there faster than any opposition."

The king nodded. "The computers are obvious, and now with your generators, something we are aggressively pursuing. But the roads? Yes, I understand what you said, but is it that important?"

"Getting to the battleground first is critical. If your enemy gets there first, then the sooner you deny them the chance to build up defenses, the better off you'll be. You can't let a border conflict be decided against you because a river is flooding or the ground is too rough to bring your supply wagons into place.

"You have to build good roads and bridges before they are needed. In addition, you can't let various factions of the kingdom become isolated. Easy merchant travel within your borders will keep everyone united.

"There ought to be a military unit, under the crown's guidance, whose sole purpose is to repair the Old Road and learn how it was built. Then whether there is war or peace, this unit of engineers should build great roads and bridges and keep everything in repair."

Harmon nodded to himself. "It sounds good, but expensive. I'm sure there will be voices against it."

Ohen said, "General Jonah liked the idea of good roads, but resisted the idea of pulling any of his soldiers away from battle. This isn't a problem someone like me can solve. It's a leadership decision."

After awhile the king thought about it and Ohen raided the pastry tray again, Harmon asked, "So, is that it. Your grand scheme?"

"Well, there is one other component."

The king sighed, "Let's hear it."

Ohen leaned forward. "Any nation can trade with their closest neighbors, and if they have a port city, they can trade all over the world to get the supplies they need."

"Like Candor and Margareta."

"Yes. Freedom of the seas is a great strategic advantage."

"So that's why you brought Admiral Falcone into your circle. There is a great deal of gossip about the army and the navy working together."

Ohen was surprised, "Oh? Why is that?"

Harmon chuckled. "The army and the navy are competitors for royal funding. And you have to understand that when two enemies start to work together, a person suspects that just maybe they're conspiring against them."

The king shook his head, "Nobody understands what's going on, but they've seen Jonah and Falcone together and speculation is rampant that it has something to do with the tall foreign advisor. Barclay, you have a lot of new enemies."

Ohen sighed. "I wasn't aware."

"And that's what I suspected. You are a great advisor, but you lack a sense of politics."

Ohen said, "The general said I lacked the ability to tell a good lie."

Harmon nodded. "Maybe the same thing. So, is that the last of your grand vision, using the navy to cut off Candor's supplies?"

"Oh, it's a bit grander than that."

"Tell me."

"Well, just like Admiral Falcone is trying to secretly hobble the trade to Candor, Xanthe has been hobbled for decades now."

"What?"

"A strong force of pirates in the Northern Ocean has systematically blocked all trade with Isidis. Your supply of carbonates—limestone—has been cut off. And I'll note that the road-and-bridge-building effort would be greatly helped if Xanthe had those supplies to make concrete.

"With computers to assist, the Xanthe navy should be able to capture many Margareta ships and increase the size of the navy. With careful intelligence and a growing number of computers to coordinate the naval fleet, Xanthe could control all shipping in the Central Waterway and expand to remove the pirates in the Northern Ocean. In the years to come, Xanthe just might totally control the seas, putting it in a dominant position over all the kingdoms of Mars."

King Harmon took a pastry from the tray and munched on it.

"Barclay, you are going to have so many enemies!"

"Oh?"

"So am I, for that matter. You've just handed me the control of the whole planet on a platter."

Ohen could read his thoughts. The king was reassessing the strength of the various nobles and speculating that the military might soon surpass the current duchies and that he'd need to be granting titles and lands to people like Jonah and Falcone. Who should he usurp to make that happen?

The king met his eyes. "Having a foreign advisor in the middle of all this is a big problem. I'm also going to need to repay you for all that you've done.

"I have a niece in need of a husband. Are you ready to settle down?"

Ohen was caught off guard by the offer. He didn't need an explanation of how significant that offer was.

"Um. I would have to think about it. I haven't given up my goal to travel to Luna and Earth."

"I'd really hate to let you go."

Ohen shrugged that off. "I'm less valuable than you think. The hard part, getting the computers out of the warehouse and into service, is already in other people's hands. The 'grand scheme' as you call it has already been revealed and I really don't have any part in its execution. It's all up to you and the military."

The king pointed to him. "And that's why people want you dead. You really don't have a clue about what you've already done, do you?"

Ohen shrugged. "Probably not."

"From the moment you gave me that personal computer, everything changed. I suddenly had a lot more power."

"But you're the king."

"Yes, but the way it's always worked is that I get my information filtered through the military and through my bureaucrats and from the nobles. Now, I can get a lot of that information directly, in the privacy of my room. And I can also give orders that bypass those same gatekeepers. Many of the nobles whose power depended on them having the 'ear of the king' now find themselves cut out of the loop. And everyone knows you are the person who made that happen. No one knows what new rabbit you might pull out of the hat and it makes a number of powerful people very nervous.

"Some people are saying that it might be better if Barclay had an unfortunate accident."

"Oh."

The king nodded. "It's not just being kidnapped for your knowledge. Your very presence is destabilizing.

"So … if you wanted to become part of my family, that could be seen as a stabilizing factor. Under my thumb, so to speak."

Ohen sighed. "It's a lot to think about. I've been walking through a pleasant forest, unaware of all the wolves circling."

"Something like that. I'm open to other suggestions. I really do owe you a great deal, especially if Xanthe can become dominant as you predict."

Ohen said, "I could just vanish, I suppose."

"Don't try anything stupid. Staying on the job gives you a great deal of protection."

"But I should watch my back." He sighed. "Maybe I should have visited Luna first. But I just know I would have tried to land on Earth, not knowing that there is some kind of force preventing that."

"Well, I'm glad you came to my kingdom first. I shudder to think what the world would be like if you arrived in Candor, or Tempe, or Margareta."

The man wasn't stupid. Ohen had let slip enough hints that King Harmon knew that somewhere, there was a spaceship that Ohen could access. Still, he didn't want to press that. It was important for the kingdom to be on Owen Barclay's good side.

A Little Paranoia

After leaving the Tower, Ohen had his clairvoyance working hard, trying to sense anyone following him. Mars was a different world and a different culture, and sometimes he forgot that.

He avoided the dorm altogether. That was too predictable.

On Ha, and across the U'tanse culture, there were a limited number of fictional novels, inspired by the few mysteries that had come across space from Earth in the grocery trucks hijacked by the Cerik. Those Earth stories had never become more than curiosities, since the culture was so different from real life. Still a few writers tried their hand at puzzle stories—who did what, and what was hidden behind tight ineda?

Still, in those stories, there was no violence. The rare murder was likely slow poison. Ohen doubted that any of the stories he'd read could help him in his current situation.

He'd already faced people who wanted to beat him, stab him, or even cut his head off. Luckily, nobody had been able to get close enough to follow through with the thought.

It was disturbingly easy to sneak into the Meti workplace. There was a guard, but he wasn't really paying attention. Ohen moved when the man's attention was elsewhere. He was quickly in his private shed and began pedaling the generator.

Admiral Falcone hadn't sent him any message about the progress of their attack on the Margareta ship, not that he'd expected any. The king was right. The army and the navy rarely cooperated. Likely not even the general had been notified.

But Ohen had left commands to photograph that area of the sea every thirty minutes while Phobos was in the sky and there was light from the sun.

Viewing the three white dots that departed from Timbuktu, he could see the photos in sequence and follow them. The sequence was erratic, with long gaps, but Ohen could still track them.

Abruptly, with the long shadows of a morning sun, there were four ships, three in a triangle surrounding one in the middle.

The battle must have been over within a couple of hours, because he could see that two of the ships must have lost sail, because their white dots were less bright than their fellows. Four ships began sailing back to Xanthe ports, at a slower pace.

Ohen nodded to himself. The plan worked, even if the Margareta ship hadn't immediately surrendered. Soon enough they would know what cargo it was carrying, and the Xanthe navy had grown by one ship.

There was a makeshift bed that he'd used before. Maybe he could get some sleep before he was back at work tomorrow, as if nothing had happened. The trick would be getting to sleep, given all that he'd learned.

. . .

Lieutenant Pascal waved. "I was looking for you at breakfast. Where'd you go?"

Ohen waved. "Just some work at the blacksmith's. I took the opportunity to visit Market Street. Sometimes the cafeteria food gets a little old."

Pascal grinned, "Are you ready for another dinner party?"

"Don't tell me Lady Luthe is at it again!"

"I'm not sure, but she starts gathering the guest list for the next event just as soon as the previous one ends. She did ask if you'd be available any time soon."

Ohen shook his head. "I'm getting some complaints."

"Everyone expects you to work late hours seven days a week, don't they?"

"It feels like it sometimes."

. . .

Ohen was using the protractor to estimate the travel distance from the port of Timbuktu to Peridier on the Isidis Gulf when General Jonah walked into the map room and gestured for him to follow. Ohen set aside his tools and walked out.

They entered one of the smaller work rooms and the general latched the door.

"Barclay, I've got an initial report from Falcone." He described the successful attack on the Margareta ship with a bit more detail than Ohen had been able to puzzle out on his own.

"The navy is pleased. They've ordered one more computer that can display the maps and five more with voice-only capabilities."

Ohen nodded. "They want to do more attacks."

"Obviously, but I don't know how fast Meti can produce those generators. And I can't just turn the whole production over to the navy. I've got troops of my own that need those computers."

Ohen leaned back in his chair. "I guess it depends on what the cargo was. How critical is it to the Candorian military?"

"Falcone reports that they captured gunpowder, cotton cloth, and iron pipes. The Margareta captain said he had expected to return with silver bars, dried fruit, and nuts."

"Local Candorian produce in exchange for critical war supplies then. Probably the iron would go to their smiths and become firearms."

The general nodded, "And I want the navy to capture all that stuff to shut down the Candorian push, but the more I can directly control our troops, the more effective they will be. We've lost too much territory to the Candorians already. We need to take it all back."

Ohen understood Jonah's position. He'd been at the same status meetings as well. The land war was uneven, Candor had taken much of the Dorsa lands in the west, even through they couldn't do anything to expand any closer to the Xanthe heartland. As far as his clairvoyance and photos from Phobos could determine, the B3 boat was still hidden. But right now it was definitely behind enemy lines. There was no way he could get back there on his own. He worried some Candorian scout would discover it and damage it, trying to get in the door.

"On another topic," the general said, "the spy you described is someone we know, a low-level agent of Tempe. We've been letting him operate, hoping he could lead us to other members of his group, but if he's following you, then perhaps we should close him down."

Ohen frowned. "Why would Tempe be interested in me?"

"Any number of reasons. You're odd, an orange in a crate of apples. Perhaps they even have an agent among the nobles and have heard of what you're doing for the army. In any case, they don't need to know any more about you than what they've already learned."

"What should I do?"

Jonah smiled. "You could be bait. Are you planning to go to any more of those Chimbote parties?"

...

In spite of Ohen's objections, Lord Casey insisted on picking him up at the gateway to the sprawling Fort Dell beside the Tower.

Casey smiled, "If you aren't going to buy your own horse, then don't gripe when people come get you. The Narrows is too far to walk."

Lady Luthe's latest event was a party at the Hessian Gardens, a royal enclave on the banks of the Narrows, where the lake that filled the central depression of Orson narrowed down to the Shalbatana River channel that flowed northward toward the ocean.

It was late in the afternoon, and lanterns were being lit along the major streets. Ohen had checked Casey's thoughts, and the man appeared totally ignorant of any spies or plots surrounding Owen Barclay. At worst, he was feeling a little guilty about taking Duke Paul's money for a task that had generally been a pleasant excursion for himself and a grand opportunity for his sister.

But, perhaps he should be asking for more details to spice up his weekly report to the duke.

"Barclay, do you get any opportunity to see the city, or do they keep you locked up in the Tower all the time."

Ohen smiled, "Oh, it's not all bad. I do get to run a few errands from time to time. All of them in walking distance, though."

He honestly thought it might not hurt to mention the blacksmith, since Duke Paul was already aware of the secret plan to resurrect the old computers—that's what triggered Lord Casey's mission in the first place. However, there was a familiar thought pattern close at hand. The Tempe spy was riding on the wagon as a hired footman, struggling to listen in to the conversations in the cab.

There was also another wagon following behind them. Eyes were watching that same footman.

Ohen tried to keep his mind off of the drama outside. He really knew a lot more about the military's plan to capture the spy than he had been told, so it was important that he not show any sign that he was aware of what was happening. Certainly he shouldn't let Casey read anything from his expressions.

There was also the possibility that someone could get hurt in the process. He really didn't need to show signs of distress if he picked up the telepathic echoes from that, and he wasn't sure he was a good enough actor to get away with hiding his reactions.

He tried to get back on topic.

"Lord Casey, you shouldn't waste your time ferrying me around all the time. I'm sure you have a lot more important things to be doing with your time."

Casey laughed. "Oh, believe me, you've more entertaining than anyone else in this city. Who else has stories of other worlds and demonic space beasts and a long lost tribe of humanity searching for a home? Really, who else can compare? Baron Kerching and his struggle to grow cotton on his land? No really, there's no one else I'd rather travel with."

Ohen smiled, he had a story for the man. "Well, at least the baron has cotton seeds."

"What do you mean?"

"My ancestors, trapped on the world of Ko, had only the supplies from two grocery wagons at the beginning. Luckily there were corn kernels and rice and a few other food items that could be used as seed for future crops, but although there might have been some cotton cloth, there certainly were no cotton seeds, so for all our history, we were limited to native plants that could be grown for fibers."

He rattled on with what U'tanse history he knew, and Casey was fascinated, happy to have more details for his spy reports to the Duke of da Vinci.

Soon, they drove up to the entrance to Hessian Gardens, a lavishly decorated expanse with large columns and elaborate stonework. They stepped out into the entrance way, decorated with flowers and lit by strings of lanterns. Lady Luthe called out to her brother and waved them over. She was surrounded by a cluster of other party-goers.

Ohen made sure he didn't accidentally lock eyes with the footman. It was hard enough ignoring his presence when the man was so focused on him.

Quickly, it took all of his attention to greet the others, some he had already met and quite a few that were looking forward to seeing the giant for the first time. Ohen had a few phrases he learned to use when making a first impression on the guests Lady Luthe had invited.

It was shortly after someone called out to come see Phobos glistening over the river waters that Ohen was startled by the panicked thoughts of the Tempe spy.

Off in the parking area with the other wagons and their crews, the man was being surrounded by soldiers in uniform. He knew exactly what was happening. Hurriedly, he reviewed the simple life story he'd memorized, telling of an ordinary Xanthe worker who had hired on as a footman.

Other than some tight bindings on the man as he was hurried off, there was no one hurt, for which Ohen was grateful. He forced his attention back to the group who had clustered around him, listening to his tales. None of the guests noticed the brief disturbance off near the carriages.

There was a theater stage as part of the place, and half of the guests went over to sit down for the performance. Others stayed and talked.

Ohen asked, "What is a Shakespeare?"

The man laughed, "Shakespeare! William Shakespeare. He's a classic writer, from long before the Plague. Long before the Star, really. I thought everyone knew about the Shakespeare plays."

Ohen shook his head. "Sorry. My knowledge of human history before the Star is limited to what one man wrote down from memory. He was a scientist, and engineer. I guess it's not too surprising that there are whole areas of the past that he never thought to mention."

The man held out his hand, "I'm Frank Ash, by the way. I'm a merchant specializing in hardwoods, fruit and grains. Anything that ships on the river, actually. I'm just here so my daughter can hunt for a husband."

Ohen chuckled. "There's a lot of that. I think that's the only reason for most of these parties."

"You could be right. And from what I overheard, you're a visitor from another world?"

"Yes, Owen Barclay. I got swept up in the middle of this Candor war and chose to side with Xanthe."

"That's amazing. You arrived on a spaceship? That hasn't happened since the Plague."

Ohen nodded. "Yes, I'm stuck here for a while, it appears."

Mr. Ash rubbed his forehead. "I guess that explains what I heard several months back."

"What's that?"

"Oh, it was posted at the port. Some official notice. It said that anyone who saw any new spaceship should report it to the nearest military outpost. People treated it as a joke. Lots of people have seen spaceships, but a new one? That's not likely."

Ohen leaned forward. "You've seen a spaceship?"

Ash nodded, puzzled at his reaction. "Of course. There are a lot of them. Hundreds of them across the planet. Of course, they're all just idle landmarks since they were shut down at the time of the Plague."

"Where? I'd love to see one."

The merchant shook his head. "Mr. Barclay, you're right in the middle of them."

"What?"

Ash nodded and walked over to the stone wall and rapped his knuckles on one of the huge cylinders that formed the centerpiece of the wall. "This is one of them. All of these big pillars are spaceships. Like I said, they went idle during the Plague."

Ohen turned his clairvoyance on the cylinder. Plain as day, it was a metal structure with storage levels inside, and some kind of mechanism at the center that could easily be a TP engine. The stone wall was just something that had been built up around it and the others at a later time.

"This is some kind of space port."

Ash nodded. "That's what I've heard. It was a big field where these spaceships could land and offload their cargo, but then it was just useless land and they turned it into the gardens."

Ohen placed his hand on the metal. "It's amazing." He nodded to Ash. "Thanks for telling me. I guess people have been looking for my spaceship ever since I told my story. They never mentioned that to me."

Ash said, "Oops. They didn't say not to tell you."

Ohen nodded. It was reasonable the military would be looking for his boat. But if they were just looking for these tall cylinders, they'd never recognize his craft even if they were right there looking at it. They were completely different designs. He'd even made the same mistake, never recognizing these cylinders for what they were.

Unsettling Presence

As much as Ohen wanted to sneak back to his hidden computer and ask about these cylindrical spaceships, the plan was to return to the Tower and check in after the Tempe spy had been captured. After a party that seemed to drag on way too long, Lord Casey tapped him on the shoulder. He was frowning.

"Barclay, I've got a favor to ask. Would you mind going back to Fort Dell with Lieutenant Pascal in his carriage? There's something that came up and I need to help my sister."

It was the first time Ohen had caught Casey lying to him. He had been notified about the footman being arrested and needed to speak with the others and also with the carriage company. He was in the dark and intended to get to the bottom of the situation.

Ohen could only wish him good luck silently. "That's fine. I'll track Pascal down."

It wasn't difficult. However, Casey hadn't bothered to confirm his lie with his sister and she casually contradicted it. Ohen pretended not to notice.

Pascal's ride was just an open carriage he drove himself. There was room for Ohen to ride beside him, barely.

"How can you afford to attend all of Lady Luthe's parties?" Ohen asked.

Pascal shrugged. "I don't have much of anything else to spend my pay on. Besides, it isn't much."

Ohen tried not to dig too deeply into the man's thoughts. Questions about money turned the soldier's thoughts to how much it might cost to maintain a home for a new wife—not that he had any chance with Lady Luthe or any of her friends either.

If it were only that simple for a U'tanse. I don't dare get into a romantic relationship. Having a random child with a normal human could be disastrous.

The U'tanse were only able to survive as a race because every mother was able to select the genetics of her child. And every infant telepath had to be raised under careful circumstances to preserve the child's mental stability.

Ohen knew it had to be done, but he'd never received that genetic training. It had always been the women's domain. Until his people returned for him, he had to remain celibate. He shouldn't even be thinking about such things.

They parted at the stables used by the officers and Ohen raced off in the dark to get to the Tower. He really had no questions for the security officers, just giving them what answers he could. He confirmed that the spy had been listening in on his conversations, although he couldn't tell them exactly how he knew it. Not that they cared. They had their man and they were confident he was guilty.

Ohen could tell they were ready for him to leave. They had their job to do and he wasn't any part of it. He thanked them and left.

It had been a long day, and he really needed the sleep, but he knew he wouldn't be able to sleep until he talked to the computer about those spaceships. Taking the unlighted streets and navigating by his clairvoyant sight he made it to Meti's place and began pedaling his computer.

"Computer, are the large cylinders in Hessian Gardens spaceships?"

"Yes."

"Are they active?"

"No."

"What happened to them?"

"In the early stages of the Plague, when it was clear that nearly everyone on Mars had the infection, Project Central ordered a planet-wide quarantine. No ship could leave. That order has never been rescinded."

"Are the ships damaged?"

"Most are not, although there were some exceptions. However, in the emergency situation, and with no competent pilots available, the ships were not archived. All power eventually drained away and not even their computer control systems respond."

That answered his most pressing questions. If there had been power cells that had maintained power for the centuries that had passed, then he might have been able to tap that energy to use with the communication computers. But with no power, there was no way to take any of those ships back into space to recharge them, either.

"Computer, if power could be fed back into one of those spaceships, could it fly again?"

"Technically, yes. However, the planetary quarantine order has never been lifted, and the ship's computer would refuse the commands to fly."

Ohen shook his head. It was again a significant difference between these ships and his own B3. His computers were just dumb assistants used to make some tasks easier. It sounded like these Martian ships were controlled by the computers, and were really in charge. The pilots just made suggestions.

"Can I lift the quarantine order?"

"Such an order must come from Project Central."

"Is there anyone left alive in Project Central?"

"No. Not since the Plague."

Ohen sighed. There were hundreds of spaceships on Mars and none of them could be used because of an obsolete order. It was such a waste.

Not that I'd have a clue about how to fly such a craft. They're nothing like my boat.

...

It was like going back in time a few months, General Jonah was focussed on pushing back the Candorians, but now he had more troops that he could communicate with directly as they moved. The dozen or so officers concentrated over the maps of Eastern Xanthe, trying to predict the enemy's movements and where to find their weak points.

Ohen's suggestions were slightly different from many of the more senior officers.

"We can't afford to lose Stege. If the Candorians can capture and fortify that city, then it'll become their new base of operations," said Major Brown.

Ohen tapped the screen. "Chia is much more important. Take a look at where the Old Road branches here. Both branches were cut during the floods of two hundred years ago, but the southern route through Chia was rebuilt by the merchants wanting to maintain trade with Orson. Moving troops and supply wagons through the Stege route would take an extra day due to the road conditions alone.

"We can support Chia more efficiently, and if the Candorians took it, then they would have easier access to the repaired Old Road."

He would have continued, except there was a rap on the door. This was supposed to be a closed meeting. Everyone's voice went still. A lieutenant closest to the door opened it and took a paper from the young messenger. The boy saluted and left.

The lieutenant glanced at the seal and the name and handed it over to Ohen.

Ohen recognized the royal seal and showed it to the general.

Jonah sighed and waved him off. If the king wanted to talk to Barclay, there wasn't anything he could do about it.

Ohen left the meeting and found a corner where no one could see him.

The message was short. Come back to the same meeting room where they'd spoken the last time. No time given, so the king must mean immediately.

What's going on? After all the secrecy last time, this will get the gossips' tongues wagging.

He hurried to the staircase. There was no time to wait for an elevator.

By the time he arrived, panting, at the correct floor, the guard nodded to him and said, "Go on in. He'll be there soon."

Ohen was grateful for the few minutes to cool down, resting in the private room. Sadly, there was no tray of pastries this time.

King Harmon entered thirty minutes later with a pleased grin on his face. "You'll never guess, Barclay."

Ohen tried not to cheat. "Probably not. What is it?"

The king eased into his chair. "After our last meeting, I had an odd thought and went to my computer. You know how you can ask if a person has a message number?"

"Yes."

"Well, I asked the computer if there was an identifier for the ruler of Luna or the ruler of Earth." He chuckled.

Ohen leaned forward. "And?"

"The computer said to wait for an answer. Several minutes later, it said that there was no known ruler of Earth, but there was a ruler of Luna and the computer gave me his number."

"Really? So there are people using computers on Luna, too."

"It appears so."

Harmon put his hand to his chest. "So I sent a message to the ruler of Luna. I introduced myself as the ruler of Mars and said that I was interested in opening a friendly line of communications between our two worlds.

"It took him a few days to respond, but today there was a message from Richard Neeley, Emperor of Luna. He greeted me and said he was pleased to hear from Mars and was curious about our history since the Plague."

Ohen sighed. "So, that's amazing. Two worlds in contact for the first time in hundreds of years. That's certainly historic. What are your plans?"

Harmon smiled, "That's why I wanted to talk with you again. How did you get to Mars? Can you leave?"

Ohen sighed. "I've been expecting this. I've never really wanted to talk about my plans, for obvious reasons."

"But you did land in a spaceship, right?"

"Yes."

"You say that there are no others of your kind here on Mars or on the other planets, so is your spaceship still intact? Can you fly away?"

Ohen knew he couldn't lie.

"Technically, I should be able to leave. There are many practical issues, however."

"Is it just my permission? You were captured, I understand. With an official release, could you just walk back to your ship and fly away?"

"Well… it would be a long walk, and through Candorian-controlled lands. Like I say, there are practical issues."

The king nodded. "I see. Well, just assuming that those problems could be solved, I've toyed with the idea of sending you to Luna as an ambassador from Mars. You could see for yourself how this other world lives and send me reports. Maybe there is a possibility for trade. Maybe they have science that we have lost."

Ohen smiled, "And you would have the destabilizing foreigner out of your hair."

"Well, there is that."

Ohen considered it. "I would need help getting there. Military help, and I was just in a meeting where we were discussing the difficulty of meeting the Candorians head on. General Jonah might not want to waste his resources getting rid of me. He has said that he values my input. He might not want to let me leave."

The king said, "I know people on both sides of this question. You do have enemies."

Ohen nodded. "I would like to move on to Luna, and still maintain good relations with Xanthe. This sounds like a good deal for me, but it will take some thought to make it happen. I may need your help to navigate the political and military conflicts."

The king nodded. "As long as Xanthe can stay on track to become the dominant kingdom on Mars, I'd love to have your people grateful for Xanthe's help as well."

Ohen could read several layers to his thoughts. Having other worlds recognize King Harmon of Xanthe as ruler of Mars was a card he might be able to play in the future. And Harmon was totally honest that he wanted to be on the good side of the U'tanse. If Barclay or another of his kind decided to back some other kingdom, it could be disastrous.

Deep down was a memory of a discussion Harmon had with several other nobles. They had recognized the value of Barclay's innovations, and wanted him killed to keep him from helping anyone else.

...

General Jonah shook his head. "Absolutely not. I'm not ready to turn you loose on a whim. Besides, it would take too much force to fight all the way back to Dumont and then we'd just have to pull back. We'd never be able to sustain a push like that. It's just too expensive in lives. We could lose a whole city over this if Candor took the opportunity to move in wherever we left unprotected."

Ohen nodded. "Are you okay with me thinking about less expensive options?"

The general breathed out. "You say the king suggested this?"

"Yes. I'd be doing a task for him and removing my unsettling presence from the political scene."

"Unsettling? Well, you are that!"

Ohen chuckled. "You've already gotten the most out of me already. He just doesn't want to have to pay me off with lands or a title. Letting me continue my journey is a cheap way out, he figures."

Jonah was frowning. "That may be. Our troops are getting more efficient. Once we push the Candorians back, several officers will be sporting fancy new titles. That's the word, at least."

He sighed. "But I still don't like losing you."

"Well, unless I can figure something out, I many not be able to leave. I don't relish the idea of hiking all the way back to Dumont through hostile territory."

A Strong Hint

"Okay," Pascal bumped his arm. "What's going on?"

"What do you mean?" Ohen concentrated on his breakfast, wondering if he had time to make a second pass through the line.

"Don't try to hide it. Rumor has it that the king called you out of a meeting and then you had a one-on-one with the general. Something is happening."

Ohen sighed. "And I can't tell you. It may turn out to be nothing. Sometimes ideas never make it to the planning stage."

The lieutenant gave him a look. "If you say so."

Ohen ate in silence for a bit.

I'm doing it again. When there's a chance I'm going to be leaving a friend behind, I start to put up barriers ahead of time.

"Pascal, what are your long terms plans?"

"What? I don't know what you mean."

"Are you going to be an officer for life, working your way up the ranks? Do you have family waiting for you to come back home?"

Pascal shook his head. "I've got family back in Camichel, but when I received the invitation to train at the capital, everyone congratulated me, happy that I was on the pathway to a good life. They don't expect me back. It's not like I have a family title or anything. My father is a merchant, but he has three other children to get established in the world.

"I suppose I would be pleased to work my way up to a captaincy, but that would take some luck." He sighed. "That's my plan, make friends and connections and pray for luck."

Ohen smiled, "You're not fishing for a front line commission?"

Pascal glanced around to see if anyone was listening. "Sad to say, I like paperwork more than the opportunity to see battle. Don't tell anyone."

"I'm hardly in a position to judge. The only time I've been close to fighting, it made me sick."

By the time they finished and walked out into the courtyard, Ohen opened up enough to mention that he had a younger brother. "Of course I haven't seen him in ten years or so. Make that six Martian years."

Pascal asked, "No sisters?"

"Sad to say my family prefers boys."

"Like you have any choice in the matter."

Ohen just nodded, having momentarily forgotten that ordinary humans indeed had no control over the matter. His own family had preserved the height and size of his ancestors deliberately, and there was reluctance to have tall daughters. His own mother and grandmother were all much shorter. It was only the men that were bred for their size.

"Barclay! Pascal!" There was a shout in the distance. Just outside the archway, Lord Casey was hanging onto his wagon, waving.

Ohen asked, "What's he doing here?"

"I have no clue."

The both of them walked over through the archway. Only military wagons were allowed inside.

Ohen whispered. "I think Lady Luthe is with him."

Pascal stepped a little quicker.

Lord Casey stepped down from the wagon and met them.

Ohen offered his hand. "What are you doing here?"

Casey took it, and then said, "I just had to come and apologize. I've just learned that the footman that I had hired was actually a foreign agent come to spy on you. It's unforgivable that I put you in harm's way."

Ohen shook his head. "That wasn't your fault at all. There's no need to apologize."

Pascal looked at Ohen. "A spy! What spy?"

"Oh, just someone from Tempe, I think. That's what General Jonah told me. I really don't think I was in any kind of danger. They arrested him at the garden party."

"And you didn't tell me?"

Ohen shrugged. "I didn't think it was that important."

"Well I think—"

Ohen reacted. A sharp image appeared in his head, one of the three of them, hovering over the barrel of a rifle. The shooter was focussing in on his head, taller than the other two.

"Down!" Ohen shouted, grabbing both of them by the arm and trying to drag them forcibly off to the left, where there might be shelter.

Bang! And there was a sharp pain in his leg.

No, that's Pascal's leg. The telepathic echo didn't make it any less painful.

There was a shriek. Luthe heard the shot and saw them all fall. She fumbled with the wagon door's latch.

Ohen shouted, "No! Stay in the wagon!"

But she wasn't listening.

"Let's get Pascal to the wagon."

Casey was still in shock at what had happened, maybe not realizing Pascal had been shot, but Ohen's words made sense.

The gateway was suddenly filled with people. The guards were out with their own guns, searching the surroundings for the shooter.

Ohen knew roughly where he was, on a rooftop to the west, but he was much more concerned with getting all of them out of sight. The assassin was concerned with getting himself to safety, and not really sure whether he'd hit the right target or not.

"Lady Luthe!"

She locked onto his eyes.

"Pascal has been shot. We have to get him into the wagon out of sight. Casey is unhurt."

She nodded and climbed back inside. Ohen lifted Pascal bodily up after her.

Casey grumbled. "The driver's run off. I'm never hiring anyone from that place again!"

Once they were all inside. Ohen grabbed Pascal's leg. He screamed.

"Hold on, I'm just stopping the bleeding."

Luthe took Pascal's arm. Ohen was focussing his clairvoyance into the man's leg, sensing what he could. There was a slug of lead embedded in the muscle tissue. There was considerable tearing of the tissue, but the bone was intact.

There was a guard at the door. "Is anyone hurt?"

Lord Casey said, "Yes, Lieutenant Pascal has been shot. The driver's gone. Can you get someone to take us to the doctor?"

The guard nodded. "I'll drive you there."

Ohen was conflicted. They were close to the fort's hospital, but he didn't really have a lot of confidence in the local doctors' abilities. He could probably get Pascal healed with his limited psychic skills, but it would be very hazardous to get labeled as some kind of magical healer.

At the hospital, the doctor was experienced with gunshot wounds, but put off by the lord and lady accompanying him.

Ohen got the doctor's attention. "I could feel the bullet embedded in his calf, about this deep." He spread his fingers. His hand still red with blood gave him a little believability. "I don't think it hit the bone."

The doctor's thoughts seemed competent. As long as they got the bullet out with sterilized instruments and didn't cause too much additional damage, Pascal should be okay.

The doctor made them leave.

Casey was holding his sister. He apologized. "She's a little faint."

Ohen said, as confidently as he could, "I really think he'll recover from this with no permanent damage. I'm just glad the two of you are okay."

"Who was that shooter?" asked Casey.

"I have no idea. I have been told I have enemies. I fear they were trying to shoot me and missed. Maybe I'd better not be attending any dinner parties for awhile."

That got a slight laugh.

Ohen said, "I have reports to make. You two need to get back home and out of this madhouse."

Casey nodded. "And I have some strong words for Hessian's Travel."

...

After Ohen made his report about Lieutenant Pascal bravely taking a bullet to protect Lord Casey and himself from the assassin, the general had to be talked out of pairing him up with a bodyguard.

"Believe me, I'm totally convinced that someone wants me killed, as distasteful as that is. Still, I've been on the lookout for enemies before and I can move faster without having a bodyguard to deal with.

Jonah nodded. "I want you to spend more time planning your exit from here. I can't have people shooting at you. I'd rather you vanish."

Ohen nodded. "Some exit that won't take too many resources. I'll think of something."

. . .

A spy from Tempe. A spy from the king's cousin. And now, an assassin hired by persons unknown that had managed to escape unseen. The capital of Orson didn't feel like a very safe place. He had to make his escape.

For now, being a telepath had its advantages. That assassin, by concentrating on his target—Barclay—had effectively been shouting his name. That was how telepaths called to each other—forming a clear mental image of the person you wanted to talk to. Telepathy was a listening skill, rather than a speaking skill, but sensing that strong image of yourself in the background telepathic noise was a useful way to initiate a conversation.

The disadvantage was that now that the news of the attempted murder was spreading far and wide, many people were thinking about him strongly. It was just more noise to be filtered.

For most of the day he was in the map room, taking a good hard look at the western half of Xanthe, hunting for an optimal route. Then he visited the hospital again.

Pascal was alert and grumpy. "This thing hurts!"

"How did you expect a gunshot wound to feel? Like a bee sting?"

Ohen didn't mention that he was suffering from it as well.

"Oh, by the way, in my report you saved us all by your quick thinking and taking the bullet to save us."

Pascal winced. "I doubt I can pull off the hero act. You are the one who pulled us down."

Ohen nodded. "Yes, be modest, just like that. Take the win. Lady Luthe was very concerned about you."

There was a slight smile on the wounded man's face. "I do seem to recall some acts of charity from her. I can't deny that."

Ohen did his best to examine the wound. The bullet had been extracted with not too much more damage. With psychokinesis, he was able to kill off a couple of minor infections. There wasn't much more his skills could handle. Pascal just had to heal naturally.

. . .

That night, Ohen managed a sleeping room in the Tower and spent some time during a Phobos pass to use one of the computers. He scheduled a number of photos he could examine later.

After a couple of days, the attack was fading from people's minds. Ohen was still staying alert for other enemy's thoughts, but he was able to get back to his normal schedule. He visited Pascal once a day, and so apparently was Lady Luthe.

With a bandaged leg and a cane, the lieutenant was soon able to leave the hospital.

Ohen was pleased that his repetition of the story that Pascal had been the hero was working. He wasn't sure what Lord Casey remembered, but Lady Luthe was happy to accept that tale to organize her confused memories of the incident. She requested that Lieutenant Pascal stay as a house guest at their place as he recovered.

· · ·

General Jonah mumbled, as he looked over the large map showing a heavily forested region. "The Tangles has made a decent border between Tempe and Xanthe for a long time. I'm not sure there are any trails heading east to west through that area."

Ohen said, "I think it's my best bet. It's far enough north that there isn't likely to be a significant Candorian presence. I've taken a good look with current photos from Phobos of this area and with my memory, I'll have no trouble finding my way through here. All I'll need is a good strong horse to carry me and my stuff. If I can carry one of the computers, I can report what I find as well."

"And how much horse riding experience do you have?"

Ohen sighed. "A few hours."

"I wouldn't send anyone on a trip like that with no experience. You're always pestering me to build good roads, but there aren't any roads in the Tangles. Riding a horse around a manicured trail isn't the same as making your way through uncharted forest land.

"And sending you with a computer? We're barely putting two computers into service a week, we need every one of them put into the hands of an active military unit."

The general shook his head. "Barclay, you're not a mountain man. You're large and strong, but the first thing you did on Mars was knock yourself out by hitting a tree branch. You're an indoor man. You tell the story of growing up on that moon where there really wasn't any outdoors. Know your own limitations, man!

"Until you can come up with a better plan, you need to stay here."

Trip Planning

Having tasted the idea of breaking free and returning to B3, it was hard for Ohen to concentrate on his job at the Tower. General Jonah was just beginning his process of equipping troops with the new computers, and that process wasn't something that could be handed off. The computers were still so rare and valuable that, one at a time, a troop would be ordered to return to the capital where a communications officer and two or three strong soldiers were trained in how to use and care for the computer and generator. They were also given strong instructions on how to destroy them if there were any chance of them being lost to the enemy.

Most of the troops had no idea that this was going on. Supposedly this was just a time for resupply and their officers to be updated on the war effort. The computers were supposed to be hidden from friends and enemies alike.

A second Margareta ship was captured and the report was much like the first one, only this time the cargo ship had been surprised and taken without much of a fight. Admiral Falcone's tactics were getting better. The requests for more computers was repeated.

Jonah was resistant to the idea of giving the navy priority. "My troops have already won two major battles due to the extra coordination the computers can bring. We need to build on that advantage rapidly, not slow it down."

Ohen didn't get into that debate. He'd done his part getting the naval expansion started, but the pace was for more experienced people to decide.

He looked over a large paper sheet map marked with the past month's worth of land battles. The southern extent of the Maja valley was shaping up to be the new boundary line between Candor and the Xanthe-controlled lands. He wondered if that was Candor's end game, to make Xanthe accept the new line between the kingdoms. It would certainly leave several major cities like Chia and Stege far too close to enemy lines.

That would leave lots of places like Dumont and Marion open for Candorian settlers. The loss of such a large land area, even though it was lightly populated, would be a heavy blow to Xanthe. Certainly Ohen didn't expect King Harmon to accept a defeat like that.

Looking at the map, however, it did seem that the Candorian forces were concentrating on beefing up that line. In contrast the Xanthe forces were having to spread out more thinly, being prepared to defend any new incursion in a new direction.

He spoke. "There needs to be a second front, to force the Candorians to divide their forces."

Major Brown nodded. "Sadly, there are no allies in that area we can call on."

The conversation shifted to how a smaller force might force through a gap in the Candorian-held lands. The problem would be that they would be encircled almost immediately.

When he compared the limited paper map with the big map under glass, he had a feeling something was off. He'd examined that area recently with current photos and some things had changed. His memory was good, but he still couldn't identify what was bothering him. He needed another look at the recent images.

When the meeting was over, he went to the secret image-analysis room where the extra computer was kept, but General Jonah was already ahead of him, intent on doing some research of his own. Ohen didn't want to get into that.

Since the assassination attempt, he hadn't gone back to Meti's place, but unless it had been discovered, he still had his private computer hidden there. Ohen waited out the day until sunset and then with his paranoia and his inner senses on high, he followed the darker streets until he reached the area.

There was the sense of a familiar person. His first impulse was to duck out of sight, but it was Raymond Wills. He stood up straight and moved out of the shadows.

"Barclay!"

"Hey, keep it down, will you?"

They shook hands. Raymond shook his head. "I was wondering if you were ever coming back."

"It was a close call. Can we get out of sight?"

Raymond frowned. "What's going on?"

Once they went to the workroom, Ohen gave him a simplified version of the story.

"Someone shot at you! Why? Because you invented the generators?"

"That's part of it. There's politics involved as well. I got too friendly with some important people. You need to be careful, too. You've been told to be quiet about the computers, right?"

"Oh, yes! Meti hammers us all on that. If anyone finds out what we're doing, the money will stop." Raymond grinned. "I got a raise over this."

"That's good. But you know, there's a good chance I won't be back. I'd better clean up all the stuff I left behind."

Raymond shrugged. "I was going to grab all that gear for myself if you didn't. I'm going to miss having you around to pester about all this electrical stuff."

"Well, don't you get access to the computers when you hook up the electrical connections? You could send me messages—just for testing purposes of course."

They laughed.

"I may just do that. 'Owen Barclay' right?"

"That should do it."

They chatted a bit. Ohen left most of his notes and all the battery prototype stuff to Raymond. Without making a big deal of it, Ohen stuffed his secret computer and the generator in a large tote bag while Raymond was reading through the notes.

"Owen, do you think we'll ever get to the point that a guy like me could have a computer of his own?"

"It's a tough call. You, being an electrical expert, might be able to make the case that you needed to have one for your work. You can ask a computer all kinds of questions, like how many turns of wire at what diameter you'd need to produce the right amount of power. Things like that.

"But the average guy might not be able to get one. Nobody is making new ones anymore. There's a limit to how many of the old dusty ones can be brought back to life, here on Mars. I think they'll always be rare and valuable."

Raymond sighed. "I think so too. But I like that idea that I'll need one for my work. I've got more design ideas, and having help with the math stuff would be great."

His thoughts showed that he'd noticed Barclay packing away the computer, but he didn't figure it was any of his business. He just wished he was someone important enough to have a computer, too.

They shook hands again and Ohen began his dark-alley trip back to his dorm room. Once there, he had to find a place to stow and use it.

The room had originally been designed for two, but he'd had to scoot the bed at an angle and use a little table to extend it's length enough for him to be comfortable. At least he didn't have to deal with a roommate.

The generator, during his first trial, made enough noise that it intruded on the thoughts of one of his neighbors, so he limited his use to pulling down one of the current images of the Tangles that he'd requested before.

It was just enough to identify the features that had bothered him before. At several places in the southern band of the Tangles forest, there were features that looked like freshly cleared land.

He settled back on his bed, cleared his mind, and tried to locate what he'd seen in the photo.

. . .

Convincing the general took some effort.

Jonah shook his head slowly, "That's a lot of effort for something so uncertain."

Ohen tapped the screen. "I don't think it's that uncertain at all. These are refugees, the farmers and the townspeople that had to run when the Candorians forced the Xanthe troops out. They went north and hid in the forests. They've set up these camps for mutual protection, but every day, it gets colder. Winter is coming and they had to leave all their crops behind.

"There are probably quite a few men there, ready and able to fight, but they have to protect their families.

"If Xanthe troops showed up with food and confidence that they'd be pushing the Candorians back down to their valleys any day now, many of them will be ready to join up to help—as long as they are confident that their families will be fed."

The general leaned back. "I doubt we could feed them all. Getting wagons through there would be difficult."

"Then do it in stages. Show the effort, make a big confident splash with the easternmost refugee settlements and work westward when you can.

"If they see your confidence, then you'll have the second front we need to divide the Candorians."

Jonah looked at him, folding his arms, "And you'll get to go back to Dumont, won't you?"

Ohen decided the time was right. "And you really want that to happen."

"I do?"

And then Ohen spelled out his last, best, offer.

. . .

"Are you still using that cane?" asked Ohen.

Lieutenant Pascal sighed and leaned a little heavier on the cane. "Not while I'm on duty, but my leg is still a little weak. I'll probably be done with it in another week. It's healing up fast."

"That's good."

Pascal's thoughts momentarily dwelt on how soon he'd have to turn down the Lady Luthe's invitation to stay at their house. If he was healthy, he had no excuse to continue.

At Ohen's instigation, the two of them were standing at the front gate in the evening light, waiting for the rental wagon to arrive. Pascal looked around, not really looking for another gunman, but remembering when he was shot.

He looked at Ohen, "What prompted this visit to Luthe and Casey?"

Ohen shook his head. "Not here."

The messenger arrived, driving the light-weight rig Pascal was renting. The Chimbote's mansion was in walking distance, but not for someone with a healing leg. Since Pascal had chosen to return to work, it was his temporary solution to stay at the mansion and continue to receive Lady Luthe's hospitality.

They rode to the mansion in just a few minutes. The doorman was quite familiar with Pascal, but went to announce the arrival of Owen Barclay.

Both siblings came to greet them.

Ohen said, "I'm sorry to show up like this."

Lord Casey shook his head. "There's no problem. You had an open invitation. We will have to throw the kitchen staff into a panic, but they're used to that."

"Please, nothing extravagant. I came here for a nice talk, rather than a big meal, this time."

Lady Luthe whispered to Pascal, asking what was up, but he just shrugged.

They went to the dining room a little later, after the cook managed to extend the dishes a bit.

Ohen smiled as he smelled the food. "I'm really going to miss this."

Lord Casey asked, "Oh, Luthe can always hold another party."

Ohen shook his head. "No, I'll be leaving soon, and I may not be back."

Pascal asked, "What do you mean?"

"I mean that after I take care of a mission here in the next week, I'll be leaving to continue my journey."

Casey asked, "Leaving? To where?"

Ohen smiled. "I'll be heading to Luna, to meet the Emperor of Luna."

Luthe dropped her fork. "What?"

Ohen gestured. "I must ask all of you to keep this from the gossips, at least until King Harmon announces it himself. The king has been in communication with Luna via his computer and has arranged for me to visit."

She was still at a loss. "You mean like flying up into space. For real? Not just a fantasy story?"

Ohen took a bite from his pasta. "Yes, up into space, traveling many millions of kloms."

Pascal said, "So you've had a spaceship all this time."

Ohen nodded. "It's rather well-hidden, and difficult to get to, but yes. It's waiting there for me to wake it back up."

Lord Casey asked, "Why are you telling us? Isn't this a rather big military secret?"

"Well, I'm afraid the first step in my journey is to leave Orson without alerting all my enemies to what I'm doing. I proposed that if my good friend Lord Casey invited me to spend a little while with him at his home in Chimbote, then that might supply an adequate cover story.

"In reality, I'd meet up with a military escort once we're partway there and go on with the mission I really must finish before I leave.

"Lord Casey, do you think you could help me with this?"

Heading West

Lord Casey was obviously uncomfortable as they rode the closed carriage out the east road out of Orson.

Ohen asked, "Are you worried about leaving your sister alone?"

Casey shook his head. "She's hardly alone. Anne Jefferson is staying with her as chaperone while I'm gone, and of course the lieutenant and the house staff will be there in case she needs them. She wasn't really interested in a short visit home."

His eyes went to the roof. "At least there aren't any spies trying to listen in on us this time." It only made his feeling of depression more intense.

Ohen put the vague feelings together.

"Lord Casey, you aren't at fault for the Tempe spy."

"It's not that...."

Ohen nodded. "I've been aware of your arrangement with Duke Paul since the beginning."

"What?"

Ohen waved his hands. "I was warned about the politics between the royals and I spend hours every day staring at maps. It wasn't a big stretch to see that Chimbote was dependent on its powerful neighbor to the north. Then, when out of the blue, I received the dinner invitation, well... I kept my eyes open.

"Personally, I think you're trustworthy and I don't really have any objection to having my taste in steaks and my after-dinner tales reported to Duke Paul. I'd never have asked you for this favor to sneak out of town if I worried about the duke knowing about it."

Casey sighed. "I haven't been comfortable with this. I thought it was just an easy way to make it in Orson, and of course nothing could stop Luthe from coming along. I just don't like the actual spying part."

"Well, I'm sorry that I'll be leaving. Will that be a hardship?"

They talked for a few hours, making their way out of the Orson crater, following the road to da Vinci.

"You're really going to fly off to Luna?"

"That's the plan. Eventually, I'd like to visit Earth as well."

Casey sighed, "That would be wonderful."

Ohen shook his head. "Not for you. Earth's gravity is three times stronger than what you've grown up with here on Mars. Everything you do would be three times harder."

"Oh! Would you be okay?"

"I should. I grew up with the same gravity as Earth, so that's what I'm really used to. That's why I'm so strong here on Mars."

"And Luna?"

"Gravity would be half as strong as Mars."

Not too far from where the main road branched to the agricultural settlement of Dia-Cau, the carriage halted.

"Owen Barclay?" asked a man in leathers.

"Yes, that's me." Ohen stepped out of the carriage.

They said he was big. The man had his doubts about his new orders. Babysitting some foreigner was bad enough, but they were going into the Tangles based on his information. It could be a disaster.

"I'm Terry Carlyle. Terry, Terr, Carlyle—it's all the same to me. Do you have baggage? It'll have to ride on your horse."

"I've only got one bag. I'll get it." Ohen didn't really have many possessions. A couple of changes of clothes, a coat he hadn't worn yet, and they were all wrapped around his secret computer and a few odds and ends. He pulled the large bag, one-handed from the boot of the wagon.

He waved goodbye to Casey. It had been good to clear the air with him.

The wagon was waved off and Ohen tried to put it out of his mind. Nothing was more important than this mission.

There was a big Creme Draft horse. He secured his bag and stepped up into the saddle. He hoped the limited riding experience he'd accumulated would be enough.

Terry obviously didn't think so. He kept the smile from his face, but the thoughts were clear. **He's going to be saddle sore for sure by nightfall.**

Ohen nodded that he was ready, and they headed off, just the two of them on horses. Instead of heading to the east, they really needed to cross the heartland of Xanthe a thousand kloms westward before they could meet up with the troop and supply wagons. It was going to be a long, hard ride, even if the most of it would be on good roads.

Their first destination was a ferry across the Shalbatana River.

Terry wasn't one to talk, and Ohen was comfortable with that. The scout had already been briefed on him and he had his misconceptions. Talking wouldn't fix those, Terry had to see him in action.

Ohen just hoped he could handle it. The saddle sore warning was helpful. He was able to take precautions, both with changes to his blood circulation and simple things like standing in his stirrups from time to time. It was something he had to adapt to. He would be days in the saddle.

They reached the ferry crossing fairly quickly. Following the scout, they seemed to be traveling much faster than he had on the practice trails he'd used before. The horses seemed to be gliding through the air, rather than slowly walking. He wondered what their sustainable pace was. They were, after all, beasts that could run long distances in Earth's gravity. Even bred here on Mars, their genetics were capable of much more.

They dismounted and Terry took care of the fare. They led their horses onto the wooden planks and Terry warned him to keep his horse under control. There was an iron railing near the side, so he wrapped the reins around it.

Terry put his hand on his horse's flank.

Ohen did the same with his horse. The large horse was used to being touched and his thoughts were only slightly unsettled by the feeling of the waves underfoot. It had ridden ferries before.

Ohen hadn't. This was the first water boat he'd ever ridden, at least that he was aware of. Perhaps one of the wagons he'd ridden on had used a ferry, but if so, he didn't remember it. The Old Road all the way from Dumont had bridges over the rivers it had crossed.

The Shalbatana was fairly wide at this point, although not the lake it had been back in Orson. He could imagine building a bridge here would be an ambitious effort.

As they rode across the river, pulled by long cables, Ohen couldn't shake the grin on his face.

Terry asked, "Haven't you ridden a boat before?"

Ohen chuckled. "Not one like this. I don't get out much. The maps I've memorized are often quite detailed, but it's nothing like smelling the air and feeling the waves for yourself."

Terry shook his head. "And you're headed for the Tangles? You must be crazy."

Ohen shook his head. "In my own way, I'm an explorer."

Terry stifled his urge to laugh.

. . .

They were crossing through populated Xanthe, frequently passing through villages and farmlands. The road wasn't quite as smooth as the Old Road, but it was maintained.

And they got to stop at places that served hot food. Ohen dug into his stash of Xanthe script to order extra and treated Terry from time to time.

Terry was grateful. "Thanks. I've got a limited budget for this trip."

"It's no problem. Back in Orson, there were people who bought my dinner just so they could hear my stories. It's my turn to do the same. How long have you been a scout?"

The wiry man brushed his finger through his gray-streaked hair. "Oh, I don't know, fifteen years or more. I haven't been in the Tangles for three years. It was pretty tough-going back then."

"There are several trails to Tempe on the maps."

He nodded, "Yes, but nobody's ever had a reason to go west through there."

"Nobody until the Candorian invasion."

Terry nodded. "I read the briefing. You think refugees have set up camps there."

"Several of them. And they didn't want to mess with the Tempes either. Some moved up the existing trails and then found their own routes east and west."

"I don't know how you can possibly know that."

Ohen shrugged. "I'm not perfect, but I had a reputation at the Tower for guessing what people might do."

"I guess. Somebody had to believe you, or this trip would never have been put together."

. . .

"What's this smell?" asked Ohen, as they crossed a mountain pass west of Nandy, after taking the northwestern branch of the road.

"Smell?" Terry stopped and sniffed the air. "I smell pine, that's it."

"Pine? As in pine trees?"

"Yes, the sap is resinous and at times, the scent goes on for miles. We're getting into more forested lands."

Ohen took another breath. "It's wonderful. Do other trees have their own scents?"

Terry laughed. "Yes, they do. You've really never been in a forest?"

"If I have, I wasn't paying attention to the scents. The vast majority of my life has been spent indoors. All this is new to me. What do the other trees smell like?"

"I don't know, in words. I just recognize the scent."

. . .

Days passed. They stocked up supplies in Drilon and had to get a horseshoe replaced in Kolonga. Although Terry didn't really want to talk about where they were going, just asking the questions got him to think about the details. That was enough for Ohen to visualize the ford on the Maja River that Terry wanted to use. There wasn't a bridge or ferry to get across on that part of the river, but Terry had crossed there before. They'd already waded across many smaller watercourses.

Ohen frowned. "Horses swim, right?"

"Yes, even loaded down like this and riding them. I guess you've never done that before?"

"I can swim, but I just worry about Merry."

He'd named his horse Meringue, then it quickly simplified. The horse must have had other names, but quickly got used to being called.

Terry called his horse Bud, but wasn't terribly attached to it. After all the years he'd been a scout, he'd met and lost many horses. Terry thought of Ohen as a kid in a way.

Eventually, they arrived at the Maja. Terry kept them out of sight for a while.

"In peacetime, there are log rafts that go up and down the river. The big ones go north to the ocean."

"Granite?"

"Yes, how did you know? But some come upstream with trade supplies."

Ohen frowned. "How do they go against the current?"

"I've seen oarmen. Sometimes they use poles. On some stretches, there are places that can tow your raft with horses on shore."

"Do they use sails?"

"Rarely. It's hard to keep control, so I've heard."

But now, the raft business had dried up, probably out of fear of Candorian attacks. They were north of reported battles, but Chia and Stege were the economic centers to the south, and they were practically under siege. That was what this mission was supposedly all about.

The ford was wide. The river spread out and was shallow in many places. There were marked pylons that showed where it was deep enough for the rafts. They waded in. Ohen tried to keep his nervousness under control so Merry wouldn't get spooked.

"Just follow me," called Terry.

"Okay."

They went into the deep stretch. Ohen gasped. "It's cold!"

Terry laughed. "Try it in the winter when you've got to dodge the ice floes."

It reminded Ohen of the official reason for the trip. Winter was coming, and those refugees were farmers and merchants—not used to hunting the forests for game to keep their family's fed.

"Do the wagons float?"

"Of course! Who'd build a wagon that couldn't ford a river?"

Those city wagons he'd rode back in the capital probably couldn't, but that was different.

When they came ashore on the western side, Terry was anxious to get them back into the trees. Ohen scanned the area with his clairvoyance, but didn't sense anyone.

I should have been doing that all along. It would be stupid to get himself captured, again.

Terry had his own senses on alert. They were no longer in safe, Xanthe-controlled lands. He wanted to join the troop just as soon as he could.

They rode a few miles in and Terry stopped to examine the ground.

"Is that our group?"

He looked up the road. "Should be. Tracks aren't that old. If we ride hard and don't take breaks, we can catch up with them before nightfall, maybe."

And the scout was right, they rode another three hours on a trail that Ohen had seen on the maps, and other than stops to let the horses water, they kept at it.

The smoke from a campfire gave them the first warning. Terry held up his hand. Ohen eased Merry up beside him.

"They're close," the scout whispered.

Ohen nodded. He'd located them via clairvoyance, but wasn't inclined to reveal that.

They walked their horses slowly until Terry silently pointed to the tracks and led them off on a side trail barely wide enough for a wagon to make it through.

In a secluded meadow, the four wagons were visible, circled together. Almost instantly, two riders were beside them, escorting them in.

"Carlyle."

"Harris." Terry returned the greeting.

Nobody talked to Ohen. They'd been expecting a stranger. A foreigner. Some kind of a map expert. Nobody knew that to expect of him.

Other than one person. Ohen caught a very different train of thought as he dismounted and walked toward the wagons.

He walks funny, like with a bounce. Maybe I can use that when I need to take him down.

Ohen couldn't identify who it was, but someone had a very different agenda, and that included knocking him down and taking him captive.

The Northern Camps

Most of the men were dressed like Terry, in leathers. Captain Sean Jenkins was just as rough-looking as his men, but wore a military shirt with his brass star at the collar.

Jenkins scratched his beard. "I was wondering when you were going to show up." He gestured to a small fire ring where they could talk without the rest of the men listening in.

Terry grinned as they walked. "I could blame it on the desk jockey here, but the real reason is we had to swing by Kolonga to get a shoe replaced."

Jenkins looked at the stranger. "I was told to wait for you. I don't suppose you can tell me where we're going next?"

Ohen nodded. "Yes. Continue north on the same trail that led you here for another forty-two kloms, then take a trail that follows a creek to the west for about eight to ten kloms and you'll find the first refugee settlement. I know where the others are as well."

"And how do you know this?"

Ohen shook his head. Theatrically, he looked around to see if others were listening. "I'm not allowed to discuss this with anyone other than General Jonah at the Tower."

Captain Jenkins nodded. The general was making some very strange and risky changes lately, and the battles were proving him right. Jenkins had his suspicions, especially now that he'd been given the little canister with a crank on the side that he couldn't tell anyone about.

But trusting this stranger was a hard step.

Ohen put out his hands to soak up some of the warmth of the flames. "You might want to send a scout to confirm the location. Perhaps you might even give the refugees warning that we're coming. It would be best if we didn't start shooting at each other."

"I have confidence in my men."

Ohen nodded. "That's good. Those refugees need to see the confidence boiling off of you. They need to believe that they can return home soon."

Jenkins frowned. "How confident are you?"

"Very confident. The Candorian supply lines will be drying up soon."

"How…?" He didn't complete the question. This Barclay character wouldn't answer.

Ohen nodded. "All that's needed is a second front. Your troops, and whatever volunteers you can inspire to join you, will make the Candorians realize they've left their western side undefended. At the same time, the main Xanthe forces from the east will attack. The Candorians, running out of supplies, will have no choice other than to return to the south."

"How can you be certain that they have left their back side undefended?"

"I know. There are very few Candorians left in the towns they've conquered. It's so bad for them that the Xanthe captives are on the verge of rebelling on their own. Returning refugees would make all the difference."

The captain frowned and looked at the scout. "What is your estimation of his claims?"

Terry laughed. "He's an innocent in these woods, and barely able to stay on his horse, but he's not stupid. He knows stuff I'd never expect a Tower officer to know. I'd have to believe him."

Jenkins stared at the fire. He took a breath. "Okay then, pick someone you know and go make first contact with this refugee camp. Leave in the morning."

Terry nodded and went back to the circle of the wagons.

With just the two of them there by the fire, Captain Jenkins asked, "I was told to trust you. Trust isn't easy."

"I completely understand your position. But you should know that I do know a few things. You have paper maps of the region? I need to add a few things."

"Like those other refugee camps?"

"Yes, and a few suggested places where Candorians are weak and your troop and the volunteers could make the biggest impact."

Jenkins had his own theory. Somehow the Xanthe command had tapped into a network of spies spread throughout the land the Candorians had captured, and that this Barclay person knew a lot of valuable information.

Ohen had that information, but he'd never reveal that it had come from photos from Phobos and his own clairvoyant and telepathic scans.

. . .

When Ohen rode into the refugee camp with the wagons, he was nearly overwhelmed by the fear, hunger, and hope that the displaced people radiated. The news had spread rapidly that King Harmon had shipped wagons of food for them. There were many who were also just waiting for the catch. What were those troops going to demand in return?

Captain Jenkins was clearly in charge and Ohen insisted on it. He didn't want any more people asking questions about him. Still, there were some who were curious about that tall guy in the back in the city clothes.

Overnight, Ohen had spent some time trying to identify potential enemies in the troop. He had it narrowed down to about four that had the right kind of suspicions of him. Until someone started planning more direct action, he couldn't sense more than the general feelings about him. Nor could he identify why people were planning to capture him.

Was it a spy or spies from other countries that had infiltrated this group? Perhaps someone native to Xanthe, but loyal to one of the different factions? The worst case would be someone acting under secret orders from the general himself.

Ohen believed Jonah's thoughts, but he just hoped that he could be trusted. The man did have untrained ineda that could hide secret plans he didn't want Barclay to know about. Maybe they did have a bargain that would let Ohen leave Mars, but the general wasn't happy about it.

But regardless of who was planning against him, it was plain nothing was immediate. Did this enemy know Barclay was planning to make an exit for Dumont when the refugee situation stabilized? Did they know he had a spaceship of his own?

He had to face the mistakes he'd made. It was widely known that he claimed to be from another world. Many thought he was crazy, but space travel was a real thing from history. It wasn't an unbelievably crazy claim.

And if he was from some other world, he needed a spacecraft. Any of the factions or other countries that had been alerted to the existence of Owen Barclay just might be willing to kidnap him in order to get his boat.

. . .

There was a common thought he'd picked up several times from the crowd. **We could be home by Christmas.**

He saw Terry walk by. He gestured.

The scout asked, "What's up?"

"Tell me about Christmas. I've heard of it, but my people never celebrated it."

Terry winced. "Strange. Everybody celebrates Christmas in the winter and Advent in the summer. From what I heard, Mars years are twice as long as Earth years, so we split the holiday up into two different ones. But really, much of the same traditions happen in both holidays, so it just the 'summer Christmas' and the 'winter Christmas' for most people."

Ohen nodded, "So it's an important holiday."

"Sure! It means a lot."

That clarified some of the feelings he was intercepting. The weather was getting colder and people were thinking about winter coming. Some were feeling the loss of being homeless. The idea that they could be home by Christmas was contagious.

Four months was an optimistic time frame, but it was a possibility. Many of the people who had fled the invasion had decided that protecting their family was more important than fighting. If they had confidence that loved ones were going to be fed and protected, they just might be more enthusiastic about joining the volunteer forces to push the invaders back out.

Ohen needed to have another talk with the captain and casually mention a few things he'd 'overheard' in the camp.

. . .

Captain Jenkins rushed things. He let the refugees know that he had several other camps to visit and had to leave soon. Some had thought all of the wagons were for them, but the captain said no. "There will likely be more supplies coming, but I can't let the others starve so you can stay fat and happy here through the winter. The situation down south is changing too rapidly. I need to finish making contact with the other camps and start moving my soldiers into position."

"How long will this last?"

"It depends on how many volunteers join up."

The refugees had to make some decisions. The troops wouldn't stay and protect them, but it sounded like they were in no danger from the Candorians. Some had to stay and protect all the families while others could go harass the invaders.

If they did their part, maybe they could be home by Christmas.

That night, Ohen monitored the captain's thoughts as he secretly cranked his computer and reported in to his commander. Things were going as planned, but a second troop with supply wagons should be sent as soon as possible to keep the refugees confident of a quick victory.

. . .

The second refugee camp was a little harder to reach. The troops had to cut through trees near a small river before they could reach the north-south trail that these other families had used. The displaced were more exclusively from farming areas than the first camp, but the story was the same and the volunteers from the first camp were the most enthusiastic recruiters for the second-front force.

As soon as they reached the third camp, the captain confirmed that a second supply shipment from King Harmon was already on its way to keep his people from starving. The recruitment pitch was becoming second nature.

Ohen realized he'd already done all he could to organize the effort and he needed to move on to part two of his mission.

Jenkins frowned. "I'm not used to people in my group just deciding to leave."

"You know I'm not doing a thing to help. You've got it all under control. I've updated your map. It's time I continued with my part of the mission. I can do this myself, but General Jonah was insistent that I have a guide. But that was before I really knew how to ride a horse."

"So you want to take more people with you as well?"

"No. I'd rather go alone. I just have to be clear what my orders were. I'd advise you to check with the general yourself if you're uncertain."

Jenkins couldn't admit that he had the capability to call the Tower, but he was sure that Barclay knew about his canister. He sighed. "I'll think about it. Don't go running off unless I give permission."

Ohen nodded. "I wasn't planning on it." That was half a lie. It was always an option.

That night, the captain contacted his commander again. By morning, there was a reply. He ordered Terry to choose one or two soldiers to go with him, to escort Barclay on the next leg of his journey.

By the time Ohen was officially notified, he was already packed and ready. They left shortly after noon.

Terry pointed. "That's Lem Kircher—Kitchen, we call him. And Dawson."

"Hey, Dawson! Do you have a first name?"

The quiet man shook his head.

Ohen nodded, "Kitchen and Dawson. Thanks for coming along."

They retraced the old trail south. Terry said, "Maybe I should go ahead and scout ahead."

Ohen shook his head. "No Candorians in the area. We should just make kloms while we've got light."

"Are you sure?"

Ohen nodded.

Terry asked, "You've really got all the maps memorized?"

"Better than the captain's maps. I know right where to go, and when to avoid the Candorians. But you're probably the expert on where to find shelter and forage for the horses. The maps can't see smaller stuff like that."

Terry tried to get his head around it. He'd never seen the detailed maps in the Tower, so all he ever knew were the ink sketches that got handed out to the troop commanders.

214

"Well, don't make a mistake. I don't relish the idea of the four of us riding up to a Candorian patrol. We'll run out of ammunition pretty fast."

Ohen nodded. "That wouldn't be my idea of a good day either. I'll keep you informed if we get close to any hazards."

It was the second day when he waved Terry down.

"What?" Terry pulled Bud into a trot.

Ohen pulled closer. "You're planning to follow this trail up the creek to a pass, right?"

"Thinking about it, yeah."

"I suspect there's a Candor guard station there. Only about two or three of them, but I'd suggest an alternate route."

Terry frowned. Kitchen and Dawson pulled up to see what was going on.

Dawson's thoughts intruded, **Are we close now? This isn't near Dumont. I need to look for columns.**

Ohen marked Dawson as the one who planned to kidnap him. And he was expecting a spaceship. Was the plan to capture his boat? And who was behind it?

Terry shrugged. "Okay, I guess I know another way around, but it'll take us a little longer. If there's only a token force, and they don't know we're coming, we could take them out."

Ohen shook his head. "No. Someone would notice if they went missing. That would alert other Candorians that we're in the area. It's better if no one knows we're here."

Terry nodded and pointed, "Another twenty kloms this way, then. We'll stop for water at the creek."

They moved on, but in addition to scanning the land for Candorians, Ohen also needed to be sensitive to Dawson's thoughts. Could Kitchen or Terry be part of the scheme?

Second Mission

Dawson never talked around the campfire, but he listened to everything. He was especially alert when Terry questioned him about their route, how he was able to know where the Candorians were hiding.

On the forth day, they had to skirt a large crater where the Candorians had taken over the village and made it into a staging center where fresh troops and supplies from the Candor arrived.

Ohen had them hide a couple of times to avoid security patrols. They left, making their way cross-country to the southwest. This development hadn't been in place when he was first captured. Only after the Candorians had taken Dumont had they been able to move into this area.

The rapid invasion was more impressive, now that he was able to see the results up close. He suspected it was only possible once the shipments from Margareta had begun to arrive. An army had to be supplied, or it would stall out.

Just has he had that thought, he sensed even more Candorians, about a hundred horsemen with supply wagons. Merry could tell he was distracted and fell off the pace.

Ohen shouted, "Terry!" Faces turned back.

When he waved his arm, they pulled to a stop, waiting for him to pull up beside them.

"We're going the wrong way. More Candorians up ahead, on a side road. I think it's the route they take from the canyon lands to the Old Road."

"But you said to go this way!"

"I know, but I had the schedule wrong." That was a lie, but they needed some story to believe. "We'll have to race at full speed to cross ahead of them or wait until they pass."

"How many?"

"Should be a hundred. Something like that."

Terry frowned, "How much time do we have?"

"The road is five kloms ahead. They should reach that point in an hour."

The scout nodded. "Then we race for it. Let's get out of this place. We can't be caught between the two groups." Kitchen nodded with him.

Terry looked around at the faces. "Don't slow down for anything. I know there's a forested patch on the other side. Make for that. We can't leave a trail of dust for them to follow. Sunset will give us cover."

They urged their horses into a gallop and pushed on.

Ohen worried about the dust, but his memory of the photos agreed with Terry's experience. On the other side of the north-south road, the scout led them to a stream bed and they splashed through it for a couple of kloms, hiding their tracks.

By sunset, they were safe in the trees, far enough so that no stray sound or smell would catch the attention of an experienced Candor scout.

"No moonlight for a while, and we'll do without a fire tonight."

Ohen was tired. He'd been doing with the same rations as the others and it was getting to him. He pulled his blanket and tarp from his bag and found a place with more fallen leaves than stones. At least he could sleep.

But three hours later, Merry's uneasiness brought him awake. Someone was sneaking through the camp. Ohen probed for thoughts. It was Kitchen.

I've got to see what's in his bag! If he has maps and schedules of current Candor activities, then I have to get a look at it.

Ohen cleared his throat. "What's wrong Merry? Did an owl bother you?"

Kitchen froze in his tracks, confident he was hidden in the darkness.

Ohen pulled out his flint striker and sparked a few times until the oil-soaked wick on his pocket lamp flickered into a tiny flame. Kitchen turned and moved out of the sudden light. He couldn't do anything if Barclay was awake.

Ohen took a few minutes to stroke the horse. Merry was content.

It was nice to be able to read the horse's thoughts. He took some extra time to make sure that she didn't have any hidden injuries. Ohen would be demanding some extra effort from the mare very soon now.

· · ·

Morning light brought a frown to Ohen's face. He'd intended to sneak out before dawn and get a head start on the others, but he was the late riser. He checked his bag, but nothing was disturbed, although he'd apparently slept soundly and Kitchen could have returned.

The man had been looking for papers, but if he'd seen the computer and the generator and the other wires, he'd have gotten a clue Ohen would rather no one see. But his gear was still wrapped in layers like he'd left it.

They headed out, still on track to approach Dumont from the southeast. Ohen had coached Terry to take this route, partly to avoid Candorians on the Old Road, but also as misdirection. He never intended to go to Dumont. B3 was hidden near the village of Marion south of there.

In all their planning, he'd always mentioned Dumont, as if that was his destination. Had Kitchen and Dawson gotten that information from Terry, or had they been independently coached? He hadn't gotten a clue from their thoughts, yet.

But today was the day. He needed to get free from the group and make straight for B3. He had to get there alone to reactivate the electronics now that the batteries had certainly drained. And he didn't need someone standing behind him, ready to claim the boat for someone else.

He had a place in mind. The highlands where he'd landed had a gentle slope toward Marion, but there was a cliff to the river valley to the east. His route toward Dumont followed that river valley.

"Terry!" he called, after riding a couple of hours. He rode up, with a tight frown on his face.

"What is it?"

Ohen put his hand to his stomach. "I've got to stop for a few minutes."

Terry winced. "Bad food?"

"I don't know, but I've got to stop! I'll catch up."

Terry sighed. "Okay, but don't be long."

Ohen nodded, flicked the reins and guided Merry over to a secluded cove of trees. Confirming that the others were riding on ahead, if a bit slower, he unpacked his bag and slung it over his shoulder.

"Go on, Merry. That way!"

The horse was confused but decided there was forage over there for him and walked away.

Making sure that the bag was balanced reasonably well on his back, he took a few trial jumps.

I've gotten a lot weaker pretending to be a Martian.

His jumps lacked the distance he'd managed when he first arrived, but he was still stronger than most and could make distance in this rough terrain. He needed to climb the cliff as rapidly as possible and get entirely out of sight before they came back for him.

Ohen put his mind to the effort, climbing and monitoring the distant thoughts of Terry and the others. Shortly, the scout decided he didn't want to get too far ahead and stopped so that their horses could drink from the stream.

Ohen had hoped for more time.

When he reached the top of the cliff, he was confident a horse wouldn't be able to follow. He needed to cover ground now.

His clairvoyant sight brought B3 clearly into view. There were tree branches that had grown over one side of it. *I'll have to break free, but that shouldn't be hard.*

But then he saw something else, a stack of branches up against the side of the boat where someone had made a shelter. Someone had found it!

He just hoped they hadn't damaged it.

Expanding his senses, he could tell that there were perhaps three people within a few kloms of the boat. No one was there at the moment, but someone from Marion had discovered it.

He ran faster, each step arching across the grassland. A horse would be faster, but as long as he was on the top of the plateau and they were down in the valley, he could outrun them. Hopefully, they didn't even know which direction he'd gone.

Down below, he sensed that they'd discovered Merry wandering alone. Now their search would intensify. He needed to be at the boat!

He paused to drink from his canteen. He was burning up, running at top speed, carrying a bag. He was disgusted at how weak he'd gotten, just doing paperwork day after day. He needed to exercise more.

He had to swing in an arc to avoid one of the Marion people, shepherding a flock of sheep, but he was able to stay out of sight.

And then, memories came back. He recognized some of the landmarks from his first day on Mars. He was getting close.

He leapt harder. And there it was, he could see it with his eyes. He pushed through the trees and his heart raced as he put his hand on the metal. He was home.

The rude shelter someone had built was just to protect blankets and supplies. He didn't know if anyone actually slept there recently.

He hurried around to the door.

There were scratches on the metal, but not bad ones. The Delense ceramic coating would heal itself before too long, even in an Earth-like atmosphere. That was one of the things he'd insisted on in the design. The old Cerik boats had used a version that healed in the atmosphere of Ko, but not in Earth's atmosphere. That had cost them a couple of boats back during the time of the Star.

The lock didn't respond when he pressed the buttons in order. He nodded. The battery was dead.

He closed his eyes and put his palm flat on the surface. Sensing the mechanism just under the hull, he used the same trick he'd used on the jail cell, moving the little parts with his psychokinesis. He was grateful that he'd used a simple lock. It had just been an afterthought in the design. It took longer because the striker had to move a greater distance, but it wasn't difficult.

There was a click and the door opened. The air was a little stale. The airlock was pitch dark inside. He opened the door as wide as he could and went inside and then opened his bag.

Working more by clairvoyance than the weak light coming through the trees, he used one of the tools he'd swiped from Meri's workshop to dismount a lighting fixture. Connecting wires from the pedal-powered generator to the boat's wiring, he removed the voltage limiter and leaning against the wall, he pedaled as fast as he could.

In a minute, indicators on the airlock controls started flickering. If he ever redesigned the boat, he'd add a safety battery that was never used for anything, other than to bring the system back to life. But who could have predicted this?

Don't be stupid. Engineers are supposed to predict everything, even the impossible.

After fifteen minutes, he was able to bypass the airlock safety and open the inner door. He moved inside. There was a little light from various indicator lights, but the air was bad. Probably some food he'd left out had oxidized or something, he just left both the inner and outer doors open for now to let the boat air out.

He moved the generator inside to a more comfortable position and re-wired it. Settling in with a bottle of water and favorite snacks from his boat's stores, he sat in a comfortable chair and pedaled the generator.

The next order of business was getting enough charge into the battery system to activate the power cell conversion circuit. That would quickly bring the whole system back to life. Until then, he didn't even want to waste power on the overhead lights. He kept his eyes on the control panel, waiting for the power level to reach the critical level. The voltage level crept up far too slowly for his taste.

He sensed Terry's thoughts in the distance, worried about him, and angry that he'd been tricked.

Sorry, but that's how it had to play out. I'd rather have come alone.

His legs ached after pedalling for over an hour. A light began blinking. It was time. Without stopping his pedaling, he flicked the switch. The converter came alive and in less than a minute, the batteries were flooded with the charging current from the main power cells. The B3 was fully functional.

He sighed and let the generator stop. Now he had to fix all the wiring.

The inside wires were restored quickly and then he went into the airlock to re-install the light fixture.

He was barely finished when there was a click. Dawson was there in the outer doorway holding a pistol aimed at him.

Stupid. If the general has an ineda, then other people could as well.

Dawson was a quiet man, he didn't speak much and he hardly had any internal dialog either. With a natural ineda, he'd been able to sneak up without any warning.

Ohen said, "You found me."

"You left a trail. You didn't even try to hide it. What is this place? I was expecting a spaceship."

He was leaking thoughts, now. He was puzzled by the artificial lighting. He'd expected a towering column just like all the other spaceships. He was alert for any attack by the big man.

Ohen smiled. "Oh, this is a spaceship, just not one like you're used to. Let me put these tools up and I'll show you."

Dawson gestured with the barrel of his pistol. "Move slowly and don't try anything."

Ohen moved with comical slowness, moving through the inner door and setting the tools down on his bags. Dawson followed him in.

Ohen asked, "Who are you working for?"

"None of your business." **The duke.**

He'd almost expected that. The king's cousin probably had many spies all through the kingdom. The military, especially, were loyal to the kingdom, but whether to the king himself or to some other noble family was a different question. Someone had leaked the full story of Barclay's origins to the duke and had Dawson and perhaps others in place ready to take advantage of his exit plans.

"What do you expect of me?"

Dawson was a little puzzled. He was supposed to capture Barclay when he returned to his spaceship, but whether he'd have to carry the giant tied up on his horse all across hostile territory back to da Vinci or....

Ohen said, "Are you planning to make me fly my spaceship to your destination?"

Dawson nodded. "Yes! Fly it."

"Okay, but I have to finish my repairs. I'd rather not be shot by accident."

"I'm not putting down my gun."

"Whatever you say, but you must know I'm not a fighter. Just don't let it go off by accident."

Dawson didn't say anything, but he did ease the hammer down, making it a little less likely to go off by a random shock.

Ohen said, "I need to press this button here. It's the next step in bringing the spaceship back up to full operation. Is that okay with you?"

"I guess." He still held the pistol aimed menacingly.

The instant Ohen pressed the control, the floor gravity came back on. Gravity over four times stronger than Martian normal grabbed Dawson. His pistol fell from his grip and the man crumpled to the floor.

It was tough on Ohen as well, but he was better adapted and he was expecting it. He'd never changed the floor gravity from the 1.4 standard gravity settings he'd used on his journey from the starship.

Ohen gasped. "Sorry, it's brutal, I know." He stepped over, picked up the pistol.

"What's ... what's going on?" Dawson struggled, trying to get up, but it was useless.

Ohen put his hand on the man's head, forcing him back down.

"You forgot that I'm not from this world." He put Dawson to sleep, just as he'd done to Will months before.

The Promise

Just as soon as Ohen turned the gravity back to Mars normal, he pulled Dawson back outside, reinforcing the sleep patterns in his brain. As a last thought, he put the pistol on the ground a few feet away from the sleeping man.

I don't need the thing, but Dawson is still in enemy lands.

He closed the airlock, did the last safety checks, and then with hurricane winds, B3 lifted from its hiding place, collapsing the shepherd's storage shed and breaking off a few tree branches.

Straight up. That was his intent. Ohen wanted to get as high as possible while there was the chance that there was someone else around with a twitchy trigger finger.

It was like stretching unused muscles, piloting the B3 up through the atmosphere. It wasn't long before the sky darkened and he could see the curve of the planet below him.

His visitor had thrown off his plans. It was a mental shift from being a Xanthe soldier to being a free agent again.

Should he go into orbit? What about his promise to the general?

There was nothing preventing him from setting a course for Luna and leaving Mars behind, never to return. But that wasn't really his primary mission was it?

He really needed to be on very friendly relations with the nation of Xanthe. The U'tanse would return for him, eventually. He shouldn't poison the one good political contact he had on the planet.

And he hated to ignore a promise.

So, he had a plan. Step one, go charge up the power cells on B3.

He climbed higher, well out of the atmosphere, higher than the orbits of Phobos and Deimos. He checked the positions of all the other planets. He needed to find a good alignment.

A thought occurred to him. He looked at the hand-crank generator, designed to power that computer, and then shook his head. There was a better way.

The B3 was in a stable orbit, for now. He dug out the Martian computer and took it to his utility charging station, where he could recharge small power cells in his hand tools. It took a little alignment to get the computer positioned correctly, but once he pressed the button, the Earth-designed power cell, bathed in the TP beams, charged just like his U'tanse tools.

The computer lit up.

"Computer, this is Ohen bar Clay. Do you recognize me?"

"Yes."

"I need to confirm something. I was told that Mars was under quarantine after the Plague. Spaceships couldn't leave because of that order. However, I just left Mars. Why did that rule not apply?"

There was a delay. Ohen suspected the computer was contacting Phobos for information.

The computer said, "The quarantine order was to all Project spacecraft. You craft is not in that set."

"Computer, I have also heard that no craft is allowed to land on Earth. Is that true of my ship?"

"It isn't just spacecraft that are interdicted. The order is broader than that."

Suddenly there was a human voice. Someone, voice slurring, clearly suffering from his disease gave the order. "… an interdiction barrier covering all near-Earth space. Don't let anything get through."

Ohen frowned. "And this order is being enforced. Nothing can get through near-Earth space?"

"That's correct. At the time of the order, there were many destabilized space stations that could have impacted Earth. More than just ships were prohibited."

"Computer, some months ago, I tried to set up a charging beam with Earth as one of the endpoint masses. Something happened."

"In such a situation, the Project Central computers would have detected the beam and drained the power cells on the ship."

Ohen nodded. That's exactly what had happened to him. That last order said "anything" and the computers interpreted it to include TP beams. Not only was he forbidden to use Earth in a charging beam, but he couldn't even use Earth for course corrections, and certainly he'd never be able to land there.

"Thank you, Computer. That was useful information."

There was no reply. He wondered what a thank you meant to a computer.

He went to his console and calculated potential charging positions. There was one nearby on the line between Venus and Saturn. On a whim, he asked the computer to come up with solutions. In just a few seconds, it had duplicated his list and included thirty additional possibilities using large asteroids, moons and what he guessed were orbital habitats.

I think I'll keep this computer. It's handy.

After charging up the B3 power cells, he shifted to an orbit around Mars that was near Phobos. He was still on the far side of Xanthe, so he took the advantage to shower, take a nice long nap, and relish the taste of home from his boat's food stores.

But soon the time came.

"Computer, send a message to General T. Jonah of Xanthe: Please contact me soon on a private voice call."

"Sent."

It was a little less than an hour before the call came back.

"Barclay! It's good to hear from you. I'd heard that you left Captain Jenkins's troop. Did you find your ship?"

"Yes, and while I'm willing to fulfill the rest of our deal, I need to confirm you're in a private place?"

"Yes, no one can overhear us."

"Good. After I arrived at my ship and was preparing it for flight, one of the soldiers, named Dawson, attempted to capture me and my ship, holding me at gunpoint."

"Were you injured?"

"No. And neither was he, although he was rendered unconscious for a bit. I gather that he was supposed to transport me and the ship to da Vinci."

"Hmm. That's unsettling. I'll have you know that I knew nothing of this plan."

Jonah was thousands of kloms away, but Ohen's familiarity with him and the voice channel helped him read the general's thoughts. There was no hint of deception there. Ohen just had to be sure.

"I know. However, I want to take some additional safety precautions before I finish our trade."

"That's understandable. What are your conditions?"

Ohen spelled them out. He could even hear the scratch of a pen on paper as Jonah took notes.

"Can you be ready before dawn? I'd like to arrive in the dark to avoid making a spectacle."

"I guess that's possible. So ... no one on the roof?"

"Yes, I'm a little short of trust right now. Any stranger there and I won't land. I even rode with Dawson for weeks before he turned on me. I hope you understand."

"I can make that work. I'll even circle the building with guards. Is that it?"

Ohen paused. "Oh, and a small hand-trolley would be useful."

"I can do that."

. . .

It was still dark in Orson, but on the roof of the warehouse building, the four corners were lit with pole lanterns. Ohen scanned the area with his clairvoyant sight. There was no one on the roof, nor on the floor below it. The ground floor had several troops stationed at the doors. Everything looked perfect.

Flying in the air with a boat was noisy. The tractor beams at the corner of B3 were rapidly grabbing air and pulling it downward to provide the upward thrust the boat needed to stay in flight. It cycled so fast that it made a high-pitched buzzing noise. It was sure to wake some people up.

Ohen flew in quickly and settled down on the roof of the warehouse. He had remembered that it was a sturdy building, and his sight let him center the weight of the boat over crossed load-bearing walls. There was no sign of weakness as he killed the beams and the morning went silent again.

In the distance, there were some voices, but they faded as no one knew what that noise had been. On the center of the roof, the boat was even out of sight from most neighboring buildings, and certainly invisible from the ground.

He stayed in his seat, ready to take to the skies if there was any sign that a trap had been set.

But no, the general had given his orders and probably nobody really knew what was going on. If anyone had seen the boat fly in, they didn't know what it was. No one would think it was a spaceship. It was the wrong shape.

Ohen nodded. Time to get to work. He went to the airlock and stepped out onto the roof. He looked around. Even if someone wanted to shoot him, none of the other tall buildings were close enough for an assassin to make the effort.

There were a pile of boxes next to the stairwell down into the warehouse. A quick scan showed him that there were over a hundred computers, still dusty. Most were ones with keyboards and displays, maybe forty or so were smaller canisters.

His job, his part of the deal, was to recharge all of these computers and put them back into service. It would instantly make Xanthe's military unstoppable.

He found the hand-trolley and loaded up a stack of boxes and wheeled them into B3, locking the door behind him.

For each type, he had to find the correct orientation so that the power cells inside would charge, but once he did that, it was maybe thirty seconds or so to charge a computer. He stacked the charged ones back outside and picked up more boxes. He could be done in under two hours.

The process would relieve the urgency of making new generators, but it would certainly sabotage Meti's business in the long term. Still he didn't expect the general would be satisfied by only a hundred computers. Whether charged or cranked, he'd be wanting to expand until he ran out of dusty ones.

I need to send a message to Raymond to experiment with electric motors. If he could find a way to transport large charged power cells from space to Mars, then they might be on their way to an electric economy and motors would be the next critical technology.

Dawn had arrived and he was nearly done with charging the computers when the computer spoke up.

"You have a voice call from King Harmon of Xanthe. Answer, display, or defer until later?"

"Answer."

"Hello, Barclay. Is that you I see out my window? That square thing on top of the warehouse building?"

"Hello, Your Highness. Yes, that's my spaceship. It's a different design from what you're familiar with."

"General Jonah has briefed me on what's going on. He could barely contain himself."

Ohen chuckled. "It was the only exchange that he'd accept, to allow me to leave."

"That's understandable. You've been exceptionally helpful to the kingdom."

Ohen got a hint of an underlying thought. "I must apologize for the extra security precautions this morning. I've had an issue."

The king said, "So I've heard. I wish I could rain down fire on those responsible, but...."

"It's okay. I certainly understand the political issues involved."

"You've become more adept at this over time. You seem to have a gift for understanding power struggles."

"Sometimes. But I also get the hint that when people in power give me compliments, it's just a prelude to asking for a favor."

"Oh, you're getting very adept at this. Sadly, it's my cousin again. When he heard about making diplomatic contact with Luna, he was ... insistent that an ambassador from Xanthe shouldn't be a foreigner. He makes the point that your first priority would be to represent your people, the U'tanse."

Ohen had a sinking feeling. "Yes, I see his point. However, I'm the person to go on this trip."

"I certainly agree, but what about taking along another person, a native of Xanthe?"

"I would have to be confident that my safety wouldn't be compromised."

The king said, "All these points have been considered. I do have a volunteer."

"Who?"

...

Lord Casey appeared at the top of the stairwell. "Hello, Barclay. I didn't expect to see you again. Are you okay with taking along a passenger?"

Ohen sighed. "I'm worried about you. Are you actually okay with going on a trip that just might be one-way? And what about your sister?"

He shrugged. "My job to spy on you was going away. And I'm assured by the king himself that Luthe will get my regular payments while I'm away. I'm sure she will take advantage of being the sister to the Ambassador to Luna."

"And Duke Paul?"

Casey smiled, "Both will be getting my full reports. I'm sure it would have been the same if someone else had volunteered for the job.

"And as far as a one-way trip, I trust you to keep me safe. Certainly I didn't see any other positions coming my way. This is an ideal opportunity for me."

"Okay, then. Do you have luggage?"

"Downstairs, I've been told I have to haul it up myself. Nobody is allowed on the roof until you're gone."

Soon, the last of the computers were charged. Ohen borrowed one for Casey. The rest were stacked on the roof.

With the airlock door closed behind him. Ohen pointed to a chair. "Sit there for now. We're taking off. He put the camera feed on the main display and as they took off, Casey gasped. "That's the city."

"Yes, and we're going much higher. By the way, how do you feel about getting stronger on the trip to Luna. I'm thinking of turning the floor gravity a bit higher."

"What?" He was puzzled.

"You'll get used to it. Say goodbye to Mars."

Continue the Story

The Project Saga

U'tanse of
Ko Branch

Earth
Recovery
Branch

Lunar
Alpine
Trilogy

Children
of Earth
Trilogy

www.ingramcontent.com/pod-product-compliance
Lightning Source LLC
Chambersburg PA
CBHW020551020726
47494CB00006B/2022